Praise for *Letters from Yellowstone* and Diane Smith

"If you've ever visited Yellowstone National Park or even thought about going there, you'll enjoy *Letters from Yellowstone* . . . a pleasurable story which does full justice to America's greatest natural wonderland."
—*Parade*

"Insightful . . . *Letters from Yellowstone* charms with natural surprises."
—*USA Today*

"An intrepid heroine and an ineffectual but lovable hero grapple with a supporting cast of eccentric characters in first-time novelist Diane Smith's virtuoso *Letters from Yellowstone* . . . There's surprising grit in this portrait of Yellowstone, and real charm in this quietly original debut."
—*Elle*

"I loved this book in a way that I haven't loved a book in some time. *Letters from Yellowstone* has it all—great story, engaging characters, fascinating history, science in the making, and all the awesome beauty of Yellowstone Park. But if one might be tempted to classify this novel as an idyll in the wild, think again—along with the plucky naturalists and fellow travelers, we meet railroad men and developers (in 1898!) intent on darker purposes for the Park. This may be a first novel, but Diane Smith is a seasoned observer of man's relationship with the natural world. And lucky for us, she is a completely wonderful writer who has scored one for the good guys."   —James Welch

"A beautifully written epistolary story . . . the author brings an authenticity to the controversies about scientific method and the environment as well as the expedition's finds . . . this debut novel is an intelligent story, a charmer with style."   —*The Denver Post*

"Reading *Letters from Yellowstone* was an absolute pleasure. Its heroine, Alex Bartram, a naturalist in all aspects of life, is vivid, forthright, energetic, becoming, devoted to seeing glories in the particulars, and so is the novel. Diane Smith is a natural, a real find."
—William Kittredge

"Smith manages to give each of the letter-writing characters his or her distinct voice . . . simply and brilliantly captures that time when the American wilderness was still a pristine, awe-inspiring place."
—*Rocky Mountain News*

"Like Montana's state flower, the bitterroot, this novel takes root in a cool, inhospitable environment and comes to miraculous pink bloom. It's a woman's story, but also anyone's story about ambition and science and moral rectitude. Told with wit and wisdom, it conveys the deep knowledge of a place and a time that can only be learned through love."
—Annick Smith

"A delightful trip through turn of the century Yellowstone . . . Bartram is as spunky a heroine as we could desire…the story also becomes a commentary on science and shared truth . . . Readers will find themselves caught up in the stories of these people and their lives."
—The Portland Oregonian

"Diane Smith has written a book with real magic and grace. The prose glistens and the story lingers with elegant power."
—Thomas McGuane

"Smith creates a rich world in her engaging debut novel . . . she tells this story through a series of colorful and articulate letters that give her novel something of the flavor of 84, Charing Cross Road."
—The San Diego Union

"This is a novel full of the Old West. It is graceful and enchanting."
—Tracy Kidder

"Many things emerge in this story—a portrait of scientists at work at the turn of the century, a look at the West in a time of change, the beauty and danger of Yellowstone, and the story of a forthright woman and the men who come to admire her. Smith began with a beguiling idea and has turned it into an enchanting book."
—The Arizona Republic

"1898. It is perhaps the most exciting time to be alive in the American West: the land has yet to feel the crushing advance of the agricultural and industrial revolutions; yet Native tribes have been subdued, the great herds of bison reduced from sixty million to twenty-three wild buffalo left in the vast wilderness of the nation's first national park, Yellowstone. It is into this marvelous setting that Diane Smith launches a spirited cast of characters led by her heroine, the naturalist Alexandria Bartram. One can taste the sharp anticipation of discovery and exploration blowing around every bend of the trail as these botanists and entomologists step into this fresh, largely unstudied expanse of wildlands. Smith keeps tight rein on the members of her gutsy field team whose lives every threaten to explode into the most dynamic landscape on the continent. That tension is one hell of a story."

—Doug Peacock

"A captivating novel . . . *Letters from Yellowstone* is especially memorable because it gently shows the conflicts independent women faced in the nineteenth century and, the bonds that shared experience forges between disparate personalities. And it reminds us of the joys of discovering nature's secrets."

—*The Bloomsbury Review*

"One of those rare, quiet books that simply and gracefully tells a story. Smith has a supremely natural rhythm as a writer, the letters slipping by like water, bright elements lingering long after the last page is read."

—C. S. Godshalk

"Diane Smith and other contemporary writers of the new West have a different slant on the American frontier . . . they offer new heroes and thoughtful questions about the environment, Native Americans, and feminism . . . this debut novel is a charming, probing story . . . Smith is careful with historical fact, quick with ironic humor, and adept at juggling a number of memorable characters . . . a fast-moving, well-crafted story."

—*The Eugene Register Guard*

"Serenely attentive, deliberately paced, as careful with psychology and history as it is with its botany, Smith's epistolary narrative makes a worthy addition to the expanding category of history-of-science novels."

—*Publishers Weekly*

"Colorful and credible . . . a warm, satisfying story . . . the magic of a Yellowstone summer shimmers here enticingly."

—*Kirkus Reviews*

"Smith introduces a host of memorable characters, at the same time exploring issues of the day—from ecology and feminism to the political wranglings of nineteenth-century academics . . . A thoroughly enjoyable, intriguingly off-beat epistolary novel."

—*ALA Booklist*

PEGUIN BOOKS

LETTERS FROM YELLOWSTONE

Diane Smith writes about science and the environment
from her home in Montana. This is her first novel.

DIANE SMITH

LETTERS
FROM
YELLOWSTONE

PENGUIN BOOKS

PENGUIN BOOKS

Published by the Penguin Group
Penguin Putnam Inc., 375 Hudson Street,
New York, New York 10014, U.S.A.
Penguin Books Ltd, 27 Wrights Lane,
London W8 5TZ, England
Penguin Books Australia Ltd, Ringwood,
Victoria, Australia
Penguin Books Canada Ltd, 10 Alcorn Avenue,
Toronto, Ontario, Canada M4V 3B2
Penguin Books (N.Z.) Ltd, 182–190 Wairau Road,
Auckland 10, New Zealand

Penguin Books Ltd, Registered Offices:
Harmondsworth, Middlesex, England

First published in the United States of America by Viking Penguin,
a member of Penguin Putnam Inc. 1999
Published in Penguin Books 2000

9   10

Illustrations, *Mimulus Lewisii*, *Lewisia rediviva*, *Calypso bulbosa*, and
Rosa Woodsii, all courtesy of Hunt Institute for Botanical Documentation,
Carnegie Mellon University, Pittsburgh, Pennsylvania.

Illustration, *Epilobium angustifolium*, from *Handbook of Rocky
Mountain Plants* by Ruth Ashton Nelson and Roger Williams.
Drawings copyright © 1969 by Dorothy V. Leake.
Used by permission of Roberts Rinehart Publishers.

THE LIBRARY OF CONGRESS HAS CATALOGED
THE HARDCOVER EDITION AS FOLLOWS:
Smith, Diane.
Letters from Yellowstone/Diane Smith.
p.   cm.
ISBN 0-670-88631-9 (hc.)
ISBN 0 14 02.9181 4 (pbk.)
1. Yellowstone National Park—History—Fiction.   I. Title.
PS3569.M5255L48   1999
813'.54—dc21   99–12904

Printed in the United States of America
Set in Goudy
Designed by Francesca Belanger

For Hannah Smith

There are more things in heaven and earth, Horatio,
Than are dreamt of in your philosophy.

—*Hamlet*, William Shakespeare
Act I, scene v

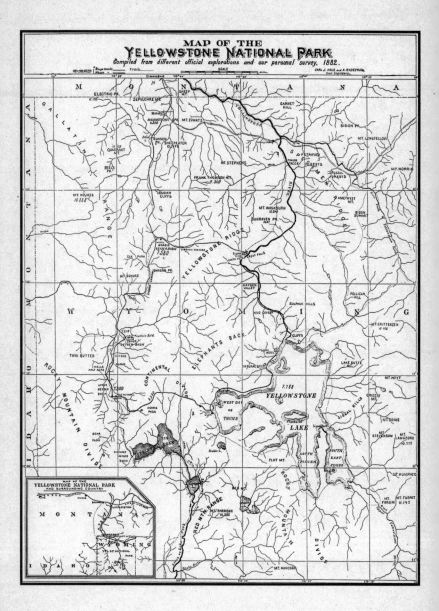

MAP OF THE
YELLOWSTONE NATIONAL PARK.
Compiled from different official explorations and our personal survey, 1882.

CARL J. HIALS and A. RYDSTROM,
Civil Engineers.

I. Mimulus Lewisii

A. E. Bartram
Cornell University
Ithaca, New York
March 10, 1898

Prof. H. G. Merriam
The Agricultural College
  of the State of Montana
Bozeman, Montana

Dear Professor,

Dr. Philip Aber of the Smithsonian made a presentation on campus last week in which he discussed your planned field study in Yellowstone National Park. Although I have studied medicine during my tenure here, I prefer the study of botany over anything else. I have a personal collection of over 5,000 specimens, some of which I inherited from a distant relative on my father's side, and have worked extensively on classification. For the last three years I have summered in Philadelphia studying the Lewis expedition, and have initiated an illustrated documentation of their collection, specializing in the Rocky Mountain species, e.g., *Lupinus argenteus*, *Linum Lewisii*, *Clarkia pulchella*, and, of course, *Lewisia rediviva*.

I have found this work to be immensely satisfying, but it has, of necessity, focused on studying species out of place and time. I am indebted, as we all are, to the earliest collectors, but am equally interested in exploring the complexities of plant life in their natural environs, and contributing to a scientific understanding of the plant kingdom. I am young, single, and without any engagement to confine me here. With your expressed interest, I could reach Montana by May 15; May 30 at the latest. Please advise at your earliest convenience as I am most anxious to make plans.

  Sincerely,
    A. E. Bartram

Howard Merriam, Ph.D.
The Agricultural College
  of the State of Montana
Bozeman, Mont.
April 2, 1898

A. E. Bartram
Cornell University
Ithaca, New York

Dear Dr. Bartram,

Your letter arrived at a most fortuitous time. I am indeed planning a scientific expedition into the Yellowstone. My goal is threefold: to study Rocky Mountain specimens in their native setting and to initiate a collection of those specimens for a research herbarium I wish to establish here at Montana College. Based on this work, I plan to prepare a complete enumeration of Yellowstone and other Montana species.

As you may know, aside from Coulter's preliminary work, little has been done to systematically collect, classify, and analyze the plant life of the northern Rocky Mountains, and much *must* be done if we are to better understand the region and its potential. I have selected the Nation's Park as a starting point for my investigations because it shelters a diversity of virtually undiscovered plant life in what could very well be the last uniquely wild place in America. But that will not last, given the tourism promotion of the U.S. government and its railroad friends. Sadly, the situation throughout the West is much the same. Agriculture may be the future of this region, but it will destroy the land as we know it. Needless to say, there is much to be done and very little time before a wealth of native species is lost to us forever.

We will establish a camp of operations at Mammoth on or about May 1, weather permitting. I suggest you plan to meet us there as soon as possible after that date. You are welcome to pursue your own interests in plant life and the environment. I ask only that you contribute to both the Montana and Smithsonian Institution's research collections, and provide me with a copy of your field notes.

Although the high-mountain country around the Park warms slowly (and this has been an unusually severe winter), I plan to start my work in the areas around Mammoth Hot Springs and other geothermal activity so we should not be too delayed. Having collected extensively around the hotpots of Northern California while a graduate student at Berkeley, I look forward to comparing the species in these northern climes.

You, too, may find this unusual environment of interest. Thanks to a federal program of road construction, the Park is rapidly becoming overrun with tourists and other travellers—they say more than 10,000 last year alone!—but I think you will find that most of the natural systems and wildlife which have evolved in concert with the geothermal areas, and which can add to an appreciation of plant life in this region, are still firmly in place. I do not know the Park well, but I assume you will also find ample opportunity to investigate the bitterroot in all its unusual stages of development—if not in Mammoth and environs then in the higher backcountry once weather and other conditions improve.

I notice that in your letter you did not call out the Lewis monkeyflower. Perhaps a specimen did not survive the multiple owners and travels back and forth between Europe that the Lewis collection reportedly made before finding its permanent home in Philadelphia. You may wish to refer to Pursh's illustrated *Flora* for additional information. The monkeyflower is, if I may say so, a lovely specimen. To encounter it at 9,000 feet is to share in some of the adventure of that first great American naturalist as he reached the elusive headwaters of the Missouri. Those compact petals and almost sensuous corolla lobes lilting along the creek-beds must have been as joyful a sight then as they are now. As you can tell, I, too, am devoted to the work of Meriwether Lewis and look forward to learning more about your studies.

Dr. Bartram, before closing I fear I must be perfectly frank with you. Although you appeal for no commitment, I would be remiss to ask you to travel such a great distance without some word about your prospects once you are here. I can reimburse you, of course, for your travel to and from Montana. I can, naturally, provide for your room and board in the field. I can also offer a small stipend, but only upon successful completion of the work, and only if the expedition proceeds as scheduled. Since you are a collector yourself, you know the financial and other hazards that await us in the field. Please understand that I cannot afford to finance any unexpected expenditures out of my own pocket. Such expenses must come from my very limited expedition funds. I had hoped to be joined by my colleagues here at the college, which would have cost me little, but due to a marriage, a death, and a trip to our nation's capital, those plans have not been realized. Thus, I find myself embarrassingly short of funds to adequately support and reward your participation.

Additionally, although there will be much classification to be accomplished during the fall and winter months, I cannot guarantee a position to you upon completion of our field work. Although I have great plans to establish a botanical research herbarium, these plans are not shared by the college president, who believes the study of botany is somehow in conflict with the educational and agricultural missions of the college. That agriculture is the growing of plants and that botany is the systematic study of those plants seems to have escaped him altogether. He is, you must understand, an historian, and as such more interested in building monuments named after the dead (dead naturalists at that!) than exposing students to living, breathing science in the here and now. But I digress.

I do hope you will consider my offer. If, under the circumstances, you feel that you are unable to do so, I will understand completely and will continue to hold you in the highest regard for your expressed interest in my work.

I remain,
    yours most humbly,
        Howard Merriam, Ph.D.

p.s. I cannot help but remark upon your name. If you are indeed a member of that prestigious family of botany, I can only say how pleased I would be to have you join our group, and I pledge to do my utmost to find an appropriate position for you here at the college. If not, be assured that the offer still stands. HGM

APRIL 16, 1898
PROFESSOR   SORRY TO HEAR ABOUT THE UNFORTUNATE
TIMING OF THE MARRIAGE THE DEATH AND THE TRIP TO
OUR NATIONS CAPITAL   HOPE THESE CALAMITIES DID
NOT BEFALL THE SAME PERSON   YES I AM A DISTANT
BARTRAM BUT CLOSE ENOUGH THAT MY FATHER WANTED
TO NAME ME AFTER DARWIN   MY MOTHER WISELY
DEMURRED   NOT YET A PHYSICIAN HOWEVER HAVING
ALLOWED MY NATURALIZING TO SUBSUME MY MEDICAL
STUDIES   WILL MEET YOU AT THE MAMMOTH SPRINGS ON
OR ABOUT MAY 1   AGREE TO YOUR TERMS AS STATED
YOURS AE BARTRAM

Howard Merriam
Bozeman, Mont.
April 19, 1898

Dear Mother,

You said you were praying for me. Well, your prayers have been answered. I have just heard from a medical student and young botanist at Cornell University who is willing to join the expedition, and will do so with little or no financial commitment on my part. And, he is a Bartram at that!

I may have told you that Miller bailed out. Too many commitments he says, now that he is married. It was a disappointment, but fortunately my work does not depend on a cartographer. That aspect of the Park has been fairly well documented by the government by now. But Gleick has been making similar rumblings, and now informs me that he is off to Washington for a month. I think his reservations are more related to the increasing severity of the president's highwaymen reports than to any time commitment at the Smithsonian. Gleick lost a friend to some sort of holdup when they were surveying for the railroad, and I do not think he has ever recovered. His lack of interest is a real loss for me. Gleick is a surgeon by training, a crack shot, and he knows the land. Besides, he believes in the value of science and is the only true ally I have on campus.

There is Peacock, of course, but he will disappear into his private world of beetles once we reach the Park. The only thing I can count on from him will be the occasional fish dinner—he is a superb fisherman. But then he should be. He is on first-name basis with all those bugs!

Ironically, I find myself now in the position of having to enlist the help of Andrew Rutherford (you remember, the weather man), who represents agriculture in all its glory and could not care less about native species. I so badly need to field a team that I might even be able to put up with that foul-smelling thing he sticks in his mouth. (These days, knowing how I feel about it, he has taken to stuffing the pipe—still burning!—in his pocket whenever he comes upstairs. Better he should catch fire than my office, temporary as it is.)

Rutherford is ambitious in an off-handed sort of way. I might talk him into giving up his daily beaker of brandy and weather checks if he thought I might name an edible grass or two after him. And back him in his fight against naming the two new buildings after Lewis and Clark. You know how I feel about the significant contributions made by the two explorers, but I am getting desperate. And these days I really do not feel up to the fight.

One thing I have discovered as I have gotten older is that I do not have the heart, or maybe it is the stomach, to take on these kinds of arguments—particularly with colleagues like Rutherford. He is one of those men you encounter in academia who find it more convenient to champion a single complaint rather than dedicate themselves to any specific field of study. For some contrarian reason known only to Rutherford himself, Lewis and Clark have attracted his particular ire.

It should be interesting when this man Bartram joins us. He apparently has dedicated his naturalizing career to studying the plants of the expedition. I did not have the heart to tell him that neither Lewis nor Clark ventured anywhere near the Park. If he does not know it now, he will figure it out in time. I hope it is not too much of a disappointment.

As you can see, I am in the thick of it here. Appreciate your letters and kind thoughts. And yes, these days even your prayers. You have managed to deliver a botanist with medical training. Maybe now you can drum up a new research facility and herbarium—named after Washington and Jefferson, of course. Got to keep Rutherford happy! To be honest, the way it has been snowing this last week I would settle for a sign of spring. See what you can do!

Love,
Howard

———— •◦•◦• ————

A. E. Bartram
Philadelphia, Penn.
April 25, 1898

Dear Jess,

I have booked passage for Montana, so before I go I would like to arrange for storage of my meagre campus possessions. Can you accommodate them? There is not much. Mostly books, and a small trunk of personal "treasures"—botanical drawings, illustrations, my water colors, &c. There is the collection, of course, but that I am leaving with Lester until my return this fall. In spite of our differences at the moment, he is a good curator and will guard it, I am certain, with his life.

The visit with my parents, as I should have predicted, has been a mixed blessing. My mother is convinced that if I go to Montana she will never see me again. "Where is Montana?" she keeps muttering. "I don't even know where Montana is." Her mournful sighs sound not unlike the last *Sialia* of summer.

Father, the great supporter of Indian rights in the West, has kept our conversations focused on Native American vision quests, their use of medicinal plants, inter-tribal rivalries now that they are confined to the reservations, that sort of thing. His inquiries only fuel my mother's emotional fire, I fear.

Underneath all his apparent scientific interest in native peoples, and the feigned concern he shows my mother, I am certain my father is pleased about my plans. He has been, after all, supportive of my naturalizing from the very beginning. In fact, at one point he suggested shipping me off to England for schooling, hoping, I suppose, I would become a latter day Franz Bauer, while keeping the Bartram name alive and well in the annals of natural history. Or maybe he did not want to clean up any more of my early, admittedly foul, attempts at taxidermy. Regardless, I wish I would have known then what I know now. I would have jumped at the chance to study at Kew Gardens, and would have made my mother's life hell if she refused me the opportunity.

So, you see, this is my second chance at it. I know you, too, think this trip is foolhardy, and that I am putting my medical career (not to mention my personal life) at risk but, to be honest, I only pursued medicine to please my mother, who always dreamed of having a physician in the family.

You must believe me when I say that naturalizing is in my blood. I do not want to live—and die—a closet botanist in New York, sneaking out to the field only when it does not interfere with my so-called real work. You, of anyone, should understand that.

Besides, I want to match the best I have against the best the world has to offer before it is gone. That is what the West is all about, is it not? Why else would Meriwether Lewis have risked his life, and the lives of so many others, if not to be the first to witness—and to *understand*—that part of the natural world which was unknown at the time? The National Park is still such an enigma—at least in the scientific world. I want to be the one who helps the world better understand it. And understand it in context—not in some book or museum. It will be a true test of my own mettle.

So please do not think ill of me for taking advantage of this opportunity. I am not deserting my career; I am pursuing my life's work. Besides, it is only for four months. I can always pick up where I left off if I, too, decide at summer's end that leaving medicine is a mistake.

Now that you hopefully understand why it is essential that I "seize the day" as they say on campus, I have to confess that I, too, have my own reservations about the trip. Professor Merriam, the head of the expedition, has written to me making the grossest assumptions about the state of my botanical knowledge. He refers me to F. Pursh as if I have never heard of him and his work; suggests I may have somehow overlooked the *Mimulus Lewisii*, which he refers to as the monkeyflower. I can only hope that he does not presume to instruct me in the field, he who writes of the "compact petals" and "sensuous corolla lobes." I fear I may be joining a party of romantic old women revelling in their botanical gardens, rather than an expedition of practicing scientists.

Be that as it may, Professor Merriam can rejoice in his precious flowers "lilting along the creekbeds" all he wants as long as I am free to practice my own brand of science while being assured of the professional recognition afforded Smithsonian-endorsed field work. That stamp of approval, coupled with my other work to date, should help me establish a real career in botany, for which I so long! As for Merriam and the rest, I have never been one to feel constrained by the limitations (scientific or otherwise) of those around me, as you well know.

So I am off! If it is convenient, I can arrange for my books to be shipped directly to your Hudson Valley address. Or, if you prefer, I will leave them in your study at Cornell. In either event, please let me know as soon as possible as I will be returning to campus within the week. I will be leaving from Ithaca to avoid any last-minute scenes with my parents.

My best to Jonathan, Lester if you see him, and to your own dear family.

I remain, as always,

    most sincerely yours,

        Alex

Howard Merriam, Ph.D.
The Agricultural College
    of the State of Montana
Bozeman, Mont.
April 25, 1898

Dr. William Gleick
Smithsonian Institution
Washington, D.C.

Bill,

Well, I have sold my soul to the devil (or James Hill, depending on your point of view). I can only hope that neither calls for payment until this fall. In the meantime, I have put together the barest bones of an expedition, to include Andy Rutherford and Daniel Peacock, the best I could do, and have notified President Healey of our plans, promising we will all be back on campus in time to satisfy our fall teaching. How I do hope you can join us!

We will be met in the field by a young scientist from Cornell and, with any luck at all, by my benefactor there at the Smithsonian—Dr. Philip Aber. Do you know him? His area of specialty is the flora of the European alpine tundra but, with his appointment to the Smithsonian, he has developed an interest in western montane environments. He has been most generous in his support (in exchange for which we will provide him with specimens for his collection). It might do us both a world of good if you stopped in to see him while you are in Washington.

The other scientist, A. E. Bartram, has studied extensively the botanical discoveries of the Lewis and Clark expedition. He is also, I might add, a direct descendent of John and William Bartram. Needless to say, I am going to do all I can to keep him working in Montana beyond the summer months. Imagine: a Bartram working in the new herbarium!

Before I leave campus, I am doing my best to ensure that there will be a new research herbarium to appoint him to upon our return. Just yesterday I had an impassioned meeting with the president in which I turned his own argument against him. If we are to have a future in Montana, we must build for it, I told him. Picture the herbarium as a library, an educational resource from which all—students, faculty, and, yes, even administrators—will benefit, a place to house and catalogue our collections, study the intricacies of the plant kingdom, and teach our students about the natural world. There is no real separation between teaching and research, or at least there should not be, I argued, and to prove my point, I have invited two students to travel with the expedition— at their own expense, I might add—to enhance their education. I have no illusions. They are simply looking for a way to get out of working on their father's ranch over the summer, but needless to say I did not tell President Healey that. I even invited him to visit our camp to see real science in action.

I know he will never abandon the safe confines of this campus— he is far too busy stabbing his critics in the back and worrying about his "New Century" campaign—but I am not going to give up. I am an educator, after all, and believe in the power of education! We will spoon feed it to him if necessary, but by d——, he is going to learn the value of research.

Which brings me in a round-about-way to James Hill and friends. I have jumped into bed with Rutherford, the Anaconda Company, *and* Standard Oil, if you can imagine the aberrant offspring of that relationship! Gives you an idea of how desperate I am feeling these days.

Since you left, the local rag has been afire with the news that the railroads are petitioning Congress for right-of-way passage through the Park. Since the railroads rely primarily upon the goodwill and false hopes of those they can dupe into moving West— coupled with the propaganda of their sponsored research in western agriculture, I might add—they are desperate for good fare-paying opportunities. What better way than a direct route through Yellowstone National Park? Needless to say, this does not go over well with the nature seekers who want to experience the Park in all its pre-historic glory, without all the fury and fumes of Jim Hill's mechanical dynamo.

There is also much political posturing going on, depending on which journal you read on a regular basis, threatening the demise of the Park, the end of the natural world as we know it, that sort of *fin de siècle* doom and gloom. Sounds like a perfect fund-raising opportunity to me, or at least that is what I pointed out to our esteemed president.

Healey needs money for his new buildings, there is some vocal and even contentious opposition to naming those new buildings after Lewis and Clark, and I am pressing for a new research facility and herbarium, which will take a significant investment—more than Healey says he has or at least is willing to commit. Why not run over three birds with one locomotive and approach the railroads for support of all this new construction? Present it to them as a unique opportunity to purchase a little goodwill in the West, as it were. We could name the new buildings the Great Northern and the Northern Pacific which would immediately defuse the Lewis and Clark argument, and there just might be enough left over in the existing building fund to support my new facility. I would even be willing to name it Hill Hall—Hill Herbarium???—if I thought it would make a difference!

I fear I may have overdone it a bit. Healey was talking much too loud for a man of his size and tipping up and down on his toes, you know the way he does, but this time he looked more like a diver about to make a dangerous or maybe even fatal leap. Time will tell where he lands—and whether or not it is with a ripple, a splash, or just a dull thud.

Pray for me, my friend. My mother does so nightly but I do not think she has much influence with the darker side of life where I have taken to cavorting. And, please, say you will join us upon your return. As you can tell, I am skirting with danger and will need all the help I can get!

Yours faithfully,
Howard

A. E. Bartram
Livingston, Mont.
May 15, 1898

Dr. Lester King
Dept. of Biological Sciences
Cornell University
Ithaca, New York

Lester:

It has been a long but exhilarating journey. I am now stuck in Livingston, Montana, while my train awaits a private rail car from Chicago which will be joining us on our journey down the Paradise Valley and into the Park. Think of it: delayed, just this side of Paradise.

So far, my western adventure has proven to be a most eye-opening experience, of which I am certain you would approve. The railroad is indeed a stononiferous organism, sending its tentacles out across the country with wanton disregard for soil, climate, or water (there is none outside of the Missouri and Yellowstone Rivers and their thin web of tributaries as far as I can tell). Pity the poor families who follow this mechanical messiah so far from human habitation in search of the elusive promised land. I fear they will not find it in the West which, despite railroad proclamations to the contrary, is as unsuited to cultivation as any desert on earth. Lewis was right: it is "truly a desert barren country." You can see it in the landscape, which is dry and desolate, dominated by a large species of sagebrush (*Artemisia tridentata,* best I can tell; I have enclosed a specimen for your review). This one species is often the only sign of botanical life to be seen for miles. From time to time, I have spotted Lewis' cottonwoods in bloom down by small creekbeds that we have passed on our westward journey. They appear to be *Populus angustifolia,* but are difficult to identify at such a distance. They are, as Lewis described them, quite reviving just to look at in such dreary country.

By calling this a desert, for desert I am sure it will prove to be, I do not mean to suggest that it is devoid of life. Raptors circle high overhead like gulls following the wake of a ship, anxious for sight of rodents and other small mammals spooked by the train. Early this morning, I spotted a bald eagle (*Haliaeetus leucocephalus?*) and later a large golden raptor (I am assuming *Aquila chrysaëtos?*), feasting on a rabbit which had ventured too close to the rails. Eagles are easy to identify, if nothing else than by their sheer size, but most raptors are so similar looking to my untrained eye I am missing an opportunity to expand my natural history knowledge. So I have a favor to ask. If you have one, could you please send a field guide that includes bird silhouettes? Or perhaps you could check with the library on campus. Mrs. McGough might agree to lend me one on account until my return. In either event, I would be most grateful if you would assist me with my western education.

For an education it is proving to be. Yesterday, a young girl of ten or eleven, knowing of my interest, lured me to the back of the train to see a large herd of what she identified as big jack rabbits bounding through a field. Sadly, she had never seen an American Pronghorn (*Antilocapra americana*—interestingly not at all related to their African "cousins"), but then neither had I, except in books. We are indeed prisoners of our ignorance—and our urban lives. Just having the opportunity to see American species roaming free on their native land is enough to justify this trip as far as I am concerned.

I have not, however, spotted even one American buffalo (*Bison bison*—what a grand, double-barreled name for what was once a grand American beast!), but not for a lack of trying. All the way through Dakota and eastern Montana, I was forever poking my head from some window, scanning a landscape so vast and open I could almost detect the curve of the horizon silhouetted against the thin, western air. But not a sign of the beasts. This does not bode well for the twentieth century if indeed 60 million buffalo can be destroyed in one generation just to fuel man's fleeting sense of fashion and his ever-present greed.

My fellow passengers, having to contend with open windows and the perpetual sight of my behind (as opposed to my be-front), are quite certain I am a fool, and living proof that B. Franklin was right: beware of strangers who keep journals. Aside from the young girl who follows me everywhere, they all keep their distance. Even her parents. Their reservations (could it be fear?) were confirmed as I have spent this afternoon in Livingston not in the admittedly charming café which adjoins the station here, but walking the tracks, digging in the dirt, probing into any space that might support life in this rich, evocative land.

I have enclosed a handful of specimens for my collection. Common I know, but of interest to me because they appear to have established a symbiotic relationship of sorts with the railroad, thriving along the areas most disturbed by rails, rock, gravel, &c. When I crossed the road into an open pasture I found not a sign of them. It would be interesting indeed if the railroad, separate from the activities of man and the plow, proves to be the greatest harbinger of change when examining the evolution of flora and fauna of the West.

In any event, treat these specimens kindly. William Clark camped on this spot (or very near to it as far as I can tell), so even if they are not of any botanical or sociological interest, they do come from semi-sacred ground. Please care for them as if they were the rarest member of the Orchidaceae.

I must end now. The Livingston station master warns me that I should enjoy this brief respite of spring since I will be transported back to "six inches of winter" once we make our ascent into the Park. I hope he is wrong, since I am anxious to get to work, but will take the long way to the post office and enjoy the sun just in case. Livingston's weather, in spite of a cruel and unpredictable wind, feels so fine.

I hope you do, too.

Alex

Andrew Rutherford, Ph.D.
Mammoth Hot Springs
Yellowstone National Park
May 18, 1898

Dr. Robert Healey
President
The Agricultural College
    of the State of Montana
Bozeman, Mont.

President Healey:

Have established temporary camp outside Mammoth Hot Springs complex. Not much to report. Butte company commissioned to provide room & board. Miners, it must be noted, an undemanding lot. Immigrants & ruffians, willing to settle for broken-down cots, rough blankets, and ragged roofs over their heads, & be glad for it. Had I known I would be setting out in middle of snow field, sharing camp with Chinaman who speaks little English, mountain man who doesn't speak at all, & two layabout ranch hand kids, would have declined your generous offer. Even promised ag extension facility inadequate for summer spent in this primordial cesspool. Seen one bubbling cauldron, seen them all.

Have made my bed, so will lie in it. Lopsided as it is. Will need supplies to sustain me, however. Please forward following:

1. two heavy woolen blankets
2. tarpaulin
3. waterproof jacket large enough to fit over my top coat
4. pair of oiled boots
5. large brimmed felt wool hat

Josephson at Bozeman Mercantile knows my size. Will arrange for shipping. Rain gauge would help allay perpetual boredom. So would brandy. Prices at railroad-owned hotel reminiscent of your tales of highway robbery.

Little else to report. Merriam not wasting time. Mean temperature 46° & barometer falling. Little to do but wait out weather.

Fool that he is, Merriam has taken to horseback searching out warmer conditions—or greener pastures. A search futile as this excursion will prove to be. Could even be dangerous, given volume of snow in backcountry. If desperate, you might want to settle for demonstrable foolishness. Leave it at that. Save us all some misery.

Physician from Cornell to arrive on afternoon train. Once here, may break camp. If so, will notify of new address so provisions can be sent.

Sincerely yours,

A. B. Rutherford, Ph.D.

2. Lewisia rediviva

A. E. Bartram
National Hotel
Mammoth Hot Springs
Yellowstone National Park
May 20, 1898

My dear Jess,

Well, I made it. Or perhaps I should say I have *almost* made it. Sitting here next to the hotel fire, with my own room, fresh linens, and indoor facilities, it hardly feels like the promised rigors of field work, but I am in the Nation's Park, and oh what a wondrous place it is! My dear, dear Jessie, how I wish you could see it.

The hotel itself is quite respectable, much like you might find in any out-of-the-way railroad tourist destination, for that is what the Park has become, even though the railroads have miraculously been kept from within its borders. In spite of all the late spring snow, the hotel bustles with the comings and goings of adventurers, photographers, writers, families, foreigners—a cosmopolitan group indeed considering we are so far away from the rest of the world. Many, I am told, enter the Park as soon as the roads are passable, and spend up to six months a year in Mammoth, convinced that the Park's sulphurous waters can cure them of the most virulent diseases. One woman invited me to join her for a swim after breakfast, but I demurred. There will be ample opportunity to soak up the benefits of the Park's waters and other wonders before I leave. The last thing I need right now is for Professor Merriam and his colleagues to see me cavorting around in a snowbank dressed in my swimming costume. It would confirm their worst opinion I am sure.

For, yes, I believe the Professor and his friends are ill disposed to my joining their company at the moment. It started with the worst possible misunderstanding when I arrived at the Cinnabar station. My train was late, having been delayed in Livingston, so it was well after dark when I arrived. The road from the hotel into the Park can be treacherous even in the best of conditions, so it was arranged via telephone message that I would be met at the Cinnabar Hotel in the morning. As promised, a man did arrive first thing and inquired after a "Dr. Bartram." As the woman at the front desk shuffled through the registrations, I walked up to introduce myself.

"Professor Merriam?" I inquired. The man turned, looked down at me through the palest, most distant eyes I have ever encountered, and then promptly returned his attention to the hotel clerk. I should have had my wits about me and quietly returned to my seat, where I could have waited for the hotel clerk to point me out. But, you know me, I persisted.

I have to tell you that I was diminished by this beast of a man, for a beast he appeared to be, all bundled in hides and reeking so intensely of ill-tanned skins that his fetid odor all but dominated the small smoke-filled lobby. But am I deterred? Not in the least. I reasoned, as only I am capable of doing, that he must have just returned from a long stretch working in the field. So I persisted.

"Professor Merriam?" I asked again, holding out my hand in peaceful offering. "My name is Bartram."

Again those pale, hostile eyes scanned the room, before darting back to the hotel clerk. I looked at her, too, hoping, I suppose, for some sort of confirmation, but she avoided us both by shuffling her registrations, still looking for that elusive "Dr." Bartram. So again I persisted.

"Are you Professor Merriam?" I repeated, placing my ignored hand on the registration desk. Well, maybe I banged it on the desk a bit for emphasis, but I was trying to get his attention.

The man looked contemptuously in the direction of my hand, mumbled something like, "I ain't Merriam, and you ain't Bartram," and then he stalked out of the hotel, climbed into a wagon, and drove off. I am certain my mouth dropped open as I turned back to the woman at the front desk who, by now, had found my name in her shuffle.

"Dr. Bartram?" she asked. She, too, sounded incredulous. I assured her there was no physician in the house, promptly paid my bill, and checked out, catching the yellow stage into the Park, where I was met by yet another telephone message from the *real* Professor Merriam, who arranged to meet me at this second hotel later in the day.

For, yes, that was not Professor Merriam, but his hired hand, who had met me earlier in Cinnabar. It turns out, however, that I am not the *real* Dr. Bartram, either, for it seems that we have all suffered from a most unfortunate comedy of errors. That we should live to see the humor in all of this remains to be seen.

As I should have expected from his initial correspondence, Professor Merriam is not at all like the mountain man with matted hair and beard and stinking skins I initially took him for, but more like any member of the faculty you might encounter at Cornell: soft-spoken, attentive, neat and tidy in a befuddled sort of way, clearly more passionate about the common names of plants than the opposite sex—destined to break many a Montana matron's heart I am certain. That I could have mistaken his hairy, fur-clad assistant for Professor Merriam just goes to prove what a fool I am.

Unlike his driver, Professor Merriam was gentleman enough to accept my offered hand and to sit with me by the hotel fire, and, in spite of my written clarification to the contrary, he insisted on addressing me as "Dr. Bartram." After the usual niceties about the trip and the adequacies of the accommodations, Professor Merriam finally blurted out that he feared he had made a terrible mistake.

"I must apologize for my driver abandoning you at the station like that but you must understand that we were expecting . . ." He hesitated, and untangled himself from a long knitted scarf which he pooled in his lap.

"Well, I guess you could say we *weren't* expecting . . ." and again his voice trailed off. This time he busied himself wiping his spectacles on the scarf fringe, taking great care in both the cleansing and subsequent replacing of them upon his nose. His is a long, narrow nose, so perhaps spectacles are difficult to balance.

Finally he looked up, his eyes squinting as if to focus. He shook his head and removed his spectacles again, tipping them back and forth to catch the reflection of the fire in hopes of finding the speck of dust or lint which was impairing his vision. Still he said nothing.

"Whom were you expecting?" I finally asked. I wanted to tell him that William Bartram, if that was who he had in mind, had been dead for more than 75 years. His father, John, for well over a hundred. But as I thought through the actual number of years, it occurred to me.

"You were expecting a man?" I asked.

He blushed and mumbled, hurriedly replaced his spectacles, and then leaned toward me from his chair, squinting and staring so intently that I felt that I, too, might blush.

"Oh, Dr. Bartram, please do not misunderstand me," he said. "It's just that we simply cannot accommodate a woman. As it is, we're three or four men to a tent. We can barely accommodate ourselves. And in this weather . . . I don't know what to tell you."

I felt so sorry for him, mumbling and fumbling and smoothing his scarf, that I wanted to lean over, pat him on the knee, and tell him that I understood. But before I could act on that most primitive feminine instinct, I realized he was sitting there with the fire glistening off his spectacles, robbing me of my opportunity. My very next instinct, a much more rational one I might add, was to lean over and pull that scarf around his neck so tight that he would choke.

Don't worry. I did not do it. I did, however, tell him that I would not leave. He invited me and I am staying. He cannot get rid of me that easily. And I told him so.

He looked up again, bewildered, said he would see what he could do, encircled himself a few times with his scarf, looked again at me very closely, coughed a time or two, and then left. And that is the last I have seen or heard from him.

So I am waiting. And will wait, at least until I hear one way or another. Please do not breathe a word of this to anyone, particularly not to Lester who has taken to sympathizing with my mother over this misadventure as he calls it. And please do not worry. I will keep them all informed of my whereabouts, but I will keep the details necessarily vague. I will let them know about the rest when things are settled. One way or another, things will work out. They are bound to.

In the meantime, think positive thoughts! Looks like I will need them.

Alex

Howard Merriam
Mammoth Hot Springs
Yellowstone National Park
May 20, 1898

Dear Mother,

Remember that Dr. Bartram I wrote to you about? Well he has arrived. Only he is a she, and now I am at a complete loss as to what I should do. I am so woefully short of staff, I would embrace the worst laggard or miscreant the scientific world has to offer but, dear Mother, what am I to do with a woman? We already have a cook.

Bill Gleick wrote from Washington to warn me of her arrival. Unfortunately, his letter has just arrived. A day late and a dollar short, much like this entire expedition, I fear. Bill is in the Capital now and, as a courtesy to me, met with my contact at the Smithsonian. In the course of the conversation, Bill politely asked after this Dr. Bartram of whom I had written so enthusiastically. Philip Aber remembered her well, according to Bill. In fact, Aber apparently went out of his way to look her up while visiting Cornell.

Miss Bartram's credentials are impeccable, and her work, albeit that of an amateur, is well respected. She has published two papers on the Bartram collection under the deceptively androgynous name "A. E." Bartram—I still don't know her given name. She has also contributed to the Nation's collection—specimens and scientific illustrations at which she reportedly excels. Although Aber did not refer her to the expedition, Bill seemed to think Aber would recommend her if asked.

In her personage I can find no fault either. She is quiet, understated, and respectful, not at all the chatty old woman that the botanical field is wont to attract amongst the female sex. Even so, if she were to join us in the field, I fear the entire enterprise would be put at risk. Where would she sleep? With whom would she travel into the backcountry? And how could she possibly endure an entire season of collecting in such primitive conditions? I desperately need the manpower but . . . you see, even the language conspires against me.

And that is not to mention my driver. Straight from the mines in Butte, he "ain't gonna haul no women," he has made it perfectly clear. In fact, he even refused to transport her into the Park. As for the others, Peacock advised that I should take advantage of all the help I can get, but then he promptly disappeared, off scouting early hatches, while Rutherford contentedly sits by the fire, puffing on his pipe, mildly amused by my dilemma. But now that his new provisions have arrived from town, Rutherford appears to be mildly amused by everything. Even the weather.

And the weather is anything but amusing. Gusting and damp at one moment, cold, still, and snowy the next. I made the mistake of asking the driver when spring arrives in this part of the country and he looked at me with that vacuous look of his and grumbled something like "this is spring." Then he grumbled and growled some more (at the sky this time, or maybe it was at his dog) and staggered off to the hotel where he spends so much time soaking in the outdoor baths that he looks more and more like a boiled lobster every day. Hard to tell if his coloring is from the curative powers of the water or the degenerative powers of drink which he also generously partakes of at the hotel. A combination of both is my guess.

The driver is not the only one who wanders back to the campsite at all hours of the night. I foolishly made the mistake of inviting two students to join the expedition to prove my point that research and field work are the foundation of a scientific education. Now that they are safely established in the Park, and away from the watchful eye of their father, these two young men appear to be more interested in sniffing around the young blossoms arriving daily at the hotel, than uncovering any botanical discoveries. More than once I have heard the cook cursing them in Chinese as they tried to sneak into their shared tent well past midnight. I must say I cannot find too much fault in their harmless pursuit of amusement. At least not yet. Other than Peacock, we all have to sit and wait until the weather shifts.

In the meantime I am busying myself noting wildlife, of which there is a growing abundance in the Mammoth area (some elk have become so tame, they have taken up semi-permanent resi-

dence at the hotel where they are fed nightly by the hotel staff).
Saw my first pair of sandhill cranes down by the river. Also spied a
goshawk circling the field where we are camped, a sure sign that it
is warming—even if the thermometer and Rutherford both deny it.

By the way, I did not shoot anything. It is strictly forbidden in
the Park and the U.S. Cavalry is now fully in charge of the administration to ensure that all visitors respect these regulations. But
even if it were legal, I admit that I am losing the desire to add to
that part of my collection. Maybe it is the bleakness of this country, almost primeval, but I am beginning to see even a solitary raptor as an essential contributor to the fragile thread of life. I
certainly do not want to be the one to start it unraveling.

So you see, perhaps having excess time on my hands is not such
a bad thing after all. I may still be skeptical about God and his so-
called creation, but I am learning to see the world around me with
older and, hopefully, wiser eyes. That anything—hawk, man, or
beast—could survive in such a bleak and unforgiving land is truly
a miracle of evolution worthy of respect.

I hope you are well and it is warmer in California than it is here.
It must be.

Yours faithfully,
Howard

p.s. Miss Bartram is short and very slight of build so would not
eat much. Given our meagre provisions and the state of our finances, that would be an asset, I must admit.

———•◦•———

Alexandria Bartram
National Hotel
Mammoth Hot Springs
Yellowstone National Park
May 21, 1898

My dearest family,
I write to you, believe it or not, from Yellowstone National
Park. Mother, one sight of this place and you would understand

why I had to experience it for myself. It is as though I have travelled back in time, to the very edge of the universe, where the earth, still in its most primordial stage, sputters and bubbles and spews out the very origins of life.

That is not to imply that the modern day world has forsaken Yellowstone National Park. On the contrary. It is like a small city here, complete with post office, hospital, laundry, riding stables, barber, and a large barracks facility for the U.S. Cavalry which administers and patrols the Park.

The hotel where I am staying is a large, very modern tourist facility, conveniently located within walking distance from the boiling cauldron further up the road. There is a spacious lobby, dining room, even a ballroom, and hot and cold running water on every floor. My fellow lodgers, many of whom are women you will be relieved to know, entertain me over dinner with stories of their travels abroad or their mishaps in the Park. These women appear to be an adventurous lot, arriving before the six-day coupon tours commence, often travelling on their own or in small groups of like-minded souls, demanding equal time in the hot ponds, which are otherwise monopolized by the men.

When I tire of my dinner companions and their tales, I can retreat to the lobby with a cup of tea or a glass of English sherry, and enjoy a good book (right now I am reading a history of the Park written by the resident historian, another regular in the dining room). While sitting thus by the fire, a young pianist, knowing of my love of Schubert, selects his lobby repertoire as if to entertain me alone. I feel as though I have been transported to the wilds of New York City—not the wildest West.

If I long to view the Park's wildlife I have heard so much about, I simply step outside onto the verandah and there I am joined by more wildlife than I know what to do with. Just last night, for example, nineteen elk (*Cervus elaphus*) lingered on the cavalry's snow-covered parade grounds just outside the hotel, their moist, warm breath mingling with the steam from the hot springs behind them. It was a lovely sight, until I realized that these handsome and stately creatures have been reduced by habit and convenience to begging for handouts, a degradation encouraged by the hotel staff which throws out table scraps after dinner.

The Park's other persistent and virulent form of wildlife (a subspecies I have Linnaeanized *Homosapiens horribilis* but who are identified locally by their common names of Whiskey Jack, Lord Byron, Geyser Joe, Handful of Dollars, &c.) can also be viewed after dinner, congregating in or around the hot baths up the hill from the hotel, or in the hotel itself, caging drinks and entertaining guests with their tall tales. One claims to have fallen into Old Faithful only to be spit back out at Beehive Geyser miles away! Another told of how the birds in Mammoth drink so much hot water, they lay hard-boiled eggs.

"You watch for 'em, next time you're out there, little lady," one told me. "Hard as rocks those eggs are. Hard as rocks."

Not to be outdone, a third leaned over to a particularly gullible-looking young woman sitting next to me and warned her quite sincerely of the dangers of wading in Alum Creek.

"Why, it's so potent," he cautioned, "it turned my first set of horses into Shetland ponies, just by settin' foot in it," he said.

At this point the young woman's mother intervened, suggesting that if the creek were as powerful as he suggested, then the teller of the tale would no doubt benefit from soaking his head therein. Great laughter erupted amongst the group, but the storyteller had the last laugh when a large jar of beer appeared at his table not long after the mother and daughter returned to their rooms.

This natural ability to entertain and successfully beg, borrow, and steal from tourists must be yet another form of specialized western selection and adaptation, not unlike that demonstrated by the Park bears (*Ursus americanus, U. cinnamoneus,* and *U. horribilis* if you can imagine!), which have learned to rummage through the garbage dumped behind the hotel for their benefit—or, more likely, for the benefit of the hotel's guests. They have even learned to beg at the kitchen pantry door (I am referring now to *Ursus americanus,* not *Homosapiens touristii americanus!*) and take apples and other treats directly from the hands of fools (for only fools would be so foolhardy!).

Thoreau was right. We are at risk of civilizing our native species right off the face of the earth. We must all work to document this last wild place in America before it, too, is gone from us forever. If the fauna is so easily domesticated, can the flora be far behind?

It is unclear what accommodations will be made for me to join the scientific expedition, which has established a temporary camp outside of the Mammoth Hot Springs area. The organizer, Professor H. G. Merriam, is working out the details for my joining them now.

I think you both would like him. He is quiet and mild-mannered, so should be easy to work with. He also appears to worry a lot and to take his scientific calling seriously, in spite of his irritating penchant for common names. Father, you would be interested to know that the Professor spent three years teaching on the Crow Indian reservation where he apparently developed an appreciation of medical botany, primitive as it is. Like you, he is interested in native cultures and *Weltanschauung*.

His colleague, Andrew Rutherford, is a large, red-faced man who clearly enjoys the hotel and all it has to offer. I must admit I cannot imagine him enduring the rigors of field work, but perhaps he has another assignment in mind. An entomologist, Daniel Peacock, has left for the field, so I have not had an opportunity to meet him, but I have seen the expedition's two student assistants, with the unlikely names of Stony and Rocky Cave, who also spend their evenings at the hotel. They, too, seem serious in their pursuits. The group has hired a driver and cook from the mines in Butte so I am sure that even when they leave the luxuries of this part of the Park behind them, accommodations will be more than adequate.

As you can imagine, I am anxious to join them in the field, but it has been such a harsh winter, and cold, blustery spring with much snow still on the ground, that we cannot even begin to explore much less collect. In the meantime, I am determined to enjoy my warm room and the luxuries of the hotel, and to do my own exploring of the natural wonders of the Park. There will be time enough to "rough it" in the pursuit of science!

So you see, dear Mother, and Father, too, there is nothing whatsoever to worry about. I am warm, safe, and enjoying myself immensely.

I hope you are both well. I miss you, love you, and wish you were here!

Most affectionately,
    your loving daughter,
      Alexandria

                    Andrew Rutherford, Ph.D.
                    Mammoth Hot Springs
                    Yellowstone National Park.
                    May 21, 1898

Dr. Robert Healey
President
The Agricultural College
    of the State of Montana
Bozeman, Mont.

President Healey:

Dr. A. E. Bartram has officially arrived. Happy to report Bartram is a Miss. Not a physician. Not even doctor at that. Merriam prepared to send her packing. No female facilities. But she is not deterred.

My notes from the day:

8:55 a.m. Miss Selma Zwinger, lady naturalist and world traveller, arrives. Pitches small cavalry tent, cot, bedding, & camp stool with much ceremony on edge of clearing. Informs anyone who will listen (just me & Cookee in hearing range) that accommodations are for Dr. Bartram. As you know, my accommodations inadequate, but Butte miners live like princes & kings compared to average cavalryman if this gear any indication. Once all in place, Miss Z departs with equal flair.

10:20 a.m. Horse arrives. Delivered by Capt. Alexander Craighead from headquarters. Tall, handsome chap with large mustaches who claims keen devotion to botanical sciences. Stays for coffee, then leaves. No sign of Miss B.

12:05 p.m. Small bundle of poetry arrives, tucked inside fishing creel. Grey-beard transporting same identifies self as writer. Looks more like aging priest with long white locks and long black garb. Catches breath by fire, looks around for Miss B, then leaves.

1:45 p.m. Delivery wagon from nearby ranch arrives. Prime cuts of beef on ice. Cookee beside himself shouting in Chinese something about bears. Rancher driving wagon shares tobacco & whiskey. Makes me question value of higher education when even cowboys smoke & drink better than I do. Claims to know Park backcountry like back of hand. Offers his services. Says he could be valuable asset. Then leaves. Still no Miss B.

3:30 p.m. Female delegation arrives with kettle, ceramic pot & sandwiches. Make themselves at home. Brew tea, make small talk by fire. Expecting Miss B & will wait until she arrives. No sign of her. They are not deterred.

5:15 p.m. Miss B arrives. Dressed for parlors in Philly not campgrounds in Park. Long hair neatly pinned. Boots shiny. The two louts lug gear. First work I've seen out of them since we arrived. Accommodations do not phase Miss B. Stacks books, travel case, equipment alongside tent. Will not fit inside. Miss B smiles & sips cold tea as if laced with fine brandy. One night in this weather will dampen good humor is my prediction.

6:00 p.m. Young women leave as Merriam arrives. Spies horse hobbled behind Miss B's tent. Wants to know who will feed it.

7:00 p.m. Merriam paces all night. Can't sit still. Even at dinner. Young louts devour steaks. Miss B joins us at table, but says little except to Cookee who she compliments in Chinese after dinner. First time I've seen him smile. Has solid gold tooth. Right in front.

8:00 p.m. Miss B borrows candle from Cookee, says goodnight to anyone who'll listen, crawls into tent. Merriam walks. Louts sneak into town. I stay put. Too much snow & mud, even if brandy at hotel far superior to what you've supplied.

Tell Little Allen at tobacconist on Main to send month's supply of usual. Same address for now. Put it on my account. Send better brandy. Put that on yours.

 Sincerely &c,
  Andrew Rutherford, Ph.D.

 8:30 a.m. Merriam & I breakfast alone. Louts sleep in. Miss B, horse, gone by time we're up.

———◆———

A. E. Bartram
Mammoth Hot Springs
Yellowstone National Park
May 22, 1898

Lester King
Dept. of Biological Sciences
Cornell University
Ithaca, N.Y.

Dear Lester:
 Please send a field guide or other materials on montane mosses. They thrive adjacent to the hot springs and I am assuming they do equally well in spring snowbeds which are beginning to thaw. There are a number of brightly colored lichens, too, about which I am woefully under educated. Please, please send references.
 Alex

 p.s. I am so happy!

———◆———

Howard Merriam
Mammoth Hot Springs
Yellowstone National Park
May 23, 1898

Dear Mother,
 You will be relieved to learn that I have not turned Miss Bartram away as planned, and that she is now fully ensconced into

our camp, with her own tent, bedding, and other feminine necessities delivered (without any charge!) by a woman naturalist who considers herself a patron of the sciences. This leaves me little choice but to accept Miss Bartram's presence and welcome her into our group. It would be unethical and, I dare say, unwise at this point to do otherwise.

Miss Bartram has been most gracious in accepting my generosity, and has settled in with little ceremony and even less disruption to our lives. She has even been considerate enough, given our meagre provisions, to return the horse delivered for her use, claiming it would prove to be an inconvenience, and that she prefers to walk to her destinations.

So far, she has spent most of the daylight hours away from camp, systematically collecting moss, lichens, grasses, anything growing this early in and around the hot springs adjacent to the hotel. When wading in the warm, murky waters she does not appear to be in the least bit hampered by her skirts, which she keeps hitched up around her knees in a most efficient-like manner. In the evenings, she works by lantern light copying her field notes and initiating her illustrations which have a precise, albeit feminine, quality. Copies and duplicate specimens she shares with Rutherford who, she apparently assumes, is the expedition's record keeper. He appears to revel in the assignment, and has taken to keeping his own daily journal and weather book.

While at the hotel, Miss Bartram made a number of friends and acquaintances, many of whom now make a regular pilgrimage to the hot springs area, travelling up the hill in shifts to deliver tea, sandwiches, and gossip from the hotel by day, and to our camp to monitor Miss Bartram's progress each night. Although she is most gracious to all, she is a tireless worker and does not appear to enjoy the constant interruptions.

Last night at dinner, she mentioned to Rutherford that she is thinking of moving further up the valley and following some streambeds off the main road. Of course, I can never allow her to break camp on her own. For one thing, there is too much danger for a woman, with the bears and the vagabonds and the uncertain weather. There will be plenty of opportunity to venture into the backcountry when we will all be there to protect her. Besides, my plan is to maintain a systematic methodology when collecting, an approach which requires us all to work in one well-defined area at a time. We are a party now and must stick together in all that we do.

Even though she claims to be anxious to venture further into the field, once we do break camp here I am certain Miss Bartram will miss the companionship of other women. I think Rutherford will miss them, too. Even the Cave brothers, the two students who are travelling with us, have taken to spending more evenings in camp than away from it now that we have female company.

The only one in our party who will not miss the constant flow of feminine visitors is Jake Packard, our Butte driver and guide. He and his dog have made their own camp on Beaver Creek, refusing to join us even for meals. I am to get a message to him at the hotel when we are ready to move camp. Otherwise, he has made it clear he wants nothing whatsoever to do with us.

The weather is warming considerably and, thanks to a west wind last night, the clearing around our campground is now completely free of snow. Rutherford complains bitterly about the mud, but then Rutherford will always find something about which to complain. I see the changing conditions as a sign we will be working soon. I am ready to get started.

I will keep your advice about Miss Bartram in mind, whose name, by the way, is Alexandria Elisabeth although she refers to herself as Alex. I doubt that she will last the month, particularly when faced with leaving the conveniences and conviviality of the hotel. However, while she is my guest here, I will do my utmost to be considerate of her and her special needs.

Love,

Howard

A. E. Bartram
Mammoth Hot Springs
Yellowstone National Park
May 27, 1898

Jess!

I am settled, working, and, as promised, writing to keep you informed of my where-abouts and my what-abouts. Thanks to one of the world travellers I met at the hotel, a Miss Zwinger by name, I am now comfortably accommodated in Professor Merriam's camp just outside of Mammoth Hot Springs. I have a lovely cavalry tent all to myself, into which I crawl at night feeling quite privileged and pampered, since the rest of the party, even the Professor, is forced by limited funds and facilities to share. I feared that my special privileges would alienate the rest of the party but, with one exception which I will reveal momentarily (just as he has revealed himself to me!), they have been quite gracious about my good fortune and have welcomed me into their group as if they were expecting me all along.

Professor Merriam has been most accommodating. As long as I cost him little or nothing, keep to myself, and do not bother or talk to him, he appears content to leave me to my own resources, since planning and administration consume most of his attention right now. He spends a good deal of time in the Park headquarters and at the hotel, so I have very little interaction with him anyway. In his absence, I will do my utmost to earn his respect and scientific admiration.

Andrew Rutherford, on the other hand, has a private reserve of some foul-smelling alcohol, reminiscent of the earliest preservatives we used to work with in the laboratory, so he does not bother to leave the confines of the camp. Instead, claiming the weather is either too cold, too wet, too windy, the ground too muddy or too snowy, or the barometer or thermometer threatening one of the above, he keeps to the fire. Instead of venturing into the elements, or simply touring some of the marvels of this place, he has generously offered to catalogue and maintain my contributions to the expedition collection. Or at least he will manage them until field conditions improve and he can begin the collection process himself, something he insists he is planning to do eventually.

Dr. Rutherford is an agriculturist by training—a villein who failed at farming his family's land, due to the vagaries of poor weather and probably poor management given what he has revealed about himself so far. Instead, Dr. Rutherford has pursued this alternative profession in academics with a passion, hoping, I assume, that young prospective farmers and ranchers might learn from his mistakes. I cannot help but believe that the same passion might have saved his family's farm, but he now sees his future tied to his western agricultural students. Their success apparently will be enough for him.

However, even if he lacks the temperament for applied economic botany, he has survived the mental molding which accompanies a graduate education and has, in the process, developed some quality academic skills. He is a quick learner, and follows my studies and the illustrations of my small discoveries with great attentiveness and interest.

Daniel Peacock, the entomologist, has made one brief appearance, returning from the field only long enough to safely store his collection of bugs (which Dr. Rutherford reluctantly has agreed to curate), restock his provisions, and catalogue a stash of trout, which he then stuffed with *Allium cernuum* (or possibly *A. Schoenoprasum*—they must taste very much the same) and grilled on wooden racks woven specially for the purpose. The sweet taste of onion is particularly inviting, and enhances the smoky flavor of the fish. I think we all secretly look forward to another visit from Dr. Peacock and a respite from the Chinese cook's adequate but unimaginative fare.

Unfortunately, Dr. Peacock did not stay long enough for me to learn much about his studies. Our campground has turned into quite a social place, and he appears adverse to any socialization. I must admit that I, too, weary of the constant interruptions, although it is certainly flattering to have so many express an interest in me and my work. We will be breaking camp soon and I am certain the visitations will cease. It is one thing for visitors to walk down the road from the hotel at tea time in the name of science, but quite another to travel miles into the backcountry without the aid of roads or guides. As for me, there will be time enough at the end of the season to discuss my work, when I have something worthy of sharing.

That is not to say I have not started collecting. I have. The hot springs area above the hotel is a diverse landscape of multi-leveled terraces of hot water falls, steamy semi-circular pools of red and green and yellow, and singular underground springs which percolate from the earth like a pot put on the fire to boil. The water carries with it a milky-white substance of calcium carbonate and, when it shifts or retreats, it leaves behind strangely formed travertine aprons and solitary projectiles some as high as thirty or forty feet.

Hayden, or more likely one of his party with poor eyesight or a vivid imagination, dubbed one such travertine cone the Liberty Cap, after the hats worn during the revolutionary war. The name has stuck, but I will admit to you alone that it looks more like a 40-foot phallus than any hat even the most outrageous revolutionary would place on his head. I find it greatly amusing that the women staying at the hotel cluster below the projectile to have their photographs taken. For liberty, or at least that is what they say.

The Liberty Cap is at the base of the hot springs area where I walk each day in search of specimens. As you can imagine, the sulphurous water is deadly to animal and plant life (pale white tree skeletons stand like sentries marking where the water once engulfed them before retreating), but even in such poisonous and dangerous conditions, much richness and diversity of life is beginning to reveal itself in the land adjacent to the hot pools. I could spend the entire season just chronicling the emerging flora, as it adapts to changing conditions. Because the water and, thus, the land, shifts and moves unpredictably, sometimes as often as day-to-day, it is reminiscent of the beginning of the earth. Or maybe the end. If ever I am to understand the plant kingdom in all of its complexity, and truly internalize the lessons Darwin had to teach us all, it is here, where all of creation constantly changes and struggles to adapt and survive. Even me. Which brings me back, in a stumble-down sort of way, to the Liberty Cap.

Yesterday, on just such an exploration, I ventured west from the Mammoth main terrace, and passed a large, round, mountainous deposit of travertine and slowly moving water streaked and mottled with an oozing amber and orange. As I walked past the mound, I spotted something growing next to a tree below me, so I cautiously left the path and ventured toward it. The air was preternaturally still and, other than the constant bubbling and boiling noises, there were no other sounds. The earth's crust is thin and unstable throughout this area, so I was focused more on the ground immediately in front of me, with my concentration only briefly interrupted by the occasional squawk of a solitary *Pica pica*, a cry which is in itself unsettling.

As I cautiously crept down the last six or seven feet toward the prize, my foot slipped on an unstable rock or bit of loose sand, and I went tumbling down a steep incline toward Bath Lake. I could not have choreographed it better. After skidding and scraping my left side against a fallen tree, I bounced once into a sheltered snowbank and landed miraculously at the foot of the expedition's mountain man driver just as he had slipped out of his buffalo and elk skins, but before he had had an opportunity to slip himself into the water. Now it is customary, I am told by my companions at the hotel, that when women wish to swim in the bathing lake they throw rocks ahead of them to warn of their imminent arrival. I took this quaint custom to new heights. I threw myself!

It must be said that the gentleman in question appears to have a phobia about women. As I may have told you, he refused to transport me into the Park from the Cinnabar station and has declined to re-enter our camp since my arrival. I suppose if I had screamed, or fainted, or cried with shame at my dilemma, his worst suspicions about entertaining a woman in the party would have been confirmed, but at least his world view would have been left intact. I am afraid I looked up at him in all his glory with a total lack of interest, at that particular moment more concerned with the specimen I had missed further up the hill. This only added insult to injury and I am sure will do little to improve our relationship. I can only hope I do not run (or fall!) into him again for a while.

Once I limped back into camp, Kim Li, the Chinese cook hired for the field study, provided some foul-smelling botanical salve for the scrape on my knee and thigh. Not wanting to offend him, I thoroughly washed the affected area and lightly applied his medicine. This may be more a case of performing the proper procedures followed by a folk remedy which can do little or no harm, but I am happy to report that both physician and patient are more than satisfied with the almost immediate healing results. If only Kim Li could deliver a similar potion to calm the savage breast, if not soothe the bruised pride, of my new buckskinned friend.

Until he heals, or at least for the next few days, I think I will avoid the hot springs area altogether and, after delivering this letter to the post office in the cavalry complex, will proceed down the Gardner River. Although pockets of deep snow still lie in most of the protected areas, I am told that *Ovis canadensis* populate the cliffs above the river. Once we hit open land, there may not be another opportunity to view bighorns or any other cliff dwellers, so will walk along the river while I have the chance. And you never know. The Gardner is wide and marshy in places, so might even see an *Alces alces*. I have seen them on several occasions in New England, but to see them here in the West, and in the Wild, would be a most wondrous sight. And I will not give up on the *B. bison*. They have not all been destroyed, I am told. You just have to know where to look for them.

If you see Lester, please tell him I am fine and will be sending packages of specimens soon. He has kindly forwarded a travelling library which should prove to be immensely helpful once in the backcountry.

I hope this letter finds you as well and happy there as I am here.

Yours most faithfully,

Alex

Dr. Philip Aber
National Hotel
Mammoth Hot Springs
Yellowstone Park, Wyo.
May 28, 1898

Mrs. Philip Aber
Dupont Circle
Washington
District of Columbia

My dearest love,

How happy I was to find your letter waiting for me upon my arrival, the sweetness of your hand bringing you so close to me here, even though I am so far from you and our dear, dear children. Imagine, then, my disappointment that not a word was written about joining me here. How I do hope, my darling, that you have not reconsidered. I think you will find the destination well worth the journey, and not too overwhelming, even for the children, if your mother and dear, sweet sister agree to accompany you. Of course, I shall accommodate them here as if they were my own family, which, of course, I consider them to be.

I have rented for a month a suite of rooms at the Lake Hotel, commencing the first of June. Although the hotel is not officially open for commerce until then, my instruments are being unpacked there as I write. Our rooms overlook Yellowstone Lake, a wide placid expanse over which the sun rises each morning and sets at the end of the day. With my laboratory situated next to our living areas, I will never have to leave your side and we can watch the sun and moon circle us without a care in the world. The children can play on the shore of the lake, and when the weather is particularly fair, we can spend the afternoon touring the Park's thermal wonders. The children will marvel, as I have, at the geysers and deep, boiling pools. But marvel as I do, I cannot enjoy them without you, my better half, my eyes on the world, my life, my love. I do hope you are proceeding as planned for I so need you by my side.

I am quite certain you will enjoy your stay here. The fellowship and civility of the Park hotels will remind you of our years in Europe and of the many world travellers we have met on our own journeys before the blessed arrival of the children. Since my own arrival here I have met an Englishman about to embark on a walking tour of the Park; a group of lady naturalists who, I must admit, would no doubt bore you with their incessant chatter at dinner about a world far in excess of their naturalizing abilities; an accountant from Wyoming who is cycling through the Park with a club of like-minded individuals; a Chicago journalist who is in the Park to write about the planned rail expansion, travelling, I might add, at the expense of the railroad!; and an aging poet and naturalist by the name of John Wylloe, of whom you may have heard. The ladies inform me he is a close friend of T. Roosevelt, and much admired by nature lovers from around the world.

Yesterday morning I breakfasted with an engineer from Helena, Mont. who is negotiating a U.S. Government lease to develop a commercial elevator to carry visitors from the top of the Grand Canyon of the Yellowstone River to the Canyon floor some 1,000 feet below. This awe-inspiring engineering feat, it is widely believed, will prevent the more foolish of the world from descending the canyon walls on their own volition, an act which has resulted in more than one body tumbling to an untimely death on the rocky crags below.

Just this morning I accompanied my mealtime companion to witness for myself the power of the gorge which, even I must admit, does present the viewer with a powerful attraction. Without thinking, I found myself clambering out onto a rock outcropping to better witness the river at the falls, since a light but persistent rain was obscuring my view. As I ventured to my desired outpost, a dreadful wind whirled around me, transforming each drop of rain into a small pellet which flailed against my face. I stood there stunned, by the wind, the rain, the vastness of the chasm stretched out before me, fully and calmly understanding how easy it would be to hurl myself into the crevice below. You see the effect even a short separation has on me. I am not myself without you.

My dear, dear, darling, you must join me at the earliest possible moment. I have a professional commitment to remain here long enough to set up operations and yet I cannot face another day here without you. Please send word that you are on your way or I really shall hurl myself into the next rocky abyss.

My love to your mother, your sister, and our dear children. And most of all, my love to you, my darling, my pet.

Your devoted servant,
　　Philip

———◆———

Andrew Rutherford, Ph.D.
Mammoth Hot Springs
Yellowstone National Park
56° noon; .19″ precip 24 hrs.
May 28, 1898

Robert Healey
President
The Agricultural College
　of the State of Montana
Bozeman, Mont.

President Healey:

Exciting a.m. in camp. Dr. M & our Miss B leave camp for pts unknown. She in search of flower growing on rocky slope, he allegedly to protect her. Neither returned by end of day.

Can't find drunken driver to bring them back, no sign of Peacock for days, & cyclists in residence already off to beat weather. Have enlisted help of rancher who sent her on quest to begin with.

Two nights ago, bearing steaks for layabout louts, rancher claims to have seen emerging bitterroot, flower of great interest to our Miss B. Rancher offers transport & expert guiding. Miss B smiles, asks a few questions, declines. Next morning before breakfast both she & field bag gone. Weather from north. Rain imminent.

Prof. in real fury over breakfast. Sets out to find her. Now both gone. When rancher arrives this a.m. with more beef for camp, raining steadily. Learns of our Miss B's departure. Gallops to rescue.

Capt. arrives with government-sanctioned rain gear minutes later. Learns of our missing Miss B. Now U.S. Cavalry in act. No doubt two arguing at this minute in pouring rain who will sweep Miss B off feet & onto trusty steed. Both read too many poems by that philosophical grey-beard who hangs around hotel bar. Still, good to have more than one on look out just in case. Weather could turn for worse in less than moment's &c. This is spring, I remind both rescuers as they gallop out of sight.

Scheduled to move camp later in week. Entire Cody, Wyo., bicycling club now camped in our clearing. Englishman determined to walk grand loop through Park in record time threatening to join us as well. Lady naturalists in daily attendance. Not to mention mealtime visitors, like Capt., for coffee in morning, and rancher with Montana steaks at night. Philip Aber, from Smithsonian, lurking around camp asking lots of irritating questions, day & night.

Too many interruptions to suit the Prof. Too much attention for our Miss B.

Yours,

A.R.

p.s. Brandy supplies running low. Replenish c/o hotel in Mammoth. Will send louts to retrieve & to forward new address when have one.

———— ❖ ————

A. E. Bartram
Mammoth Hot Springs
Yellowstone National Park
May 31, 1898

My dear, dear Jess,

I have just returned from my first, genuine Yellowstone field experience and can honestly say that these are the days for which I have been living. Not that they have gone as planned, of course, but then one should almost plan for the unexpected upon entering the field. There are so many things that can go wrong. But, oh, there is so much that can go right!

First the right. Knowing of my interest, a local rancher who was dining with us mentioned a south-facing slope where I would find *L. rediviva* beginning to flower. It seemed too good to be true, particularly with the weather being as it has been, but just in case I took note of the location, and decided the next morning to set out on foot to see if I could find the place he described, if not the plant in question.

As I have mentioned before, Professor Merriam may be resistant to my presence in his group but he accommodates me because I do not ask anything of him nor do I bother him with the details of my comings and goings. So on this particular morning, I set out unannounced at daybreak, with a small provision for my day's meals kindly provided by the Chinese cook, Kim Li. I also carried my field journal, a handbook, my field lens, pencils, paints and brushes, and a small jar of water. And, even though the weather was particularly fine that morning, I took the simple precaution of packing a coat. I did not want to offend Dr. Rutherford who had warned at dinner of an imminent change in the weather, and this time he seemed convinced that he was right. Had I known I was not to be alone on my quest, perhaps I would have been better prepared.

By the time I reached the head of the trail leaving our camp's clearing, the sun was beginning to warm the sky into the truest, palest blue, not unlike the first spring blooms of *Myosotis*. I shall never forget it, not the blue, not the warmth, not the feeling of freedom of being out on my own, and certainly not what followed.

As I headed up the mountainous incline, a dozen large white handkerchiefs or flags ascended over the horizon, glistening in the early morning sun. Then, just as miraculously, they descended, like a signal of distress or a sacred ceremony which employs scarves with great finesse. I stood spellbound as the flags rose again, in total rehearsed uniformity, flickered for a moment, and then collapsed upon themselves behind the ridge. I watched from the trail as the strange morning ritual fluttered again and again against the high horizon, the white of the flags iridescent in the morning light.

Thinking I might catch the performers, or at least witness the activity at closer range, I hurried up the trail toward the spectacle, just as the handkerchiefs or flags or scarves waved at me one final time, retreated behind the ridge, and then were released in unison into the wakening sky, where they fluttered, rose, and formed a perfect V shape directly over my head. They circled once, bright white, then grey, then white again in the sun, and were gone.

Jessie, in all of my admittedly limited work in the field, I have never experienced anything like this. I can say, quite truthfully, that coupled with my hurried ascent up the trail, and the genuine confusion as to the nature of what I was witnessing, the sight took my breath away. But more importantly, it filled me with a sense of wonder which, as a naturalist, I had yet to experience. In his *Voyage of the Beagle*, Darwin wrote that "the day passed delightfully" but then he goes on to say that delight is a weak term to express the feelings of a naturalist who, for the first time, has been wandering by himself (or herself!) in a forest. Darwin's forest was in Brazil. Mine is closer to home. But that overwhelming feeling must be very similar, and not unlike what primitive believers must experience when overcome with what they believe to be God, but which, at least for me, is the first and full appreciation of the wonders of the real, physical, living, breathing world. It is that moment in a naturalist's life, and we are all naturalists if we open our eyes, when the curtain lifts around us, and it is good, so good, to be alive.

Of course, you know, with your extensive knowledge of these things, that what I saw was not made by man nor God, but exquisitely made by natural selection: *Pelecanus erythrorhynchos*. Lewis encountered five thousand of these birds clustered together on a sandbank in the Missouri River and he shot one to take home as a specimen. Can you imagine the sight alongside the river when his shot rang out and 4,999 white pelicans rose in unison overhead? It must have been rapture. Pure rapture.

I have since learned from Dr. Peacock that pelicans soar on the warm, rising air which carries them over the mountain ridges as they migrate into the Nation's Park. But this is one time, at least for me, when the ability to identify and classify the experience is simply not enough. Understanding the science enhances but does not replace what I witnessed that morning. Finally, I have internalized what I have sensed all along but did not fully understand: that I need to experience the natural world in its context, not in a book, not in a laboratory, not under a microscope. That is not science, but mere learning.

With my "pelican epiphany" behind me, I climbed easily past the first rocky ridge and, with a lightness of heart and step, maneuvered over, through, and around pockets of crusty snow which still obscured parts of the trail, particularly in the sheltered areas. At the crest, I walked out onto a mountainous basin, which was surprisingly like our dinnertime visitor had described it. I confess that I have ignored this rancher for most of my stay here, thinking he had little to contribute to my work. I cannot even tell you his name. Yet in spite of the fact that he makes his living raising and slaughtering meat for Park visitors, he clearly has the time and inclination to be an excellent observer—even in these backcountry environments where there is nothing financial to be gained. I will listen more intently to his stories in the future.

The sky overhead was clear, the air cool but warming, and there was no wind, so I assumed I had plenty of time before the heavy, grey clouds threatening to the west and north would become a problem. I climbed to a ledge where a large boulder provided an expansive view and as I settled myself onto my rocky throne, there, at my foot where I could have easily crushed it, was a solitary *L. rediviva* just beginning to open to the morning sun. At first glance it was, as Nuttall described it, low-growing and cactus-like. On closer examination, however, the *L. rediviva* revealed itself to be so much more—a perfect and quite unique 1½ inches of pale blush of rose, borne atop a leafless scape.

Without hesitation or deference to scientific protocol, I unsheathed my knife, cut the plant from the ground—easy to do given the gravelly conditions—and removed a thin, two-inch root, not at all the thick, fleshy tuber I was expecting. Of course, even in its premature state, I had to sample what the Indians consider a sacred and sustaining food. Just like Lewis before me, I found it "quite nauseous to my palate." I fear I would have to be near starvation before I would resort to any such sustenance. But then Indians collect the root before the plant flowers, when the roots of mature plants are thick and starchy, and the periderm reportedly easy to remove. Perhaps then the plant is more palatable and "reviving."

Regardless, the very same plant was there in my hand, full of potential life, just as it had been in the hand of Meriwether Lewis on his journey and, after shipping said specimen east, just as it had been in the hand of the seed merchant McMahon who had detected signs of new growth on the fully dried specimen, the same specimen which had been tipped more than once into the river and stored in its cross-country journey in less than ideal conditions (Lewis was a fine naturalist but having worked with his collection in Philadelphia, I can assure you he was not well equipped to preserve botanical specimens).

McMahon, sensing life in what should have been a long-ago dead and stored specimen, planted the root, and watched as it proceeded to grow—thus, *rediviva* or coming back to life. The plant grew but never flowered, and eventually perished in the hothouse climate of Philadelphia, which lacks the dry, inhospitable conditions this highly specialized plant needs to survive. I was so overcome by the richness of the story resonating in that slip of a plant in my hand that I was tempted to hold it high over my head, an offering to the sun, to somehow appease the gods of botany for taking a lone specimen in the field. You can see what is happening to me here. I am losing all sense of scientific protocol.

I then recalled that Professor Merriam mentioned at dinner that it is native custom to place a small bead or token in the hole of the first root taken each season, so I cut a button from my sleeve and planted it like a pearly seed into the ground where the plant had once been. I may not have found the root to be palatable sustenance, but with it there in my hand I was feeling quite revived.

Until, that is, I saw someone ascending the trail down below me.

At the time, I could not tell who it was, only that he was clearly headed in my direction. I quickly slipped the plant, root and all, into my field journal and climbed higher yet onto the ledge, slipping myself behind a large outcropping of rock. It was not until the visitor crossed into the basin that I recognized Professor Merriam.

I know now, as I am the first to admit that I knew then, that I should have declared my presence, but I was not yet ready to surrender the day to another's company, nor was I ready to return to camp with the possibility of more *L. rediviva* awaiting. So I did something very foolish. I simply watched as the Professor crossed the basin and entered a forested area to the south of me, and then I skirted the ridge above him, travelling across another open basin to the west. Considering the consequences of my selfish actions, I can make no excuses, but it seemed to me at the time that if Professor Merriam insisted on leaving me to my own devices, then I should leave the Professor to his.

On the next ridge I discovered a cluster of six more *L. rediviva*, which I decided to illustrate in their relationship to each other and their surroundings before removing specimens. This was my second mistake because, as I sketched, I was so concentrated on my work that I lost both sense of time and all sense of the weather. The sky blackened, but it only intensified the pale rose color of the flowers against the grey rock. The temperature dropped dramatically, and yet that, too, only served to heighten the seeming frailty of the plant and challenge my limited ability to adequately illustrate what I saw before me. I pulled on my coat and tried again to fully capture the delicate stamens which, even without my hand lens, were visibly quivering in the wind.

And then the snow started, light flakes which at first just fluttered through the sky and melted, but soon fell heavier and wetter in my hair and face and eyes and onto my journal where each wet flake pooled and then puckered the porous paper. I pulled my journal closer to me on my lap and gathered my coat around it, trying to position myself between the plants, the journal, and the snow and the wind, but still the snow fell whiter, colder, soon obscuring the plants in a heavy, wet blanket.

Knowing I could not delay my return to camp any longer, I brushed the snow away from one flower and, with my knife, proceeded to dig out the root. The soil here was also gravelly, and surprisingly dry, but the plant was well established, and I scraped and scraped at the rocks until the knuckles on my right hand began to bleed. I remember thinking as I dug that you would have to be starving indeed to work so hard for a plant which tasted so foul. But then maybe the natives are as determined in their pursuit of survival as I was at that moment in the pursuit of my science.

In fact, I was so focused on my task that even though my name was being spoken, it was as if it were coming to me from far away, or from somewhere else altogether. I did not really hear it.

"Miss Bartram," the distant voice called again.

Only then did I look up from my digging to discover that the basin below me had been transformed from a rocky, barren expanse into a soft sea of white through which a solitary figure trudged.

"Miss Bartram," the voice insisted. It sounded closer now. And familiar. "I have been looking for you everywhere."

Professor Merriam looked terrible, soaked through, with snow clumping on his hat and along the shoulders of his thin woolen coat. Even that ratty old scarf of his appeared to be of little help in keeping out the cold, but still he held it tight against his throat with one red hand, while the other hand was thrust deep into a pocket for whatever damp warmth it could provide. Without the mobility of his arms, he stumbled up the incline unable to even catch himself if he fell, which he did right before he reached me.

I offered to help him to his feet, but he ignored me, righting himself before roughly brushing the snow from his jacket and hat and hands. It was then that he really looked at me, maybe for the first time. I know it was the first time I really looked at him, for I realized then that he was not nearly as old nor as tall as I had once believed, but smaller, younger, not unlike Meriwether Lewis himself with his distant, almost sad eyes, and pallid complexion which was made even more vulnerable looking by the wet and cold. I am sure I did not look much better, my hair and face and clothes dripping with snow. I smiled at him which, I fear, only made a bad situation much worse.

"Miss Bartram, can't you see what's happening here?" The color momentarily returned to the Professor's face and eyes. "You're putting yourself, and me, in fact our entire enterprise at risk. You must return to camp immediately." And then, noticing my hands, he cried, "And look at you. You're bleeding."

Now I admit to you, as I would never admit to him, that the weather was indeed bleak. But the day was still young, and there seemed to be plenty of time to complete my task, and still return to camp before dark. As for the scrapes on my hand, they were a minor inconvenience, although they looked much worse, dramatically marking the snow with drips of blood. Still, he had no right to talk to me in that fashion. And I told him so. I would finish gathering my samples, and then I would be happy to catch up with him once I was ready to go.

This suggestion did not go over well. He insisted that I leave at that moment, in his company, and to expedite our departure he ripped the blossoms from their snowy bed and discarded them in his pocket.

"Now let's go," he said, handing me his handkerchief for my hand, "before the weather gets any worse."

I suppose I could have let him go on without me, but at that point there was no reason to do so. Besides, the weather was deepening and there did not seem to be much point in arguing about it. So, like a naughty child, I trailed behind him as he descended the ridge and headed out toward the forested area from where he had just emerged. It was there that I did resist, knowing that we needed to proceed parallel across the basin, and then down, if we were to find the trail which would lead us back toward our camp in the Mammoth area.

"No, it's this way," he insisted. "We're going down the way we came."

Now as I am sure you can imagine, I was hardly in the position to inform him that I had seen the way he had travelled, and it was from the opposite direction, so I did my best arguing for the way I had entered the basin, which was along the side of the ridge, not directly down it. But he was not interested in my route. We were going his way, and there was to be no discussion about it. So meekly I followed, feeling guilty and foolish, but simmering, too, at the way I was being treated. Yes, I did get myself into this weather, but I was quite capable of getting myself out from it. Which was more than could be said for the Professor.

We headed down a rough, rocky incline which was even more

difficult to navigate because of the now deep, slushy snow. My boots were completely wet through, as was my hair which I tied back into a knot to keep it out of my face. But as ridiculous as I looked, I was not nearly as bad off as Professor Merriam, who huddled inside his thin woolen coat, his scarf held tightly to his throat. He was wet and cold and, in spite of what I had assumed was a reasonable constitution, seemed to be genuinely suffering.

We proceeded straight down the ridge, through a tight ravine, and onto another ledge where there was less snow to contend with, but the wind was ferocious, whipping what little snow was left in the air right through our clothes. Now I, too, huddled into my coat, pulling the collar and shoulders up as far as possible to shield my neck and ears. As the wind grew progressively more severe, I retreated into my coat, pulling my chin and nose under my collar, casting my eyes directly in front of me. Which is how I missed his fall.

I am still not certain how it happened, but before I could do anything to prevent it, Professor Merriam had slipped from the ledge and into some trees maybe fifty or sixty feet below me. He cried out once, a long, anguished moan, and then there was no sound except for the wind which whipped and wailed through the trees, cold, wet, and vengeful.

I had no choice but to go down after him. There was not enough time in the day to return to camp, and return again with help, since the only way to do so would be to climb back up and across the mountain, which at that point seemed an impossibility. So I clambered down the cliff after him, discovering that if I placed my field bag in my lap, I could hold my coat and skirts around me and use them like a sled on the snowy decline. It made my descent quick and easy.

Professor Merriam had not been so lucky, having tumbled until he rolled under a snow-encrusted tree, where he was still lodged. He was not unconscious, but the fall had taken his breath away, and he had landed on a branch which had punctured his arm.

I helped him sit up against the trunk of the tree, pulled off his coat, slit open his bloody sleeve with my knife, and then used my water jar to rinse the wound which was deeper than I was expecting. I then used the handkerchief he had given to me earlier to bandage the puncture which continued to bleed heavily. Having nothing else to work with, I then cut a strip from the bottom of my dress and used it as a make-shift tourniquet. Far from ideal, but it would have to do until he could get more professional help.

The hollow under the tree was like a tent of sorts and I figured that if we had to, and it was looking more and more likely that we would, we could spend the night there, but only if there was a way to block the wind from whipping in the snow.

I left the water jar with Professor Merriam, who was still dazed from the fall but not, I hoped, from loss of blood, and, using my knife, started hacking branches from other trees in the area to create a wind break outside our little shelter. It worked pretty well, the snow drifting against the branches as I stacked them. I dug a path on the opposite side to re-enter the relatively dry area under the tree, a thick-branched *Picea*, and slid a few more branches in to provide a bed of sorts above the damp ground. Given the circumstances, the only thing missing was a fire, and we would be quite comfortable.

Professor Merriam watched me crawl into the tight space, and scurry around on all fours like a busy rodent, a wet rodent at that, but he said nothing. I could sense that he hated being stuck with me in such close quarters, so I avoided his gaze altogether, keeping to the task at hand. When I finally did stop to look up at him, he returned my gaze with those soft, sad, remarkably young eyes, which reminded me of the terminals we used to visit in the hospital. He could not possibly be that bad off, and I told him so.

"We will be missed," I assured him, "and you know Dr. Rutherford will send the cavalry out looking for us. He really is quite competent, you know, in spite of his claims to the contrary. We may have to spend the night, but other than a fire, we really have all we need." I pulled the bread from my field bag, and offered it to him. "See. I even brought dinner."

Professor Merriam fumbled in his jacket and pulled out an identical chunk and placed it, crumbs and all, in his lap, and tried to return my smile. He then drew matches from the same pocket, handed them to me, shivered, and closed his eyes.

Starting a fire under a tree may not be the smartest or most practical action but it seemed the only option available at the time. And it worked. I pulled needles and twigs and some loose rock into a tight circle and, after a couple frustrating tries, successfully started a small but warming fire between the two of us which I fed periodically throughout the night. Later in the evening, since I was quite comfortable and Professor Merriam still shivered noticeably even as he slept, I used my knife to cut off the skirt of my coat and wrapped it tightly around his shoulders. It seemed to comfort him if not provide real warmth.

In the morning, before departing, I re-kindled the fire and, leaving the remaining bread and water with the Professor, I crawled out from under the tree. The sky was grey, but no snow was falling, and the air felt noticeably warmer and fresh. In case the grey sky meant more snow, or I missed our rescue party if one was headed in our direction, I scrambled back up the slope and used rocks and branches to make an elaborate X, one arm of which served as an arrow pointing down to Professor Merriam's location. I then retraced our steps back along the ridge until I located the now snow-covered ledge where I had been sketching the day before. Knowing then for certain that I had my bearings, I headed for camp.

On the final ridge, where I had seen the pelican display only 24 hours before (it seemed like ages), I could see a man on horseback where I had previously seen Professor Merriam. This time, tired and ready to return to camp, I stayed put, and watched as the rancher rode steadily toward me in what was by then a light but persistent rain. When he saw me standing above him, his horse broke into a gallop.

The look on his face when he dismounted assured me that I looked quite the sight, soaked through, my long coat now torn barely into a jacket, my dress cut raggedly at the ends. I was even missing a button on my sleeve. He pulled his coat off and wrapped it around me before I could protest and started to move me toward his horse. I refused both, slipping out from under the coat and handing it back to him, giving him what I hoped were exact enough instructions on how to find the Professor. It was essential that he get there as soon as possible, and not bother with me. I would be fine I assured him.

I watched as he urged his horse along my tracks in the slushy snow, before I in turn headed home, for home it felt I was headed. Even Kim Li's tepid tea and cremated beef would be a welcome and warming sight, I was certain.

Captain Craighead was the next to come into view, galloping straight up the mountain on his U.S. Government steed. This time I did accept a coat, an extra one which he carried on the back of his horse, but urged him to follow the rancher to ensure that Professor Merriam was safe and made it to the cavalry hospital in Mammoth alive.

After that I must admit I remember little but the sight of Dr. Rutherford huddled morosely by the fire, Kim Li's tea which was, like the bitterroot, quite reviving, the heavy woolen blankets being wrapped around me as I immodestly stripped the soaking clothes from my back, and my safe, warm, comforting cocoon of a tent where I slept and slept and slept.

Was I to blame for what happened? I cannot truthfully answer that question. I feel genuine remorse about what happened to Professor Merriam, who is fine, by the way, although his arm will take a while to heal. But I know I set out for the Nation's Park to accomplish exactly what I did on that outing: collect Rocky Mountain specimens. *Lewisia rediviva* at that! I also know that Professor Merriam was quite explicit in his instructions not to bother him if I planned to stay with the expedition. Given the circumstances, perhaps I should have kept him informed, in spite of his directions to the contrary. I have since told him as much, which has led to a truce of sorts between the two of us. He even returned my *L. rediviva*. Like Lewis', they were no worse for the wear, in spite of their unconventional storage and mode of travel.

I know now as well that I can never go back to medicine. This is my life's work, and I will stay with it no matter what the personal or professional cost. Jessie, I know it is easy to say in retrospect, because what could have been a tragedy had a happy ending, but the *Pelecanus,* and *Lewisia,* even the heavy, wet snow—it was rapture. Pure rapture. I only wish you could be here to experience this for yourself, for experience it you must to fully understand it.

Your humbled but most dedicated friend,
Alex

p.s. We'll be setting up camp near the Yellowstone Lake in the morning. After that, you can reach me c/o the Lake Hotel. Please assure Lester that I will forward a package of specimens and my journal entries before we depart.

3. Calypso bulbosa

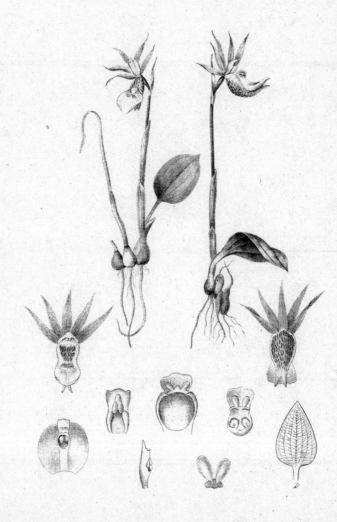

A. E. Bartram
c/o Lake Hotel
Yellowstone National Park
June 20, 1898

My dearest family,

I apologize for not staying in touch but I have been so involved with my day-to-day routine that there seems little time to reflect upon and report my work's progress. And yet, as I commit those words to paper, I realize there is much to reflect upon, as well as to report, now that the weather has warmed and the earth is beginning to respond in kind.

We are camped in a grassy meadow above Yellowstone Lake, up the road from the Yellowstone Lake Hotel. Professor Merriam had originally selected a site directly on the lake, but when the wind was not blowing full speed, the mosquitoes were, as Lewis once wrote, "quite troublesome" even this early in the season. So the Professor wisely transferred the camp to this alternate location.

It is an ideal situation. In essence, we have all the benefits of the hotel, including medical and other assistance should we ever be in need of them, without all the expense and bother of being in residence there. We are strategically located, as well, on the Grand Loop, the wagon road which circles the Park's main attractions, so most of our desired destinations are within a short walk or wagon ride. Of course, such a centralized location leaves us open to regular visits by travellers exploring the Park on their own, separate from the coupon tours. I must admit, I find the constant interruptions trying, but Dr. Rutherford and Rocky and Stony, the two students, all seem to relish the extra company in the evenings, particularly when that company includes Miss Zwinger and her lady friends from the hotel.

That is not to say that Dr. Rutherford and the boys welcome all visitors equally. Just this last week, a group of travelling Baptists set up camp immediately adjacent to our site, parking their wagons directly next to the road where their hand-painted signs proclaim, JESUS SAVES, warning all who pass by that it is time to REPENT!, and warning, too, BEWARE OF THE DEMON RUM.

Dr. Rutherford, who was raised in a strict Baptist family and is given to strong beliefs of his own no matter what the subject matter, has been in a real lather over their presence, claiming it was the Baptists who stole his childhood and, more importantly, his formative adolescence, with their anti-smoking, anti-drinking, anti-dancing, anti-card-playing, and anti-everything-fun approach to life.

He is right, of course. Children do suffer mightily at the hands of their parents, who too often refuse their offspring an opportunity to find their own meaning in life and, instead, indoctrinate them at an early age. I bless you both for not imposing any organized religion on my life, leaving me to find my own way. I am finding that path here, as the world and all its glories open before me. The natural world is my religion. I worship the random and wondrous beauty of it all.

With such a belief system I should be grateful that Dr. Rutherford has strictly forbidden the Baptists to venture, much less proselytize, anywhere near our camp, a mandate to which they have no choice but to reluctantly agree. But even if the Baptists are limited to preaching the ugliness of hell, damnation, and demon rum outside of our encampment, even Dr. Rutherford cannot stop the sweet sounds of their hymns from reaching us through the trees at night. They are not unlike lullabies, and I have learned to relish the melodies as I drift off to sleep. We all need to find joy and meaning in the world. Even the Baptists.

Our location above the hotel also allows for an ideal separation of labor, with Professor Merriam, one of the students, and I systematically collecting off the road along nearby creekbeds and meadows, while Dr. Rutherford, the other student (whomever is lucky enough to "win the toss" for the day), and the expedition driver and his dog, travel the main wagon roads in their search for specimens.

Dr. Rutherford, as I may have told you, has come late to science, being a farmer by birth and inclination, and yet he has developed an admirable collecting technique, one which I would like to incorporate into my own field work at the earliest opportunity. When Professor Merriam first proposed this expedition, he invited a cartographer to help document our collecting. Said cartographer ran off and got married instead, but he did provide the Professor with a detailed elevation map first charted by Hayden and the government surveyors. This map of Yellowstone National Park has served as a guide of sorts for Professor Merriam as he has planned his work, but it is Dr. Rutherford who has made the best—or at the least most scientific—use of it.

As I may have mentioned when I first arrived, Dr. Rutherford spent his first month here nursing the camp's fire. But he also, it turns out, spent at least some of his time, he claims out of boredom, copying to scale large sections of the Hayden map. To this grid he added known thermal features, mountain passes, major roadways, &c. At the time, this seemed a harmless diversion but he has now taken to riding with the mountain man driver on these major thoroughfares, collecting specimens, and adding them specimen by specimen to his grid, along with dates and time of day coupled with detailed weather information.

He and his assistants make quite the sight. After a late breakfast, the threesome pack their day's supplies, including a large jug of brandy or some other foul-smelling alcohol, and head off down the road. They travel in their wagon at a leisurely pace, the buckskinned driver dozing off as the horse moseys along the roadway, the student, following behind on foot, gathering samples from the areas alongside the road and the adjacent hillsides at Dr. Rutherford's command.

Dr. Rutherford, in the meantime, issues his royal mandates from the back of the wagon which he has converted into a virtual throne, complete with tarp canopy. It is while seated thus that he logs the student's findings and plots each specimen collected on his hand-made maps.

Down the road they proceed, the driver snuffling in his sleep, Stony or Rocky scurrying here and there, the driver's dog barking at their heels, and Dr. Rutherford scanning the roadsides like they were indeed his private reserve. They proceed until they reach a hot pool or stream at which point they have an agreed upon arrangement that they will stop for refreshments and, if water temperature allows, partake in a long, hot soak. Depending on the direction they head out, and the number of specimens and thermal features they encounter along the way, the three return to camp quite pickled from the day-long combination of hot water and lukewarm liquor. You can understand why such an assignment would be an agreeable one to a young college student, and why said assignment is hotly contested each morning by the flip of a coin.

As you can also imagine, it is a situation destined to drive Professor Merriam to distraction. Just the other day, Dr. Rutherford and his coterie pulled into camp after dark, the horse being smart enough or at least hungry enough to find its way home without the benefit of human guidance, since all three were sleeping soundly in the wagon. I would have laughed right out loud to see them in such a state, if Dr. Aber from the Smithsonian had not been visiting camp at that particular moment. His presence made the sight of the drunken crew even worse for the Professor who was clearly not amused by Dr. Rutherford dozing on his throne, the student curled peacefully at his feet, and the driver, stretched out in front of the wagon across his own royal seat, his hair and beard and skins dangling every which way as the horse trotted into camp. Even the dog was asleep. All four snored so loudly that they drowned out the Baptists' joyous hallelujahs which drifted into our camp through the trees.

And yet, in spite of all the grief Dr. Rutherford causes him, even Professor Merriam must begrudgingly acknowledge that Dr. Rutherford's collecting technique is producing quality results, with his elaborate system of mapping leading to some engaging evening discussions and scientific speculations about plant variety and distributions. Why is it, for example, that Coulter identifies *Pentstemon caeruleus* as a plant of the plains of Dakota, and yet Dr. Rutherford has clearly mapped clusters of the species growing alongside the mountain roads he travels? Could it be that the act of road building creates new and welcoming conditions for the spread of these plants? Or perhaps those who visit the Park carry the seeds like wayward birds, depositing them at random as they travel along the roads.

These are the kinds of questions Dr. Rutherford's maps raise, as they provide us with a broader perspective of the Park than any of us could individually obtain in the field. I hesitate to make the allusion, but it is as if Dr. Rutherford's maps illustrate the Park's flora in concert, as opposed to simply logging in each individual note.

Dr. Rutherford has also been the first to collect and identify specimens of *Castilleja miniata*, which Professor Merriam refers to as "Indian paintbrush." This is not the same species of plant I have heard referred to as Indian paintbrush in the Northeast, nor is there any mention I can find of an Indian paintbrush in Coulter. When I told the Professor as much, we proceeded to have an animated conversation (notice I avoid the word argument) about the obvious limitations of common names.

But conversing as eloquently as I could, I was unable to persuade Professor Merriam, who steadfastly believes that nonscientific names portray the "genius of the people." According to him, names like Indian potato, bitterroot, fireweed, golden eye, and death camas describe how plants are used, consumed, or propagated, how they look, or, in his exact words, "are to be avoided because of their unfortunate habit of lying in wait for some unsuspecting herbivore—man or beast." It is through embracing these names, the Professor maintains, that scientists can develop and encourage botanical awareness in amateurs and, through such awareness, enlist their help in protecting and preserving our natural history and national treasures like Yellowstone National Park.

This engaging discussion has continued sporadically on our own outings into the field, since the three of us (the Professor, the student whose luck fails him in the coin toss, and I) have been recently joined by a Crow Indian and his family. How this particular Indian came to join our camp may be of particular interest to you, Father, for you are right as always: the government is indeed forcing these people off the land and away from their traditional sources of food and livelihood.

From what I understand, it happened something like this. A woman traveller, accompanying a coupon tour viewing backcountry geysers, had wandered into the woods where she was momentarily separated from her party. She was never at risk, but she was disoriented enough so that she began to worry and probably even fear for her safety. Hearing someone approach on horseback, she was greatly relieved and hurried with much abandon toward her supposed rescuer, only to discover that said rescuer was none other than the Crow Indian. The Indian, it turns out, was hurrying himself, trying to avoid contact with the woman's party, who were waiting in a wagon parked on the road directly below them. Having missed their companion, they were calling out for their missing member.

Upon seeing the Indian, the woman automatically assumed that she was about to be attacked or worse and, thus, spontaneously regained her sense of direction and ran frantically down the hill, out of the woods, and onto the wagon road screaming for help. The Indian, no doubt as terrified as the woman, galloped silently away in the opposite direction. The woman and her friends hurried back to the military headquarters in Mammoth, hysterically informing each and every traveller they encountered along the way about the Indian war party which had invaded the Park.

Now I have met Capt. Craighead from cavalry headquarters on a number of occasions, and can vouch for his good nature and sensibility, but what could he do but head out and search for the so-called warring party? If he did not act, he would have soon had a warring band of vigilante tourists on his hands. There exists a strong sense of rightful ownership of our Nation's Park, and those claims do not include the Indians.

Two days later, Capt. Craighead and his men did indeed discover a meagre Indian encampment, consisting of a tipi and campfire high on the ridge above Mammoth Hot Springs where the young Indian, his wife, and two small children were living. The family apparently entered the Park through the northeast, in search of obsidian, a volcanic glass which is still used by natives for making traditional tools and knives and is in abundance here. By entering through the back door as it were, the family had evaded the cavalry and other Park authorities who probably would have otherwise denied them entrance. The family could have easily spent months undetected if the Indian had not had the misfortune of unexpectedly running into the lost female traveller.

As I may have mentioned to you before, Professor Merriam

taught for two or three years while botanizing on the Crow Indian reservation. Knowing this, Capt. Craighead called upon the Professor to translate for the Indian who speaks little English, in spite of having received a full "Christian" education at the Unitarian mission on the reservation. From what I have since learned from Professor Merriam, it was the captain's goal to prosecute or, at minimum, expel the young man and his family from the Park since they discovered a small bundle of obsidian in his possession. But as the Professor explained, although it is illegal to remove any physical feature from the Park, and there are no exceptions, the obsidian found with the Indian was still inside the Park and, thus, technically not illegal for him to have in his possession. Besides, the Indian insisted this was his own personal obsidian, which he had carried with him into the Park, but this would have been more difficult to prove.

To make the story even more interesting, Montana is so much like a small town that Professor Merriam knew the Indian's father, a tribal leader, who had assisted the Professor in his early botanizing on the reservation. Like his father, the son, with the curiously Americanized name of Joseph Not-afraid, is extremely knowledgeable about native plants and their traditional uses, so Professor Merriam has vouched for the young man, and has enlisted the Indian's help in identifying the specimens we collect. Capt. Craighead, to his credit, has agreed to this arrangement, claiming to be dedicated to the expedition's success.

So now Joseph accompanies us on our day-long ventures into the backcountry, with his wife, Sara, and their two small children, one of whom the woman still carries on her back. You can imagine the reaction as wagons of travellers pass us on the road. Most are thrilled at the opportunity to see real, live "Injuns," but a few, perhaps having heard of the alleged warring party which had invaded the Park, have complained to authorities. I must say that I now have nothing but respect for Capt. Craighead, who has proven to be firm in his support of Professor Merriam and his work. I only wish I could say I had similar respect for the medical botany and common names that Professor Merriam appears to be championing with this Indian.

Still, their work together has created a unique opportunity of sorts for me and my own studies. While Professor Merriam and Joseph discuss at length (and often at great difficulty given the language differences) the nutritional or medical or spiritual properties of a particular plant, I have time to illustrate flora in its natural environment. I am finding this particular task to be one of the greatest learning experiences of the time I have spent here so far. I am beginning to look at which plants grow in relation to others and in what kind of physical setting. I am also keenly interested in the different conditions under which they are growing and the dates they are in flower at different elevations.

It is clear to me now that if I could adequately document just one area of the Nation's Park throughout an entire season, I would be a long way toward understanding the development of plant life and all of its complexity. I may enlist Dr. Rutherford's novel approach to documenting our collection to help with such a project.

Unfortunately, my expanding interests and the non-scientific botanical pursuits of the Professor and his Indian friend have done little to win the confidence of the expedition's supporter, Dr. Philip Aber. He is a fine scientist and extremely intelligent and well read, but very much a traditionalist when it comes to what—and whom—should be considered "scientific." I still wonder at his apparent acceptance of me. Perhaps he has yet to notice that I am a woman. Maybe he is more interested in the fact that I am a Bartram. In either case, I can tell he is not impressed with my new work, referring to my illustrations as "group portraits." And he only speaks of Professor Merriam with contempt. Even to his face.

Sadly, Dr. Aber appears to be under some sort of personal stress, since his wife and family have yet to join him here as planned. I can only hope that his displeasure with life in general does not affect his support of the Professor and our work. While I sympathize with Dr. Aber's lack of appreciation for the Professor's interests, I believe I am making much progress, and would hate to have that interrupted.

To give you an idea of how well I am doing, I received a letter from Lester complimenting me on the quality and overall condition of my Yellowstone Park collection, if you can believe it. He thinks I may even have discovered a new genus. He is sending a sample to a contact he has at Harvard to be sure. If he is right, it could be my first genus *Bartramii* to match the B. family of mosses!

Lest you think it is all work and no play, tomorrow is the summer solstice and Dr. Rutherford and friends have planned a "summer festival," complete with music, song, and recitations to celebrate the longest day of the year. It will be our turn to blast out the Baptists with our own pagan hymns. And this is just a prelude to a long weekend of fun planned at the hotel for the 4th of July.

I will be thinking fondly of you both during the festivities, as I think of you daily, and as I hope you are thinking of me.

All my love,
Alexandria

Philip Aber
Lake Hotel
Yellowstone Park, Wyo.
June 20, 1898

William Gleick
Smithsonian Institution
Washington, District of Columbia

Dear Bill,

I write to you as a friend, for a friend I hope you are, since there is no one else to whom I can confide my situation. I am embarrassed to report that I have found myself in a bit of a personal and professional difficulty with which I am hoping you can assist.

I have had the opportunity to spend a considerable time with your colleagues in the Park and now fully understand why you chose to journey on your own to the capital rather than to venture here with your friends. Merriam has opted to ignore the ample luxuries of the Park hotels, and has instead set up a camp of operations near the Lake Hotel. He and his assistants live in the most primitive of conditions, eating poorly cured beef and game, and generally risking their health and wellbeing—not to mention my significant investment—in the name of economy, for it certainly is not in the name of science. The camp, with its worn out tents, ramshackle tables, and make-shift equipment, might be barely tolerable for a weekend camping holiday for college boys, but it is certainly not conducive to serious research.

Instead of establishing himself in some respectable fashion, and hiring underlings to venture into the field on his behalf, the underlings often stay in camp, sleeping all hours of the day, I might add, while Merriam sets off each morning with only Miss Bartram, a student, and some Indian he has picked up along the way to assist him. It is bad enough that this strange entourage brings discredit upon Merriam, who seems oblivious to the fact that he has become yet another of the Park's wonders—tourists go out of their way to view the party as it makes its way on foot along the wagon roads. But I will not tolerate the fact that such a spectacle casts aspersions on my own reputation, for supporting such canaille. And that is not to mention the questions Merriam's lack of respectability raises about the integrity of the Smithsonian Institution itself.

Worse yet, while still at Mammoth, Merriam left camp in a pouring rain to explore some remote location with only Miss Bartram to assist him. I am very open minded when it comes to science, but this is hardly a decorous situation, much less a sensible one, and was ripe for a serious mishap. Which is exactly what happened. After foolishly putting himself and Miss Bartram in unnecessary danger, Merriam apparently lost his way and, when searching for the proper path to return them safely, proceeded to fall off a cliff. It was only through the dedication of an off-duty cavalryman and some Montana cowboy, who located Merriam and brought him back to camp, that the fool managed to survive at all. As it is, Merriam now limps noticeably and carries his arm around in a sling. Not much science will result under his feeble leadership, that is clear.

Which brings me to my difficulty. I have made arrangements for my wife and family to join me here at the Yellowstone Lake Hotel. Would you call upon her and assist her in whatever way possible to ensure that she has the strength and commitment to make the journey? She is not in the best of health, with two small children to care for but, as you can imagine, I must stay here, at minimum, for the month that I had planned to ensure the expedition's success. To leave now would doom the entire enterprise, and could possibly put my own fledgling career at the Smithsonian at risk.

Thus, my dilemma. I admit to you in all honesty that I cannot face a summer apart from my family, particularly under these conditions. If you would call upon my wife on my behalf, discreetly as you must understand, it would be a great service indeed. And please, do not trouble my wife with these details. Just ensure her that she will thoroughly enjoy the accommodations of the hotels and the other wonders here in the Park.

I hope your studies are proceeding as planned and that you are not discovering your own personal or professional difficulties while in our Nation's Capital. However, should you ever encounter any problems at all while in the District or while working at the Smithsonian I hope you will feel free to call upon me as I have, without any sense of pride whatsoever, felt free to call upon you.

Yours sincerely and most faithfully,

Philip Aber

———— ◦•◦ ————

Howard Merriam
c/o Yellowstone Lake Hotel
Yellowstone National Park
June 22, 1898

William Gleick
Smithsonian Institution
Washington, D.C.

Bill:

I am writing again to try my utmost to convince you to join us here in the Park at your earliest convenience. As you can well imagine, with such a small group of men, I can use the help in the field now that it is warming. More importantly, it is the time spent outside of the field where I am at a real loss, particularly as I try to deal with my benefactor, Philip Aber. For some reason, Aber has become convinced that I am most unsuited to manage this enterprise, and so has taken to supervising and instructing me and my activities as closely as he might his youngest child. I feel like I am under the microscope here, and it detracts mightily from my work.

And work, at last, I am doing. Thanks to the excellent care provided by the medical staff at the cavalry hospital in Mammoth and, I am told, thanks to the preliminary measures taken by Miss Bartram, my arm is healing and I am more mobile than anyone would have the right to expect given the fall I took. So I am back in the field again, busily gathering samples and doing my utmost to develop in-depth knowledge of the flora in these lower elevations.

I have, by chance, encountered a native from the Crow Indian reservation who has much knowledge about traditional plant names and uses and I am taking advantage of his brief stay in the Park to learn as much as I can about plants considered useful or poisonous. It is critical that information concerning the properties of these native plants be collected now from those who have for generations needed to rely on them for food, medicine, and other purposes, since these people are being weaned from their traditional way of life and, as a result, generations of tribal knowledge will not last long. Sadly, it is not only their knowledge that is at risk. They have been herded like animals onto reserves, and I fear it is only a matter of time before they disappear from the human scene altogether.

I can tell Miss Bartram does not appreciate my interest in preserving this information, since she is very traditional in her approach to science. Except for an occasional spirited discussion, however, she leaves me to my studies as long as I leave her to hers. Rocky and Stony, the two students who are accompanying us, have also been remarkably cooperative, given the long hours and number of miles we cover each day, and have demonstrated a curiosity if not an interest in our work.

So, surprisingly, has Rutherford, who has reluctantly but dependably followed instructions and returned to camp each night with more specimens than I could have ever hoped for, even if he does follow Miss Bartram's wasteful example of preserving only one specimen per sheet. Miss Bartram, understanding the financial limitations of the expedition, has been gracious enough to furnish her own specimen sheets which are mailed to her along with other supplies from New York. Rutherford, on the other hand, dips daily into my own personal supply as he catalogues and preserves the expedition's collection. His is an extravagance we cannot afford and I have told him so.

But these minor financial worries pale when compared to the people problems I am encountering. This is work for which I have no training or natural inclination, and one which I would just as soon ignore as long as the overall goals of the expedition are being met. Aber, on the other hand, is obsessed by his need to control the every breathing moment of the expedition and insists on visiting our camp at the most inopportune times, allegedly to check on our progress but more likely to catch us with our collective pants down if you know what I mean.

Just the other night, for example, Aber wandered into camp unannounced, only to find every vagabond travelling the Grand Loop, not to mention the young, foot-loose and fancy-free staff employed at the Lake Hotel, settled in for a long spontaneous night of music and merriment in celebration of the Summer Solstice. Aber was no doubt attracted by our campfire which had grown from a few logs fed hourly, to a bonfire large enough to burn down the entire encampment given even the slightest breeze.

I assured Aber it was a spontaneous event, Rutherford being too exhausted by day's end to organize such revelry, but I was not the only one to observe that the participants all seemed to have spontaneously brought food and drink to share (there was much drink including a potent home-brew) and that each of the 50 or so merrymakers (or trouble makers depending on your point of view) had spontaneously prepared a skit, recitation, or song in celebration of summer.

Miss Zwinger, a woman who has taken great interest in our expedition and who regularly calls upon our camp, prepared a dramatic reading of Shelley's poem "The Sensitive Plant": "It loves, even like Love, its deep heart is full; it desires what it has not, the beautiful!"—a poem guaranteed to raise more than one set of eyebrows I can assure you. If hers was the limit of provocative presentations, I could have endured it, but there was more. Much more.

Another visitor, an accountant on his way by bicycle through the Park, told, in much detail, of the first discovery of Yellowstone Park. We all had a good laugh at the early reports of a bubbling hell where entire forests were "putrefied," stories so far fetched that it took years before anyone even bothered to investigate the veracity of them. And yet, who amongst us would have believed the stories if we had not seen this bubbling hell with our own eyes?

Not to be undone, a young woman travelling with Miss Zwinger advanced to the fire with her copy of Chittenden's book on Yellowstone National Park, from which she proceeded to read a hair-raising tale of massacres and pursuits of renegade Indians in the early days of the Park. Now if the young lady had continued to read to the end of Chittenden's tale, she would have revealed that even Chittenden was sympathetic to the plight of the Nez Percé who were, in the author's words, "intelligent, brave, and humane." He was also wise enough to predict that history would prove that the Indians were in the right. As Chittenden noted, the Nez Percé were making a last, desperate stand against their inevitable destiny, refusing to give up everything, including their land and their dignity, both of which had been theirs for centuries before the arrival of the paleface.

But the truth is often the last ingredient of a good story and all seemed happy with the general effect of the young lady's abbreviated tale. All, that is, except for Philip Aber.

When the next performance turned out to be a rousing rendition of "Turkey in the Straw" on a fiddle and guitar, Aber took me aside and asked if it was prudent to invite Indians into our camp given their history in the region.

Different Indians, I assured him, and different times. The run-in with the Nez Percé had taken place twenty years before. But Aber was not appeased.

"You have women here to look after, and our reputation," he added, the anger rising in his face and voice. "You can't have Indians lurking around in the trees."

"But they are helping with my field studies," I replied, anxious to defend myself and my own reputation. "The young man is incredibly knowledgeable about the plant life in this region."

"Knowledgeable?" he shouted back at me. "Knowledgeable? An Indian is more knowledgeable than you are? What are you telling me, man? That I would be better off hiring a savage to do the work I've hired you and your friends to do?"

Fortunately, by this time the lone fiddle and guitar had been joined by a small band of instruments played by the boys from the hotel, supplemented by a foot-tapping and hand-clapping tempo led by Rutherford beating a wooden spoon and a ladle on one of the cook's large stew kettles. The resulting noise (I am hard-pressed to describe it as music) drowned out our argument so the party-goers were oblivious to our confrontation. Still, I felt embarrassed that not only my credibility but my ability to lead a scientific expedition had come under attack. And by someone who has not a clue how to collect specimens in the field, preferring the comforts and daily luxuries of the hotel. I fought back. What else could I do?

"Who are you to tell me who I can or cannot have helping me?" I shouted over the clamor. "You who sit in your hotel room all day, never even venturing into the field? You have no right to tell me how to do my work, and with whom. You have no right." And then to be sure he understood my point of view, I added, "You have not earned it."

If the music had not ended at that exact moment, I am quite certain our exchange of insults would have escalated into an exchange of blows. As it was, the merriment subsided to much hand clapping, hoots and whistles, after which the noise quieted long enough for another performer to step forward into the light of the fire.

"Who is next, who is next?" Rutherford called out, banging on his so-called drum. "Step forward, and let the celebration continue."

Aber retreated to the edge of the merrymakers' circle, where he was almost hidden by the trees. My insults were bad enough but, in retrospect, it would have been much better if I had hit him and sent him packing. Maybe then he would not have witnessed what followed.

"Next," Rutherford shouted again, beating out a parody of a drum roll on his kettle.

Out of the darkness, our horseman and driver, Jake Packard, emerged. Packard is not the most social of creatures, preferring to keep his distance from the lot of us, although he has taken a liking to Rutherford and his regular liquor shipments, which he had obviously been sampling throughout the day. He held a book tightly to his chest as if it alone were providing the sense of balance he needed as he staggered toward the fire. His dog sat and waited at a safe distance.

"I have sumpen to read," he said, and the circle of revellers clapped and whistled in appreciation. The dog wagged his tail.

"I jus thought you'd wanna know what these little ladies are reading at night," he added, smiling and weaving and fumbling through the pages.

"Lissen a this," he mumbled.

Then he proceeded, not very well I might add, to pick out, word by word, the description of the sexual parts of the plant.

"Flowers open when all parts of the plant are mature," he hesitantly started. "Sumtimes," he continued, and then he stumbled, "the and-roe-eek-cum, or sumpen like that," he did the best he could with the terminology, tripping over each letter in attempt to make it sound official, but we knew what he meant, "matures earlier than the cum-and-roe-cee-um," he stuttered and spit, "soes not to inner fear with the pollen and pissels of the same flower."

He looked up and smiled.

"A pissel. I have one of them," he interjected proudly. Then he spit again into the fire.

The driver drunkenly tripped over the scientific descriptions, but the overall meaning was not lost on the crowd, which stared collectively into the fire rather than look at the matted mass of hair and shabby buckskins that wove back and forth and blasphemed in front of them. He then went on to read in much the same way how the tip of the pollen tube pushes its way into the ovule in the ovary where it makes contact with the female. Cells rupture, the sperm is released, and it merges with the egg. Standard textbook fare. Certainly nothing unusual about it.

"Well," the driver said hacking and spitting with great ceremony into the fire. "I jus wannad to share that with you."

The driver waved the book at those sitting around the circle. The dog stood and wagged his tail.

"I offen wonnered what she was doin in there in bed with a book." He laughed suggestively. "She calls it science." He spit again. "I call it inneresing."

Before the driver could continue, Rutherford was beating again on his make-shift drum calling for music, more music. The boys from the hotel jumped at the chance to perform their number, a western campfire song about the trees and breeze and the whispering pines. The driver stumbled back to where he came from, his dog following closely behind.

I looked around for Miss Bartram but could not find her anywhere. She tends to avoid these kinds of social activities, so I can only hope that she had already retired for the night, without her book, and that she had missed the entire dreadful presentation.

I wish I could say the same for Aber. He was still lurking around the circle of revellers, his worst suspicions about my leadership skills and judge of character now fully confirmed. He flashed a look of pure hatred in my direction and then he, too, disappeared into the night.

So, Bill, what should I do? I can forbid the use of alcohol in the camp, and will, of course, do that. But I also know that Rutherford and his friends will simply limit their consumption to when they are either on the road (most of the daylight hours) or visiting the hotel (which would probably be most of the rest of the time if they are not allowed to drink here). They will probably also drink in greater abandon, knowing they will have to make it through the night once they are back in camp.

Another option is to fire Packard, but if he goes, all of our provisions, including bedding, tents, and cooking capabilities, will go back to Butte with him. Then what would I do?

I can disassociate myself from the Indians, but there is no guarantee that will appease Aber at this point, and it might even put the young Indian family at risk. There are some strange people lurking around these parts, many of whom make the likes of Jake Packard look tame.

As you can see, it is the human dilemmas, not the field work or science, which puts me at a real disadvantage here. People are not my strength. If you could join us, even temporarily, I feel that a level of respectability would be restored to our group. You met Aber in the Capital. He speaks highly of you and your abilities. I think in cases like these, your age and stature would be a real benefit, providing Aber with a sense of confidence that he clearly lacks when dealing with me. If you simply wanted to visit the Park and not even worry about the field work, your presence and authority alone, I am convinced, could make a real difference.

Aber originally planned to leave the Park at the end of the month but is now talking as if he is here until the first snow falls. If he knew you were planning on joining us, perhaps that would give him the confidence he needs to change his mind and go home.

So please, please consider my offer. I have no one else to turn to and need your help all the more because of it.

Yours most sincerely,
     Howard

———————◆———————

Andrew Rutherford, Ph.D.
c/o Lake Hotel
Yellowstone National Park
Temp. 65°F., 0 precip.
June 23, 1898

Robert Healey
President
The Agricultural College
     of the State of Montana
Bozeman, Mont.

My dear President,
     Happy to report Merriam's research career fast coming to close. Has alienated Philip Aber, who threatens to withdraw Smithson-

ian funding. Ruckus & near fistfight over Indians camped in clearing & reproduction of plants. Merriam will soon have no choice but to re-join ranks of economic botanists & agriculturists. Wish I could say was my doing, but result the same. You owe me that new building as promised.

In other news, railroad active in negotiating lease of land through Park. Planning dams, power generation, large lakes. Much excitement with many swells, black coats, high hats in residence at hotel. Merriam meeting daily to talk about herbarium. Has their attention, in spite of his own dismal situation. You should be here to counter with own ideas. This is big money looking for home. Why not build them one in Bozeman?

Might find you enjoy Yellowstone. No known highwaymen. Not known as Wonderland for nothing.

Send supplies care of hotel. Would like anemometer. Windy here.

Yours reliably &c,
Andrew Rutherford, Ph.D.

———•◆•———

A. E. Bartram
c/o Yellowstone Lake Hotel
Yellowstone National Park
June 25, 1898

Jess:

I have taken your advice and written a long, chatty letter to my parents. There is no reason for them to worry so, and certainly no reason for them to be bothering you with their worries. Still, I will try my utmost to keep them better informed.

I will not bore you with my day-to-day activities, which have settled into a gentle routine. But now that we have moved to the lake and the "season" is upon us, I have had some interesting backcountry encounters and experiences which illustrate how far I have come on my journey—or how far I have fallen behind, depending upon your point of view.

First, I should point out, as I should have made clear to my parents, that Professor Merriam plans each day's outing to the minute to ensure that we are always back in camp before the first signs of nightfall. He has become almost obsessive about this, probably because he fears the wrath of Philip Aber from the Smithsonian. He not only sponsors our work, but monitors our activities closely. Should we ever be even a few minutes late, I am quite convinced that Dr. Aber would call the entire U.S. Cavalry out to prove his point that the Professor is not to be trusted.

Professor Merriam's commitment to being back in camp before dark does limit our destinations since we can, after all, only cover so many miles and still return by the light of day. But knowing exactly where we are headed and when we will return does bring a certainty to each outing which the Professor apparently finds comforting. After spending a night in a spring blizzard, I suppose I should take some comfort from it as well, although I question how we will ever manage to collect alpine species once it warms in the higher backcountry if we are confined to our camp on the lake. But those are the kinds of logistical problems that Professor Merriam must work out on our behalf. As Dr. Rutherford is fond of saying, "The Prof doesn't pay us to worry about the details. That's his job."

The other day, while on one of our well-planned excursions, Professor Merriam was collecting along a streambed with the Indian, who is his constant companion now, while I chose to climb to a shady forested area above and to the right of them. As I pushed through the trees to a clearing on the other side, I came across a small, green tent-like structure sitting just on the edge of the clearing. Curious, I silently crept toward it, not exactly sure what I was looking for, but not at all prepared for what I found.

"Shh," came a voice from inside the tent.

I stopped, of course, and listened, but I could not see or hear anything other than a slight breeze which rustled through the trees. I continued walking, quietly, toward the tent.

"Shh," came the voice again, as a twig snapped under my foot. "You will frighten them."

Again I looked around to see what or whom I might be frightening. I could see nothing. The flap of the tent opened briefly. A hand motioned me forward.

"Hurry," the voice whispered. "Just be careful," it admonished.

Silently, I inched toward the diminutive structure, which opened slightly to let me in. Because of the darkness inside the small tent, it was difficult to make out who or what was inhabiting it, but I accepted the welcome and stepped inside.

"Here," the voice whispered, grabbing my arm and guiding me back toward a narrow camp stool. "Your eyes will adjust in a minute."

I sat and waited. "Aren't they beautiful?" the voice whispered again. "A family of yellow wings."

Slowly, as my eyes adjusted to the darkness, I saw to what the soft, quiet voice referred. In the tree directly across the clearing a *Dendroica petechia* was feeding her young.

"Here, try these."

From out of the shadows emerged a pair of opera glasses, which helped to bring the young birds into clear focus. She was right, for the voice was that of a woman, the young warblers with their soft, downy feathers and urgently gaping mouths were indeed humorous if not exactly beautiful to watch.

As my eyes adjusted to the darkness, I could now also see the woman in the tent quite clearly. She smiled and, although she was at least forty, maybe even fifty, she, too, seemed young, birdlike, with tiny, wide-set eyes which darted with pleasure as I handed back the glasses. She held them in her lap and shrugged, her small head dipping into her shoulders, her eyes crinkling.

"Isn't this wonderful?" she whispered.

I looked around the small, homemade bird blind, for that was what we were sitting in, and understood that once, and not so long ago, I would have imagined such a stuffy, restricting place anything but wonderful. But now, that afternoon, it was exactly that. Wonderful.

"My name is Mrs. Eversman," she whispered, briefly offering me her hand. "Or, I should say, Mary Anne. I am here from New York to be a watcher in the woods. What brings you to Yellowstone?"

I whispered a few words about my work in the Park, and she seemed delighted, her hands fluttering lightly in the pool of her skirts.

"Oh, a scientist," she sighed, now clasping her hands as if to quiet them. "How I do admire you. I have always wanted to be a scientist, but," she added with an apologetic dip of her head, "I'm really just a dabbler. What you might refer to as a nature lover, I suppose. And now, ever since my husband died, I guess I'm also a bit of an adventuress," she confided.

She stopped as if to think what to say next, her opera glasses again scanning the trees. Taking note of the mother bird's flight, she checked a small timepiece which hung from a gold chain around her neck. She then made a notation in her journal.

"If I were a real scientist," she said, closing the book and placing the glasses atop it, "I've been told that I would stay home and pay more attention to that which is around me. Instead, I prefer to travel. Looking," she added, and motioned with her quick, bird-like hand around the expanse outside her small enclosure. As she did so, a bird in flight caught her eye.

"Ah, there," she whispered, handing me the glasses again. "In the tree, to your left. Do you see him? A mountain bluebird."

There was indeed a bright blue bird, the likes of which I had never seen. Small, almost iridescent against the green, it rested for only a moment and then was gone.

"I guess I'm too restless for real science," she said, leaning towards me to once again retrieve the glasses. She smiled, her eyes brightening at just the thought of her quest.

She was certainly not dressed for the scientific life, nor for adventuring for that matter. Compared to me, with my now ragged and filthy field clothes, she looked positively radiant, with her suit of pale blue serge, not unlike the color of a bird's egg in spring. Her shirtwaist was starched and prim, her thick brown hair, softened by threads of grey, neatly pinned. Another smile crinkled her face, her head dipped into her shoulders, and she returned her gaze to the trees.

"What a wonderful world this is," she said quietly.

I would have enjoyed sitting there all day with Mrs. Eversman, but I could now hear Professor Merriam calling me from down the hill. Since our near tragedy in the snow, I have come to understand that I really must be more responsible and responsive to the needs of my entire party. And from the Professor's perspective, right or wrong, that means knowing where I am at all times. It is not the kind of arrangement to which I would normally agree, but Professor Merriam is still so clearly uncomfortable with my presence here that I need to do all that I can to make him think of me as an asset, as opposed to a constant liability.

I could hear the Professor and now the student, too, calling again, closer this time, so I started to take my leave, regretting my departure from Mrs. Eversman and the tight confines of her blind, but fearing that their calls would disturb the birds. I felt uncomfortable, too, abandoning her there, all alone, in the woods. So, in leaving, I offered to help Mrs. Eversman back to the hotel with her things when my party and I headed back down the trail later in the afternoon.

"Oh, no," she said without hesitation. "I never go back to the hotel before nightfall. I love that hour or two before dark. The woods come alive, the birds settle, the weather calms. I never miss it."

Again the crinkle of the eyes, the small, almost apologetic dip of her head to one side, the smile. And then the opera glasses scanning the trees as I crept from the blind.

Funny, the notion people have of science. I can think of nothing more tedious than sitting for literally all hours of the day in a stuffy, dark bird blind not much bigger than a wide-brimmed hat covered with a heavy piece of canvas. And yet, there that woman sits, day in and day out, fighting off flies, mosquitoes, and the stifling heat of day, meticulously observing and documenting the nesting habits and life cycles of birds. If that is not science, I do not know what is.

I have since learned from Miss Zwinger that Mrs. Eversman has led a national campaign amongst amateur birdwatchers like herself to replace the use of shotguns with opera glasses, and to discourage the growing popularity of collecting bird eggs and nests. She has even waged war against the use of feathers in hats and has travelled extensively on behalf of her cause. This is, no doubt, from where the "nature lover" classification has come. Scientists who write for professional publication, and who prefer to tramp through the fields with guns, can be extremely cold-hearted toward those who do not pursue their own brand of science. Particularly old women who sit alone in the woods with opera glasses for hours on end.

I, for one, can certainly sympathize with Mrs. Eversman's perspective. A dead bird, no matter how beautiful and informative it appears neatly laid to rest in a drawer, is still nothing more than a stuffed museum specimen. To understand the true nature and classification of birds, you must, like Mrs. Eversman herself is doing, spend hours on end observing the living, breathing—and I might add messy and unpredictable—creatures in the field. That, at least to my mind, is real science, no matter what the other so-called scientists say.

Jessie, I know I am sounding quite didactic, but there is so much bad science or non-science wrapped in the guise of science that I cannot tell you how refreshing it is to meet this watcher in the woods. She may be sentimental about her subject, but she relies entirely on patient observation for her understanding. We need more of these so-called nature lovers in the world.

But I digress.

As I hurried around Mrs. Eversman's clearing, careful not to disturb her birds, and down the hill toward the creekbed where I could still hear the Professor searching for me, I saw John Wylloe, another of my new Park acquaintances if you can believe it, heading up the trail a half a mile or so below me. He waved, having seen me, too, and hurried up the path in my direction.

Mr. Wylloe is the writer my mother most admires, much to my father's scientific and literary consternation. I think my mother has read every book John Wylloe has ever written, both his nature essays and his poetry. He was kind enough to share a few of his volumes when I first arrived in the Park, but I must admit I find his work too sweet for my palate. However, considering all the inferior so-called nature writing—and I use the term lightly—in the world today, at least Mr. Wylloe's is based upon sound observation of the natural world. In fact, he has used his name and reputation to effectively argue against this ubiquitous kind of writing which makes for entertaining and humorous reading but is not, contrary to the authors' insistences, based on the real world. As Mr. Wylloe passionately argues (and I assume Mrs. Eversman would agree), song birds do not conduct singing schools in the woods for their young, nor do they set their broken legs with mud casts bound with grass, twigs, and horse hair. I do not care one fig for what has been "documented" in the likes of *Harper's* and *Forest and Stream*.

It is against such nonsense and the magazines that publish it that Mr. Wylloe rigorously campaigns. In fact, he has publicly taken to task George Bird Grinnell, the editor of *Forest and Stream*, arguing, quite rightly I might add, that a man in his position should know better than to print such foolishness. Mr. Grinnell considers himself a hunter naturalist, an oxymoron if ever I heard one. He is also one of the founders of the Boone and Crockett Club and established the Audubon Society, both dedicated in their way to an appreciation and preservation of the natural world. Surely these organizations cannot possibly believe that you can only appreciate and preserve that which is somehow human. That is like the Baptists maintaining that true believers can only celebrate that in which they see God.

But I must give Mr. Grinnell credit. He is wily when it comes to Wylloe. In his editorial wisdom, Mr. Grinnell has hired Mr. Wylloe to contribute to *Forest and Stream*, and is sponsoring his summer-long stay in the Park. Mr. Wylloe claims not to need the money, apparently even nature writing based on science is a lucrative profession these days, but he has taken the assignment, he says, to demonstrate to Mr. Grinnell and the rest of the popular press that the truth of the natural world, in all its interesting and unpredictable diversity, can be as entertaining as that which is based on some urban writer's imagination. What a stroke of editorial genius to send him, then, to Yellowstone National Park where the scientific "truth" is as far-fetched and fiction-like as anything the average reader would encounter anywhere in the world! I am curious indeed to learn how Mr. Wylloe will handle his dispatches.

As Mr. Wylloe advanced up the path, slower now as he

appeared short of breath, Professor Merriam emerged from the creekbed, again calling out my name. He saw me now and waved, but when he saw John Wylloe, he hesitated.

"When you have a chance," he said abruptly, and retreated into the narrow ravine.

Since Professor Merriam could rest easy knowing of my location, I waited for Mr. Wylloe to ascend the final few feet to where I stood. He was visibly out of breath, struggling as he advanced. Dressed as he was, you would need a good deal of that urban writer's imagination to see him as the Nation's leading naturalist and outdoorsman. With his long white hair and beard, black suit, wide-brimmed hat, and fishing creel, he looked more like an ancient scribe, perhaps someone from the Bible assigned to carry bad news, or one who has travelled for miles to worship at some holy shrine.

"Forgive me, Miss Bartram," he said, clearly out of breath, "but I find I still am not conditioned to these higher elevations."

Balancing himself with his hands on his knees, he lowered his head. Although I hated to see him so distressed, it was reassuring to note that even the greatest minds and talents are limited by the same physical rules of nature as the rest of us. Mr. Wylloe waited thus for a moment or two, his head bowed as if in deep concentration, took two deep breaths which he exhaled as deeply, and then raised his head slowly, like a snake uncoiling its face to the sun.

"Miss Bartram," he said, offering me his hand in salutation or perhaps to steady himself. In either case, he drew himself closer to me, taking my solitary hand into both of his. He took another deep breath, and sighed.

"I have come here to ask a favor of you," he said. "One which I hope you will be so kind as to grant me."

I told him, of course, I would do for him what I could, and he smiled, a thin, weary slit which lifted the corners of his beard for only the briefest of moments.

"I would like to accompany you, if you will have me, on your outings into the field."

I was quite taken aback, not that he would ask, for I know of his general interest in science and natural history, but that he would ask me, rather than directing his question to Professor Merriam. I was certainly not in the position to grant his favor, and I told him so.

"The Professor decides who should . . . ," I started, but Mr. Wylloe interrupted me, as impatient as he was out of breath.

"It was Professor Merriam who referred me. You see, it is you—or I should say your work—that I am interested in and, thus, it is you and your work I would inconvenience if such an arrangement were not to your liking. Therefore, the Professor referred me to you directly."

I admit, I was puzzled by the request. Flattered, of course—all I could think of was wait until I tell Mother!—but it did seem a bit of an inconvenience for all concerned. And yet, how could I refuse him his offer? He was, after all, John Wylloe.

I told him he would be welcome to join our daily expeditions at his convenience. However, I warned him, he must keep Professor Merriam informed of his desire to join us on any particular outing. It would be presumptuous for Mr. Wylloe to inform me of his intentions in this regard. It would place me in an awkward position within my group.

Mr. Wylloe thanked me, still holding my hand warmly between his own, at which point I excused myself, reminding him that the Professor had asked that I join him.

"Well, then, if it is not inconvenient," Mr. Wylloe smiled, releasing me, "I will accompany you, and we shall inform Professor Merriam of your decision together."

This, too, seemed inappropriate but I did not object. Rather, I led Mr. Wylloe down a thickly shaded path until we reached the creek. Professor Merriam looked up at our approach, but said nothing.

"She said yes," Mr. Wylloe called out, at which the Professor nodded slightly in acknowledgment, before returning his attention to the Indian.

As I advanced down the trail to where Professor Merriam was working, I started to apologize for the delay in responding to his calls, anxious to inform him of my encounter with Mrs. Eversman and her blind, but he, too, cut me short with an abrupt wave of the hand.

"No, that's not why I called," he said. "Here, I want you to see this."

He then led me to a solitary pink blossom, growing next to the stream.

"Do you know what it is?" he asked.

I had to admit, even after close inspection under my hand lens, I could not name it. Located as it was next to a stream, with three sepals and three petals, a member of Orchidaceae was the best that I could do for certain.

"Joseph has asked me not to remove it," Professor Merriam informed me.

I must have looked at him very strangely because he hastily continued.

"It is alone," the Professor explained. "And since it cannot be named, Joseph is convinced that it must be sacred."

Professor Merriam watched me closely for my reaction. Of course, that was the most ridiculous thing I had ever heard, and I told him so.

"You cannot name it if you do not take it," I reminded him. "Besides, what about the collection?"

As Professor Merriam and I talked, John Wylloe removed his boots and socks with great ceremony, rolled his pant legs to just below the knees, and sat gingerly upon a large rock, slowly easing his feet into the icy creek. Even from where I was standing, I could see them lying low in the water like two albino *Salvelinus*. He took off his hat and, again, unfurled his spine, vertebrae by vertebrae, so that his face was fully oriented toward the sun, his long white hair and beard almost translucent in the fierce light.

As Mr. Wylloe settled in, Professor Merriam conferred with the Indian in Crow, and then the two of them advanced down the streambed, leaving me, Mr. Wylloe, and the intact orchid without another word. The student looked at me apologetically, and then he, too, followed the other two downstream.

"It is a slipper of Venus," Mr. Wylloe said to me once the three of them had woven their way out of sight. "Or a fairy slipper. I have heard it called different things associated with footwear on the rare occasions I have seen them near my cabin. But the Indian is right. From my limited experience, they are rare. He may be right, too, about them being sacred, but that is beyond my ken."

With that short burst of speech behind him, Mr. Wylloe removed his feet from the water and placed them carefully, side by side, like rare specimens, upon the rocks to dry. Then he returned his face to the sun, closed his eyes, and appeared to doze.

Of course, Mr. Wylloe's information, like the term Indian paintbrush and all other such non-scientific nomenclature, gave me little if anything to go on. A fairy slipper could be anything from a *Cypripedium* to a *Lilium* to a *Campanula*.

I opened my journal and started to write a physical description but then hesitated, removing my colors from my case instead. Perhaps the process of observation and reflection needed to illustrate the specimen would help me come to better know it and, thus, identify it. At least that was my thinking.

Illustrating its precise form was relatively easy. The flower stood atop a small, sheathed stalk which barely held its own in a bed of decaying wood thick with moss. Once I pushed the debris out of the way, I could see that it also had a single basal leaf which was just beginning to emerge.

The flower itself was easy enough to capture on paper, its bilaterally symmetrical petals and prominent lip all easily translated for my visual record. It was not the flower's form which gave me pause, but rather the color, a shocking pinkish purple with tiger-like stripes tinged along its edges with a golden brown. Sensuous, succulent in the non-botanical sense, if the plant were indeed a slipper, it would be something worn by Titania rather than Puck, if I dare make such a pedestrian literary comparison to you, my dear friend, who is so much better read.

I tried with my colors to capture the plant on paper, but after more than two hours, the day was drawing to a close and my attempts were either too bland, not at all capturing the showiness of the specimen, or too gilded, losing its sense of naturalness in my clumsy translations.

Now it was I who let out a long, exhausted sigh. I returned my glance to Mr. Wylloe, who was watching me closely from his perch on the rock.

"Beautiful, is it not?" he said.

It is showy, I was thinking. A function of survival, I started to note. But for some unknown reason, I said nothing. Jessie, can you believe it? I held my tongue.

But then an even stranger thing occurred. Mr. Wylloe responded to me as if I had spoken. Or as if he had read my mind.

"I meant the setting. You look but you do not see, Miss Bartram. The dappled light, the sound of falling water, the intense green, almost devoid of color in the shadiest corners, your deep concentration. All beautiful."

It was, indeed, a picturesque setting, but I could not fully appreciate its attractions since I was too frustrated at having failed to capture the true likeness of the plant. I took my hand trowel from my bag and started to remove the specimen, when once again Mr. Wylloe interrupted me.

"Miss Bartram, you surprise me," he said.

Now I was the impatient one. Again I sighed, but this time I fear it came out sounding more like a snort. Mr. Wylloe had been most generous in his interest in my work, and in his quiet observation, never once interrupting me, focusing his attention instead on the sun, the water, a book of verse he carried in his creel. He appeared to take little interest in what I was doing—or at least he did not interrupt me to learn more about it. In fact, he was such an unobtrusive companion that for that hour or two I thought Mr. Wylloe might prove to be a pleasant addition to my day. Someone I could ignore when it suited me, but still talk to once on the trail headed home. Someone I could write home about, perhaps providing my mother with a reason to be pleased or even proud of my experiences here. In the company of such a man, she would certainly have no reason for concern. But my mother's concerns aside, I would have to discourage Mr. Wylloe's interest in my work and decline his offer of companionship if he was going to turn into a bother. From the look on my face he must have understood my concerns.

"Please, I do not mean to intrude, Miss Bartram," he said, rising from his sunny perch. He moved so slowly that I could almost detect each fragile bone moving inside his skin as he left the creek and walked towards me.

"You are young, and probably unaware of the academic life," he said, leaning softly against a tree. "I, on the other hand, am experienced when it comes to these sorts of things. You will find that the academic life is a closed world. If you plan to succeed within it, you must play by its rules."

Now I admit that I knew he was referring to the orchid, Professor Merriam, and the rest, but at the same time I did not have a clue what he really meant. The academic world, even the world of our expedition, is one of science, not sentiment, in spite of the Professor's foolishness at times. And, yes, science and the academy have their rules, but those are the rules of dispassionate reason. If he meant that I should not remove a specimen because of some Indian's idea of the sacred—well, you know me, I could not hold my tongue forever.

"Now it is you who must forgive me, Mr. Wylloe, for I wish to acknowledge and respect both your experience and your age. However, like the notion of what is sacred, this is simply outside your ken. There is room for sentiment in things like poetry," I motioned to the slim volume he carried with him, "but not science. And the academy, with all its acknowledged limitations, does not thrive on sentiment."

After a pause he spoke. "Perhaps you are right, Miss Bartram. Certainly about the science. However, I hope that even you could admit that the academy does not consist of science, or reason, or even knowledge, but people. It is people, Miss Bartram, with whom you must succeed. With that I will leave you to it."

And he did. He replaced his hat, slipped his poetry back into his creel, and withdrew, his long white hair and beard reflecting the scattered light as if he were retreating underwater.

Which brings me to why I am boring you with all of this. Jessie, I sat there and sat there like a thwarted child. I revisited the words of Professor Merriam, the way he watched me so intently, his comment that the Indian did not want him to remove the specimen, all of it, but I could no more make sense of the Professor's wishes than I could of Mr. Wylloe's. Had the Professor argued that, following scientific protocol, a sole specimen should be left to stand, I would have understood and been forced to comply with his wishes. There would have been no discussion. But this sacred business made no sense to me what so ever.

Given that, I did a very inexplicable thing. I took one last hard look at the orchid, packed my colors and journal and tools, and returned to the trail to await Professor Merriam and the rest of our group. Mr. Wylloe was waiting there as well, although he said nothing when I joined him.

As I write this I am still unsettled with my decision. Even if I did what was right, I am not at all convinced that I did it for the right reason. It pains me to admit it, Jessie, but I left the specimen behind not for science, but for sentiment. Or maybe it was my desire to finally make peace with Professor Merriam, and to be accepted into his company. I am at a loss to otherwise explain it.

That night, when I transferred my specimens to Dr. Rutherford for safekeeping, I could sense Professor Merriam watching me closely. I refused to look back at him, and since he never asked to see the specimen, there is no way he could be certain that I left the orchid behind. But he knew. For something changed between us that night. Time will tell if it is a change for the better.

If I believed in God, I would ask you to pray for me. Something or someone better save me soon, or this whole experience may end up being one in which a promising young woman goes out west in pursuit of science only to return to New York just like any other watcher in the woods, starched and prim, dressed in fairy slippers, with nothing but sentimental love of botany and a mere passion for flowers. Maybe you should pray for me after all.

Your struggling but (still) unsentimental friend,

Alex

Lester King
National Hotel
Mammoth Hot Springs
Yellowstone National Park
June 28, 1898

Dear Mr. and Mrs. Bartram,

I am writing as promised to let you know I have arrived in Yellowstone National Park, although I have yet to rendezvous with Alexandria. I have met with a cavalryman at the Yellowstone headquarters, a Captain Craighead, who will take me to her and her colleagues on Friday. He assures me that the naturalists' camp, as he refers to it, is an easy ride, and has offered to lend me a horse for the duration of my stay. I prefer, however, to wait for his guidance and expert company since I find it difficult to believe that any destination in this wilderness is an easy ride, the roads in and out of this small valley are so steep and treacherous. To make matters worse, it is now threatening to rain, which could make travel even more dangerous.

That is not to suggest to you that Alex is in any danger. The National Park has a competing wildness and a civility about it which are, in my travelling experience, unique to the human condition. Everyone I have encountered, both on the train ride to the National Park and once here in the hotel, seems to think of themselves as world adventurers, latter day Lewises and Clarks, forging their way through the wilderness and discovering new territories, without fear of the shackles society in its wisdom places upon us elsewhere. These travellers come to the National Park, according to Captain Craighead, to break free of those rules and regulations, and to set their spirits free, to find that even here, at what appears to be the end of the earth, or at least the last stop on the train, the long arm of government regulation has them in their grip.

The National Park requires this government control, according to the captain. Not a day goes by, he informs me, that some fool is discovered carving his initials into a thermal feature or chipping off a piece of a stone formation to take home as a souvenir. With thousands of visitors arriving each year, it would take no time at all before there would be little or no National Park left to visit if it were not for the law and order of Captain Craighead and his men.

Then there are the visitors who throw boulders and large pieces of timber into geyser formations to see if they can block their flow. Of course these idiots are unsuccessful and the debris, I am told, shoots hundreds of feet into the air, often endangering the miscreants themselves and innocent by-standers more than the geysers. Poachers, too, are a problem, having almost wiped out the Park's big game animals which, thanks to the military's presence, are just now beginning to recover.

The captain appears to be a young man, wiser than his years, and unsuited for the administrative life he has been assigned to here. He told me he was selected for the post without being consulted and came to the Park against his wishes. However, now that he is here, he is determined to take great interest in his work and do his duty to the best of his ability.

To give you an idea of the kind of degenerate characters he is supposed to control, let me describe a brief encounter I witnessed just yesterday afternoon. As the captain and I were conversing at headquarters, a foreign earl or count of some form of purported European royalty sauntered in under the supervision of two cavalrymen who had apprehended the gentleman and his party on the road into the Mammoth Hot Springs compound. The count in question was fortunate in that he was stopped and questioned as he travelled into the Park, rather than out of it. In his possession was a cache of preserved animals collected throughout the West, including everything from buffalo to elk to prairie dogs to prairie chickens, along with the dogs, ammunition, and alcohol needed to hunt down, kill, and preserve a good deal more.

When questioned by the captain, the count feigned ignorance about Park regulations, he was a scientist and a foreigner after all, but then he took Captain Craighead aside and offered payment for permission to, in his words, collect on the captain's private reserve. The captain declined, and with his gallant and good nature, explained the National Park's rules. He suggested, instead, that the count register his specimens with the captain's office and return for them upon his withdrawal from the National Park.

A simple request to make. Quite another to fulfill. I walked out with them as the count peeled cover after cover from wagons in which his so-called specimens were stored. There were enough preserved animals, and parts of animals including a number of severed heads, to fill a major museum. Or two.

Also in the count's possession is a full entourage of cooks, butlers, horsemen, musicians, dogs and their handler, the count's own personal naturalists and taxidermists, who identify and preserve his burgeoning collection of big game animals and birds, and assorted other young men who looked road weary if not out-right debilitated by their employ, the lot of whom sat by waiting for a resolution to be reached between the cavalryman and the count. One young man retreated under his hat and proceeded to snore, an offence for which he was rapped across the knees by the count as he showed the captain around his collection.

"As you can see, my dear sir," the count explained to Captain Craighead, "I am not a hunter. I have put myself and my men at great risk as we have ventured in the name of science into this western wilderness. You have nothing to fear from me. And the world has much to gain from my studies."

The captain was resolute. The count was welcome to leave his specimens in the cavalry's care and enjoy himself while in the National Park, or just as free to leave under escort to the Park's northern boundary. But the count did not have the option of travelling with his collection unattended within the confines of the National Park, science or no science. As far as Captain Craighead was concerned, there were no other options.

The count walked along the wagons, motioning to the piles of carcasses laid to rest in these large, mobile caskets. As he walked, examining and explaining his collection, pulling up a well-preserved buffalo head for the captain's closer examination, or unwrapping half a dozen calliope hummingbirds, their diminutive bodies falling into his hand, the count talked of the expenses associated with science, about the costs to all those involved with scientific collections, inferring, in essence, that Captain Craighead, too, must be compensated in some fashion. The captain accompanied the count along the tour of laden wagons, but at the mention again of money the captain lost his composure, and challenged the count to show him just one specimen, in amongst all the slaughter, which would help real scientists, he used those words, better understand the natural world. This was not science, the captain was certain of it, but killing for the simple joy of it.

And with that Captain Craighead raged past me into his office. With resolution reached, the entourage began re-securing the wagons and, after moving them to a shady alleyway next to the headquarters building, proceeded to unhitch and picket the horses for the night. The whole operation could not have taken more than ten or fifteen minutes but during the entire exercise, the count paced and barked orders as if he were being detained for hours.

From there, the remaining entourage, still ten or eleven wagons strong with the count's bright red buggy in the lead, proceeded down the road to the hotel, where they hitched themselves in a row and began to unload. From the captain's front porch I watched as four young men wheeled the count's piano with much effort into the hotel lobby, while another four stumbled along, the count's large iron bathtub hoisted on their shoulders. Wildness indeed.

As you can see, there are civilizing rules and regulations which, in theory at least, are looking out for the likes of Alexandria. I hope she is looking out for them. All last year, she was forever complaining about the rules and structure of the university and the limits they placed upon her, but what she has yet to understand is that it is through rules and structure and rigid protocols that we gain the freedom for creative work in the sciences. She claims to be enjoying her new-found freedom in the Park. She must be operating under the false assumption that there are no rules or limitations here to protect her from herself.

Captain Craighead has promised to escort me to Alex's camp on Friday, at which point the captain and I will both take rooms at the Yellowstone Lake Hotel. He plans to be in attendance at a large celebration in honor of Independence Day. I will let you know of my own plans after I have had a chance to speak with your daughter.

    In the meantime,
        I remain yours,
            Lester King

                H. G. Merriam
                c/o Yellowstone Lake Hotel
                Yellowstone National Park
                July 3, 1898

Dear Mother,

    The U.S. Cavalry has a saying that there are two seasons in Yellowstone, winter and July, but the weather has been at its bleakest in these earliest days of the month. It has been raining steadily for two days, so I find myself trapped inside my tent with Rutherford, his foul-smelling pipe, and his new pet raven, which Rutherford discovered standing by the side of the road, fearlessly gobbling like a turkey for the entertainment of all who passed by.

    Rutherford is convinced that if a raven is smart enough to imitate a turkey to beg treats from tourists in the Park, it can just as easily be taught how to imitate a man's speech. So every time the raven gobbles, it is now rewarded with scraps from Kim Li's kitchen and is told that it is a "pretty bird." The strategy, what Rutherford refers to as a scientific experiment, is to see if eventually the bird will not only associate the turkey call with treats, but will also learn to associate the words with the greasy goodies and, thus, learn how to talk.

    Is it any wonder that Philip Aber has his doubts about my ability to lead a scientific expedition? Not only does this so-called experiment go on for all hours of the day, but the bird travels everywhere with Rutherford, riding with him in the wagon, sometimes sitting on his shoulder or even on his head.

Journalists are arriving at the hotel to document this weekend's celebrations and plans for the electric rail line through the Park— plans which are being negotiated as I write. My greatest fear is that one of these journalists will get bored and wander into camp one day, see Rutherford talking to his raven, and the story will be plastered all over the New York and Chicago press. I will be the laughing stock of the scientific community. I can hardly show my face at the hotel as it is, since there is not a person in the Park who has not seen or at least heard about the fat man and his turkey-gobbling bird.

Of course, this weather has not helped my state of mind. Even though it is early in the afternoon, the sky is as black as Rutherford's raven so I am forced to write to you by candlelight. But the sky is not nearly as black as I feel inside.

This morning a friend of Miss Bartram's arrived, with the intention, I am certain, of taking her back home with him. He could not have arrived at a worse time. Miss Bartram is developing into a reliable and helpful assistant. She is steadfast in her commitment to science and considerate almost to a fault of the limitations of our meagre expedition. I have come to rely on her contributions as well as her good judgment in so many instances that I cannot even begin to tell you how much she would be missed, should she decide to leave. Worse yet, it is now July, which is peak collecting time in the Park. I could not possibly manage all there is to do without her.

But she is young, with her whole life ahead of her, and this is, in all honesty, no place for a woman on her own. If this friend is as serious in his intentions as he appears to be, perhaps this would be the best option for her, as disastrous as it would be for me personally. So when she came to ask permission to leave camp for the afternoon, I naturally gave my consent. I suggested, in fact, that she spend the entire weekend at the hotel. We cannot make any progress in this weather anyway, so she might as well enjoy a few days of comfort and warmth, regardless of her final decision. Besides, with the Independence Day celebrations ahead of us, this is a fine weekend to spend at the hotel. Many young people and much excitement, I am told. Given my state of mind, however, I think I had best weather the weekend here.

As if things were not bleak enough, President Healey arrived at the hotel this morning, ostensibly to check on our progress and enjoy the celebrations, but instinct tells me he is more interested in checking on tentative conversations about the herbarium I have had with representatives from the railroad (how he found out about those talks I am sure I will never know). He is, no doubt, anxious to initiate conversations of his own.

If ever there were an opportunity to raise funds for the herbarium, it is now, with every principal employee of the railroad in residence at the hotel, along with half the U.S. Congress and their staff. Thanks to a special shipment of alcohol and cigars brought in for the weekend, these gentlemen are in a good humor to bargain, and bargain they will.

I would like to think that it is those in the East who do not understand what it means to own a national resource in common for the benefit of us all, and it is these easterners who are leading the charge to buy up and sell off our country's heritage in Yellowstone National Park. But I am sad to report that it is my fellow Montanans who are right up there at the front of the line, negotiating leases for every possible money-making scheme. There is a man who wants to construct an electric elevator to transport visitors, for a hefty fee of course, up and down the Yellowstone canyon and, to demonstrate its feasibility, he has constructed a working model which he has on display in the hotel lobby. Another is negotiating a lifetime lease on Dot Island where he plans to deposit a small herd of domesticated bison, which he has purchased for this purpose from Charles Goodnight, a Texas rancher. The beasts are already on their way and are to be corralled by the lake in the morning. And then there is an architect proposing to build a large log and stone lodge on the grounds adjoining the Old Faithful geyser. Yet another is looking to lease the rights to a hot springs where he will construct a private swimming pool. All sorts of harebrained schemes are being considered. There is even some foreigner bargaining for the right to personally eliminate from the Park cougars, wolves, and other vermin as he calls them. I fear avarice and greed do not recognize state or even national boundaries.

Of course the railroad is right there in the middle of it all. In the lobby, surveys have been mounted along with artists' sketches to prove that, by damming the Yellowstone River, the railroad can generate more than adequate power to fuel all sorts of improvements, including their proposed electric rail line which will carry passengers from the northern entrance and through the Park as it stops at each major attraction. That it will also be used to carry ore from Cooke City is seldom discussed.

If there were any doubt about the need for such a service, the railroad has made a practice of transporting the dignitaries in great style and comfort by private car to the Cinnabar station, at which point they are herded like cattle into the worst wagons in the fleet and plunged down narrow canyon roads, brakes shrieking, horses stumbling, and then back up the steepest hills. One such incline has been dubbed the Devil's Stairway, since all are forced to get out and walk, even the women, because the horses cannot manage the climb with both the passengers and their luggage on board. Those with wives in attendance are now particularly well disposed to the railroad's plans I am told. It is all very sad.

Forgive me for only corresponding when I am full of bad news and trouble but I so badly need someone to whom I can confide. If Bill Gleick were here I would talk to him, but so far I have had little luck getting his attention, much less gaining his assurances that he will join us in the Park upon his return, which should be any day now. Perhaps he knows I would simply burden him with my sorrows if he were in the Park to hear them.

I can only hope that President Healey has not also learned of our setbacks here. If he discovers them, he might insist that we all travel back to campus under his command. That most certainly would be more than I could withstand.

Please put in a good word for me to whomever it is you pray. I am desperate and need all the help that you can muster.

All my love,
Howard

Lester King
Lake Hotel
Yellowstone National Park
July 4, 1898

Dear Jessica,

I am writing to you this morning, rather than to the Bartrams, to avoid any misunderstandings or concerns. If I were to write to Alexandria's family at this point in time, I would either overwhelm them with the truth or lie to them with such transparency that they would fear the worst. Alex's situation here is nothing for them to fear. It is loathsome, perhaps, but not, I think, perilous.

I arrived at the hotel near Alex's camp late in the day. It had been raining, a steady downpour, but since I was anxious to see Alex, I ventured out. As I set forth, the rain let up, but still the sky and trees and ground were damp and cold and the muck underfoot clumped to my boots, making it difficult to walk.

I trudged along a well-worn path from the hotel until I came to a muddy clearing, at the center of which a man, huddled under a greasy tarpaulin, struggled to start a fire. The man did not look up as I entered the clearing, but arranged and rearranged the wood in a futile attempt to find just the right configuration to foil the dampness.

To his left, a large hospital tent, missing half of its hardware, slumped against the side of a tree. In front of the tent, a small, filthy Chinaman stirred dishes in a pot, upon the surface of which floated the greasy remains of the previous meal. The Chinaman kept careful watch of me through narrow, suspicious eyes but otherwise did not acknowledge my approach.

Under a camp table next to the Chinaman, a raven scavenged for crumbs until it, too, saw me, at which point it let out a brief shrill alarm and disappeared into a fly tent pitched off to one side of the clearing. From this tent yet another man, wrapped in a thin woolen blanket, emerged.

It was to this man that I announced myself, and asked after Alex. He, too, was suspicious, and queried me about my business. I explained that I was a friend, and he pointed me to a small cavalry shelter tent on the opposite side of the campsite. I could sense him watching as I mucked through the clearing, lifted the flap, and stooped down to peer into its dark confines. The tent was empty except for a simple cot, blanket, and tattered buffalo hide, upon which were stacked, almost to the low ceiling, Alex's books and supplies to keep them out of the rain.

It was then that I addressed myself to the man at the fire, which had now started to sizzle and smoke if not outright burst into flame. This man's indifferent stare turned on me from behind a cloud of tobacco smoke. I explained I was looking for Alex. Miss Bartram. I was a friend.

Like the other man, he did not have any idea where she might be. Someone had mentioned at dinner that bears were feeding on fish where the river spills into the lake, and our Miss B, he referred to her thus, might be down there observing them. Miss B, as he insisted on calling her, is determined to see bears in the wild, outside of those which habituate the hotel dump site, he informed me.

Is it any wonder that Alex claims to be happy here! No one is paying a bit of attention to her, or in any way tracking her activities. She was forever complaining about the restrictions of the university and the routine of the laboratories. Here she has complete freedom of movement. That alone should be reason for concern, given the conditions under which she is living.

I never did locate her that evening. It was getting dark and the rain was starting up again in cold, heavy sheets, so rather than venture into unknown territory, I resigned myself to the hotel, and returned to her camp the next morning. When I re-entered the clearing, I again saw the fat man by the fire, which sizzled and popped against a thin but persistent rain. Next to him sat another figure, wrapped in a blanket. I assumed this was the gentleman I had spoken to the day before. When I approached, the figure turned and looked in my direction.

Alex peered out from under the blanket, first confused and then surprised to see me. No one had bothered to inform her of my arrival the night before, and she had no reason to be expecting me. But when she realized I was indeed standing there, asking after her, she was pleased, not so much to see me, I admit it, but for me to see her there, huddled next to a damp fire with a fat man smoking a pipe in the rain.

I must tell you, Jessica, she looked terrible. Thin, brown, weary, her hair unkempt and hanging in limp ringlets around her face and down her back. And she was filthy, smelling of grease, pine, and woodsmoke. Everyone talks about the warm bathing holes in Yellowstone National Park. I could not help at that moment but wonder when she has had an opportunity to partake of them. And yet, in spite of the grime and weariness, when she saw me looking down at her, her eyes, her mouth, her cheeks glowed with such pride and pleasure, even I was happy to see her there, in spite of the primitive conditions in which she was living.

Of course, I took her at once to the hotel. She did not resist, claiming that, given the weather, my visit was convenient. She used that word. But before we could leave, she went out of her way to secure permission from the other man, the one in the tent. He consented, citing not my visit but the weather. He then suggested she stay for the weekend, and enjoy the holiday and the planned celebrations. It was clear he made the offer with some reluctance, but he again mentioned the weather and he, too, used the word convenient.

I booked Alex a room, arranged for some clean, dry clothes, ordered a bath and toiletries for her personal use, and waited for her in the lobby, where I was joined by the cavalryman who had befriended me upon my arrival in the Park. Joining us as well was Philip Aber, a scientist from the Smithsonian, who is providing the financial support for the botanical expedition and its activities. When I mentioned my short visits to the camp, Aber did not even try to conceal his contempt for the conditions under which the field work is being conducted, and his professional reservations about its leadership. In fact, once his wife and family arrive in the Park, Aber told me he is planning to end support for the expedition. When I asked him when he was expecting his family, he ignored the question, asking instead about my work at Cornell.

We sat there, the three of us, talking and smoking and watching the black squall advance across the lake and rage against the windows of the hotel. Outside, travellers hurried up the hill and huddled under the hotel's covered entry way, as their bags were unloaded from wagons and from a steamboat which docked at a landing on the lake. But even under the portico, these exhausted travellers found little relief since the wind whipped the rain and cold all around them, following them into the lobby and past the heavy hotel doors which, against the wind, were difficult to close. The travellers were all wet and weary and cold from their journeys, but they were shouting and laughing and joking and stomping the water and mud from their feet, excited to be in the midst of nature in such a wild and uncontrollable state.

A red, two-wheeled buggy appeared outside the door, and a foreign count, who I met in passing when I first arrived in the Park, entered the hotel, followed by an entourage of men with trunks and boxes and other personal effects which were carried up the stairs to his rooms. Outside, the count's pack of hunting dogs yapped and howled while two men fought to keep a piano, tied to the back of one of the wagons, erect in spite of the wind.

With all the ensuing confusion and noise, I did not see Alex enter the lobby, nor did I see her join us at the table overlooking the lake until she was right there upon us. She greeted Captain Craighead and Philip Aber with a casual familiarity, and then took my hand for but a minute before joining us without the slightest hesitation or modesty.

She looked better after bathing, changing, and cleaning and brushing her hair, but still you would be hard pressed to recognize her. It is not that she has lost weight so much as that she has become more sinewy, roughened or perhaps even toughened by the conditions under which she is living here. There seems to be an air of detachment, too, from common courtesies and civilities, which have been replaced by a wildness in her demeanor. It is as if she has been held captive against her wishes while living in the East and now that she is here in the Park, she has been released from civilization, and has returned to her true, wild nature.

My companions excused themselves, Philip Aber more gracious in the excusing than Captain Craighead, I noticed, at which point

Alex turned without a word and watched the rain beat against the windows. After a moment or two, she turned to me again, her face radiant. With the wind and rain wailing outside the glass, she asked if I did not think it beautiful.

To be honest, I found the question distracting. I told her of our worry, her parents' worry, of our concern for her life and her reputation. I wanted to tell her, too, that, based on what I had seen in her camp and the conditions there, our concerns were well founded. But she interrupted me with a laugh.

She wants to have a reputation like Meriwether Lewis, Charles Darwin, and all the other Bartrams before her, she told me. She wants to understand this small piece of the world as well or better than they had understood theirs. The botanical specimens she had sent to me for safekeeping were but a small piece of the knowledge she had collected while in the Park, she informed me, and an even smaller fraction of what she planned to master before coming home in the fall.

She told of just yesterday seeing a dragonfly dipping through the misty spray of a waterfall, the water on its wings reflecting the sunlight. She crept out onto the rocks to view it closer, and saw not one but two insects, one atop the other, dipping in and out of the sunlight. They alighted on a plant, at which point her watching startled them so one flew off, leaving the other to sit alone, drying its wings in the sun. The wings were gossamer, she used that word, and had one red spot on each corner. She laughed again and said that for the first time in her naturalizing career she felt a bit like a voyeur. She used that word, too. Then she told me that there was so much to do and see and learn and experience, and so little time left in the season in which to do it all. And then she surprised me again by taking both my hands into her own and telling me how good it was to see me.

In her enthusiasm, a strand of hair had broken loose from its pins and had strayed across her cheek and mouth. I reached out and brushed it back away from her face. She grabbed my hand and kissed it on the palm, like a man would do to a woman in private. And then she laughed again, and proclaimed to anyone within hearing distance—we were, remember, sitting in the middle of a busy hotel lobby—that she was so happy and it was so good to be alive.

Before I could respond, a tall cowboy walked up with the same casual familiarity with which Alex had joined my party earlier. He knew how anxious Alex was to see buffalo, he said, and he was helping a friend transport a small herd from the rail station in Cinnabar to Yellowstone Lake, where the animals will be barged to start a private reserve on an island. There is a half a dozen head, he informed us, and they will be unloading them into corrals down by the lake in the morning. He had horses if we were interested in riding down with him to see the beasts.

Without hesitation and without consultation, Alex volunteered us both in spite of my protests. I have never been on a horse, and am not about to start now. And the back of a horse is no place for a lady. But Alex was resolute, and arranged for us to meet the cowboy and his friends before breakfast the next morning.

At dinner, Alex's good humor grew, buoyed by the bath, the warmth of the hotel, and, I would like to think, my unexpected company. She ate and drank with an insatiable ardor, and relayed story after story about the things she had seen, the people she had met, and the discoveries she had made about the world of science and about herself and other people.

She told of a party of women she met at their first camp in Mammoth and, as she related the story, the women arrived at our table as if on cue, delighted to see Alex at the hotel, and intent on making sure she planned to attend the Independence Day ball and other planned festivities. Again, Alex volunteered us both, saying we would not miss it, in spite of the fact that her wardrobe was limited. The older woman, a Miss Zwinger, responded that she should not worry about such trifles. She used that word. Something suitable would be found for Alex to wear. The woman was certain of it.

Alex looked at me, triumphant in her new friendships and full of passion for a world that, she claimed, she is experiencing for the first time. As the evening drew on, Alex's enthusiasm for her new life continued to grow. At the same time I could sense my own passions retreating. I felt overwhelmed. Diminished somehow. By the end of the evening, I can admit to you alone, I was at a loss as to how to respond to her.

This morning, rather than join me for breakfast, Alex has ventured off to see the buffalo unloaded at the steamboat harbor on the lake. She asked if I would like to join her and, when I declined, she kissed me, again in public, and clambered onto a horse in her skirts without the slightest hesitation or regret. She would be back, she informed me, her hair already beginning to loosen and fall onto her shoulders as she rode away.

So I am waiting for her here, uncertain what demands I will make of her, but more confident than ever that I need to make my demands known. It may be difficult to get her attention with all the activity here at the hotel, but I am resolute. Once I know her answer, I will then correspond with her parents. But not before. You may, in the meantime, want to let them know I have written to you and that I am in contact with their daughter.

I thank you in advance for your discretion. You have been a good friend to us both, and we both need your friendship now more than ever.

Yours,

    Lester King

— · • · · —

H. G. Merriam
c/o Yellowstone Lake Hotel
Yellowstone National Park
July 4, 1898

Mother:

I am beginning to believe that you have supernatural powers or the ear of some divine entity. Either way, I am so grateful I may yet become a true believer! It is hard to imagine that it has only been a day since I last wrote, a mere 24 hours. But how the world has changed in that short period of time! Not only has the rain let up, and the sun come out bright and full of summer, but with the early morning sunlight came word that Bill Gleick has arrived at the

Yellowstone Lake Hotel. And he has brought along Philip Aber's wife who is here, I hope, to lure him back home. This is such excellent news that I have thrown financial caution to the wind and booked a room at the hotel for myself, at least for one night, so that I might spend time with Gleick strategizing how to best salvage our expedition in the Park.

It is a perfect time to be in residence here, with the hotel staff and even the guests bustling here and there in preparation for the evening's entertainment. Just a few hours before, such excitement and joviality would have only served to mock my own sense of despair about the future of our expedition, even my future in general, but now I find the commotion stimulating, even rejuvenating, and am committed to enjoying each and every one of the day's activities to their fullest. Gleick has sent word that he cannot meet with me until after dinner, and I have just seen Philip Aber ride off on horseback to points unknown, so he is mercifully out of the way. I have, therefore, agreed to take part in a pre-celebration picnic planned by Miss Zwinger and her companions. They will be setting forth for some "secret place" they know of within the hour.

I am in such good humor that I invited Rutherford to join us, proposing that he bring along his pet raven which would, no doubt, amuse the ladies. But he is content, he tells me, to pay a courtesy call on President Healey, after which he plans to spend the remainder of the afternoon in the camp of some foreign count who, I have been told, has an abundant supply of liquor. Our driver and the two students plan to join him at the count's camp as well. There was a time when I would have dreaded the news of such a potentially ruinous combination, but it is, after all, a holiday. Might as well let them celebrate in their way, while I celebrate in mine.

President Healey would not, of course, approve of any of this, but I am not all that concerned at the moment. I am anxious for his support of the herbarium, of course, but until I can sort out the details of the expedition, and ensure its continuation and success, there seems little need to keep him informed of our day-to-day activities here. Besides, he appears to have his own plans for the holiday. As I write, Healey is standing across the lobby, handling a model of the electric rail cars being proposed for the Park, rocking up and down on his toes with one of those far away looks in his eyes. He is no doubt planning the continuation and success of his own New Century campaign, perhaps musing about some massive brick structure to be named Healey Hall. I can guarantee you that he is not thinking about a research herbarium named after Meriwether Lewis—or William Clark, for that matter.

As for Miss Bartram, I have not yet had an opportunity to speak with her or inform her of Bill Gleick's arrival. I saw her briefly as she walked through the lobby, not in the company of her friend from New York, but with that rancher who has frequented our camp from time to time. They were laughing and talking with such intimacy it makes me wonder how blind I have been, and what all I have been missing right there under my nose. But I admit, too, that I felt the slightest sense of selfish relief. If I misjudged the intentions of the gentleman from New York, or made false assumptions about Miss Bartram's intentions towards him, it may mean that she will in fact be staying with the expedition for the duration of the summer. Now, of all times, I cannot afford to lose her.

I had best keep this correspondence brief since the wagons to take us to the picnic are lining up in front of the hotel. There are at least a dozen of them, so they must be planning quite the party. In fact, I can now see several of the railroad executives, and there is a congressman, too, all getting ready to board.

I was about to write that this might be my opportunity to speak to some of these gentlemen in earnest about the herbarium but before my pen could be recharged with ink, President Healey walked out to the roadway and now he, too, is being helped into a wagon, and is taking a seat right between one of the railroad men and the senator. It looks like this afternoon will be the president's opportunity to speak of building new facilities rather than mine, for they are all laughing and appear to be in the best of humor. I will leave them to it. My highest priority at the moment is the continued success of our work here in the Park. I must ensure first and foremost that we return to campus with a full and complete collection. I can worry about where to house and work upon that collection once the summer has come to a close.

Miss Bartram, her friend from New York, and that nature writer, Wylloe, are now climbing into another wagon. I must hurry so I can join them instead. Maybe I can ascertain the gentleman's intentions towards Miss Bartram—and hers towards him. I wrote earlier that I cannot afford to lose Miss Bartram. To be honest, I should have written that I do not want to see her go.

In haste,

    Howard

WESTERN UNION TELEGRAM

JULY 4, 1898
COL BRADSHAW   INVITED TO DINNER WITH NORTHERN
PACIFIC AND SENATOR JACKSON TO DISCUSS VIRTUES OF
PRIVATE ENTERPRISE   YOU MUST KNOW I AM NOT IN
AGREEMENT   RAILROAD ALREADY OWNS ALL THE HOTELS
WHAT MORE DO THEY WANT   THE PARK BELONGS TO ALL
AMERICANS   SHOULD BE NURTURED FOR GENERATIONS
TO COME NOT EXPLOITED FOR SHORT TERM FINANCIAL
GAINS OF FEW   NATION HAS BUT ONE YELLOWSTONE
PARK   I INTEND TO ENSURE IT IS PROTECTED UNLESS
ORDERED OTHERWISE
YOURS SINCERELY CAPT A CRAIGHEAD

A. E. Bartram
c/o Lake Hotel
Yellowstone National Park
July 4, 1898

My dear Jess,

I should be extremely angry at you for not warning me of Lester's arrival, but I am so very happy these days that I cannot muster even the slightest words of reproach. This sense of wellbeing is not, I should hasten to add, because of Lester, whose un-announced arrival here has been a mixed blessing at best.

I admit it was good to see him when he walked into our camp the other day, trying so hard to be his usual professorial self, ready as always to take charge even though he was completely out of his element. Or perhaps I should say he was too much in the ele-ments, since the rain was dripping off his hat and coat and he was walking around carrying a thick layer of mud attached to his boots. Seeing him standing there, looking so out of sorts, I realized how much I had missed him, and still needed him in a strange, longing sort of way. He has been so important to me and instru-mental to my development as a scientist, that it is as if I cannot fully appreciate all that has happened to me here without experi-encing at least some of it through his eyes.

But seeing him outside the safe and respected confines of the university does put him in a new light. This morning we had an opportunity to ride down to the fishing bridge where a half a dozen *B. bison* were being corralled for shipment to Dot Island out on the lake. I admit, had I known the specifics of their internment there, I would have been less enthusiastic about seeing them. These are domestic beasts, raised not unlike cattle, but still it was an op-portunity, my very first, to see these shaggy beasts up close and I wanted to take advantage of it.

Lester would not even think of accompanying me. We had to ride horseback, which he considers ungenteel (not to mention unladylike), and leave before breakfast, another break from con-vention. He simply refused to consider the offer. So I went with-out him, in the company of a rancher, Ralph Clancy from Clancy, Montana. Imagine the size of that family's ranch! Mr. Clancy has taken a great interest in our work in the Park, and has been kind enough to supply us with fresh meat from time to time. We were joined by the two students, Stony and Rocky, who had volun-teered to help herd the bison onto the barge which will transport them across the lake.

Mr. Clancy is much more interesting and knowledgeable than I could have ever imagined, and is a walking (or riding!) contradiction to Lester's theory that it is academia that makes the man. The land is this man's university, and in his so-called uneducated way he knows more about the natural world than Lester could ever dream up in his biology labs. He was, after all, the one who knew precisely where to find the first blooming *L. rediviva* in the spring and, when I expressed my disappointment in the conditions in which these domestic bison were living, offered to show me a small herd of wild bison he knows of in the Hayden Valley. It is doubtful that I will have another opportunity to spend an entire day on horseback in search of wildlife, at least for the time being, but his offer was a generous one, and I let him know it was much appreciated.

When the rancher and I returned to the hotel, Lester was fighting off the attentions of Miss Zwinger and her companions who were organizing a last-minute afternoon picnic to celebrate that the rain had finally eased, and the summer sun was at last warm again and shining. Lester and I must both join them, Miss Zwinger insisted, and, of course, I agreed, much to Lester's consternation. I feel compelled to get Lester out of the hotel so he can better experience the Park. Besides, it would be good fun I assured him.

It was, indeed, a lovely afternoon, with good food, good drink, and good company. And, with the change in the weather, everyone was in exceedingly good spirits. Even the railroaders and financiers, who have made it a point to maintain their superiority above and beyond the rest of the sightseers staying at the hotel, were openly enjoying themselves, sitting on colorful cloths spread out upon the ground, eating cold chicken and apples and cheese and bread, and drinking freely of a wine which was so rich and deep, it tasted as if it had been fermented inside the earth itself.

After the picnic, these scions of industry took off their coats and rolled up their sleeves for an impromptu game of baseball which Miss Zwinger, like a magician, was prepared to outfit, pulling bats, balls, and a specially designed mitt for the catcher from the back of one of the wagons. Senator Jackson served as umpire. Even John Wylloe, who tends toward the melancholy side, agreed to play. I must give Miss Zwinger credit. She knows how to bring out the best in men.

Professor Merriam was more animated than I have ever seen him. In fact, he was so ebullient that he volunteered to serve as the pitcher for his team and, when the president of his college was up at bat, proceeded to deliver a fastball within a fraction of an inch of the president's ear, much to the amazement and, I dare say, enjoyment of us all. Except, of course, the president who was not in the least bit amused!

With the party thus engaged, and Lester preferring to watch from the sidelines, I suggested a short walk down to the river. He has been anxious to talk with me in private—I am certain he wants to convince me to return with him to the university—so this seemed as good an opportunity as any to let him have his say. But rather than welcome my suggestion, Lester was shocked and dismayed at what he called my proposition, and immediately declined, concerned about the propriety of leaving our party behind. He was concerned, too, he said, about what people might think if we disappeared, as he put it, into the woods together. That seemed so preposterous that I set out on my own, against his expressed wishes. As I started walking down the trail, he followed me briefly, all but forbidding me to leave, before he headed back to the ballgame and the watchful eye of Miss Zwinger. Maybe she can bring out the best in him as well.

Once I reached the river, I followed it downstream until I came to a clearing where it was joined by a small, rushing creek. From there, I turned and followed the smaller creek up the hill as it cut a narrower and narrower path through the trees. At the end of the trail, which threaded alongside the creek, I came to an open basin of large boulders into which a waterfall spilled from thirty or forty feet overhead. The cavernous ravine created by the falling water was so dark and moist and cool, I felt as if I had entered a subterranean world. In fact, it was so unlike the dry mountainous environment I have grown accustomed to during my tenure here, it was as if I might at any moment encounter Darwin himself, walking alongside the trail, observing large-beaked birds.

As if in response to my musings, a solitary *Pandion haliaetus* flew overhead, a fish firmly in its grasp. The osprey swooped to a perch above me and commenced to tear at its prey with its own small but highly specialized beak. My first thought was of Mrs. Eversman, wondering if she, too, would find such a carnivorous creature beautiful.

As I entered the deep, cool pocket carved by the cascading water, my adventuresome spirit got the best of me and I promptly climbed out onto the rocks, letting the icy water fall and splash all around me. I then did something that I am certain, if Lester learned of it, would confirm his worst suspicions about what he considers the anti-social behavior I have developed here. I removed my jacket and skirt and shirtwaist and laid them upon a rock to dry. I then loosened my hair and laid myself out, too, in a narrow patch of sunlight, closed my eyes, and listened to the living, breathing world which roared and pulsed and crashed down all around me.

I whiled away at least an hour there on the rocks before deciding I had best return before someone was sent out in search of me. My clothes were still damp, but I did my best to put myself back together again. I then retraced my steps down the creekbed until I reached the main river where I was surprised to find Professor Merriam sitting with his back to me.

He, on the other hand, did not seem at all surprised to see me there. In fact, he hardly acknowledged my approach, but sat instead watching where the two bodies of water merged, swirling together in and around some large boulders, forming a deep, mesmerizing pool.

"I'm sorry," I began to apologize as I joined him on the river bank. "I should have told you that I was leaving, and where I would be. I hope you have not been unduly concerned."

He turned and looked up at me in my thoroughly disheveled and dampened state, and did not seem in the least bit concerned.

"You're fine, Miss Bartram," he said, standing to join me. "Just fine. Don't worry about a thing."

We started walking back to rejoin our friends and, for the first time since my arrival in the Park, I did not feel an overwhelming need to tell him anything about what I had seen or what I had been doing. It was as if there was nothing I could tell him that he did not already know. The Professor seemed equally content as he, too, had little to say.

We followed the river until we could hear our friends on the clearing above us busily loading the wagons for our return to the hotel. Professor Merriam started up the river bank but then turned and looked down on me.

"I know . . . ," he said, but then he hesitated. Since he was standing above me, I assumed that when he reached out to offer me his hand, it was to help me up the incline.

With his assistance, I clambered up the bank and stood beside him. Still he did not release me.

"I know," he started again without much conviction, "that your friend, Professor King, is here to persuade you to return with him. As difficult as this is for me, I feel that it is my duty to tell you that it would be best for all concerned if you returned home in his company."

He pressed my hand softly and shrugged. I could feel the color rising in my cheeks.

"I appreciate your concern," I said, and abruptly withdrew my hand. "But if truth be known, you've never wanted me here, have you?"

"Wanted you?" he asked.

Again the Professor hesitated, looked at me closely, his eyes narrowing behind his glasses. Then he shrugged as if in response to his own question.

"Sometimes, Miss Bartram, you simply amaze me," he said. With that, he turned and walked on in silence, leaving me to ponder his words as I reluctantly followed him from a few paces behind.

When we rejoined our friends, they were finalizing their preparations to return to the hotel, shouting and laughing about Senator Jackson's questionable call at first base, and the time John Wylloe hit the ball into the river, forcing a gentleman from the railroad to wade waist deep into the water to make the play.

No one seemed to notice our return except Miss Zwinger, who simply smiled, and, of course, Lester, who gave me quite the lecture once we returned to the hotel. To hear him talk, I have become a savage or, worse, a beast, since coming to the West, ignoring well-established rules of society and abandoning all proper behavior when it comes to being in the company of men. I think if he and Professor Merriam had their way I would be banished for life to the safety of the laboratory. Or worse yet, to the confines of the parlor where they seem to believe all women belong.

Lester's concern for social convention was pushed to the limit when I later showed him the dress Miss Zwinger provided for the evening's festivities. Now I must admit, I had the gravest of doubts about what Miss Zwinger, in all her wisdom and good nature, would consider suitable for such an occasion. But I was resolute to do my utmost to please her. She had been so good to me since my arrival here, that wearing one of her frumpy old spinster gowns, if that would make her happy, seemed to be the least I could do. I am not here, after all, to impress anyone, and my wardrobe is, admittedly, limited.

Our wagons pulled into the hotel a little after four o'clock in the afternoon and, after walking through the lobby, Lester nagging me the entire way, I excused myself and met Miss Zwinger at her room as arranged. As I entered, Miss Zwinger was pulling a yellow silk dress from her wardrobe and spreading it upon the bed. I can say in all honesty that the dress was indeed beautiful, with narrow tucking down the front and tiny covered buttons from the high collar to the waist, and all along the sleeves, from the elbow to the wrist. In fact, it was so beautiful that I could not keep my mouth shut for even a moment, but had to immediately insist that such a dress was much too fine for me to borrow. I would feel too self-conscious in such a dress, I told Miss Zwinger. I would be afraid or unable to move in it, much less dance as she was advising.

"Oh, no, dear," she said, most gracious in accepting my presumptuousness. "This is my dress. I was just getting it ready for the evening. Your dress is in here."

From a large steamer trunk she extracted another dress, this one a deep ruby color, and also of silk. My eyes must have been the size of platters because she laughed as she spread the second, even more beautiful, dress alongside the first one on the bed.

"You know," she told me, "this is a very special evening, and you should be dressed appropriately. For independence," she added, and then smiled.

Jessie, I have seen women wear dresses like this, low cut and revealing of everything there is to reveal, but I could never in my wildest dreams have imagined myself wearing one of them. If anything, I have always resented the fact that women are expected to funnel their creative energy into being the showy member of the species. It is so at odds with the rest of the natural world and so distracting from our other talents.

But Miss Zwinger was resolute, and motioned to a screen at the far side of the room, behind which I retreated trying to remember my own resolution to do my utmost to please her given all that she has done for me. She wanted me to try on the dress for size, and there was always the very real possibility that it would not fit. Miss Zwinger is, after all, a very full busted woman.

As expected, the dress was too large, and revealed next to nothing since I have so very little to reveal. But Miss Zwinger was not deterred, and attacked me with a needle and thread. In a moment or two, like magic, she altered the dress and sized the bodice to just the right proportions. She then pointed me in the direction of her dresser mirror.

I hardly recognized myself. It was not the dress, although it certainly made the changes that much more striking. It was more that my body, in the short time I have been in the Park, has changed. I have always seen myself as a girl. Or if not a girl, at least a young woman, with all the plumpness and vulnerability that comes with being that age. But now there is not a trace of that childhood softness. My arms and upper chest, just barely covered by the small gathers of the sleeves, are firm and golden. My hair, too, in spite of its unkempt condition, has changed dramatically, and is now streaked with yellow, I have spent so many hours in the sun. I could not stop staring at myself, I was so transformed. In fact, I finally had to reach out and touch my reflection, just to reassure myself that it was indeed me, and not another one of Miss Zwinger's conjuring tricks.

"You cannot be a student forever," Miss Zwinger finally said, joining me at the mirror.

I just stood there. Can you imagine? I am the one who is never at a loss for words, but I was speechless, as I have found myself so many times lately in the Park. I simply did not know what to say.

"Thank you for the dress," I finally muttered. "It is beautiful."

Miss Zwinger smiled again, and thanked me in return. "You bring the dress to life again," she told me. "That's as important right now for me as it is for you."

She then motioned to the bed and moved her own dress to make room. I sat on the edge of the mattress still unsure of myself, but now more confident than ever that I would do what it took to please Miss Zwinger.

"You know," she said, carrying a small stool from her dressing table to the side of the bed, "I once wore that dress. It was Independence Day then, too, and in the patriotic spirit, the women were asked to wear red, white, or blue. Since I was contrary in my younger years, I pushed the limit, and was the only one to show up wearing something so dark. And so obviously foreign in design. It is more the color of wine, don't you agree?"

I looked at the dress, which spilled around me on the bed, the color of a deep, rich claret, almost blue in its redness, and recalled the wine from the afternoon's outing.

"Like the earth," I said. "That's what the wine today was like. It tasted of the blood of the earth."

"You have a fine palate as well as a fine eye," was Miss Zwinger's reply. "You remind me of myself in so many ways when I was your age. Unsure of my own womanhood, but outspokenly confident of everything else, including my future."

I grimaced. I wanted to befriend Miss Zwinger, and show my gratitude for all her kindnesses, but I was not in the mood to listen to a lecture, as unconfident as she might rightly think I was feeling with my womanhood so fully on display.

"Please hear me out," she said, patting me on my red silk-covered knee. "This is important," she added.

I shrugged, and the narrow silk pleats on my right shoulder slipped slightly onto my arm. I fidgeted in the dress to make it right, and then resigned myself to listen. Miss Zwinger smiled again, warmly, her eyes not unlike those of Mrs. Eversman—knowing something about the world, about themselves, maybe even about me to which I could not yet put a name.

"I know you think I'm a foolish old woman," she said, and before I could protest she continued. "Perhaps I am. I do not at all think of myself as being old, you know. In fact, I still feel quite young. But I have reached an age where I have lost my attractiveness to men. They no longer see me, or at least they no longer bother to look. It is an invisibility which we all reach as women eventually. I know this is true. And I accept it. In fact, if anything, as I have grown used to living in a world without men, I have learned to appreciate and look forward to the company of other women. I have also learned to look for other pleasures from life."

Again I tried to speak, to assure her that she was indeed most attractive—Mr. Wylloe certainly seemed to think so—but she would not let me interrupt.

"No, please, let me continue," she said. "It is foolish for you to contradict me. I know what I'm about."

She then proceeded to tell me that all her life she has had a commitment to science. Even when very young, she was forever exploring the family estate netting bugs, hooking fish, shooting birds and small mammals, all of which she preserved and stored in her room—she sounded exactly like me when I was younger!

"I cannot tell you how much I learned about life, just watching ants for hours on end," she told me. "Even as a child, I understood so much about the world simply by observing that which was around me. Around all of us." She motioned with her hand to indicate the world outside.

"But that is not news to you, Miss Bartram. You and I are kindred spirits in that way. No one but another naturalist can appreciate the joy of studying the natural world, and the passion which one experiences when you discover something new—even if it's new only unto yourself. It's as if a door opens in your soul. Or maybe it's a window."

She looked at me again, closely this time.

"I would like to say that you remind me of myself in that dress, but that would be presumptuous. I was never so beautiful. But I did have my charms. And, I hasten to add, an opportunity to marry someone with whom I was very much in love."

She stopped for a moment to give me an opportunity to ask the question that no doubt was already written on my face.

"So what happened?" I asked.

"I chose science, which I was committed to and loved even more," she said. "I could not abide the thought of giving it up."

"But surely," I countered, but again she would not let me continue my protest.

"I can assure you, Miss Bartram, that as bright and beautiful as you are, even you would find that marriage and children would effectively bring an end to your scientific studies. Men take wives to enable them to further their own careers, not to encourage and support the careers of the young women they have married, no matter how honorable their intentions. At best, you could hope to be a talented and, if you are lucky, appreciated assistant. I have seen it time and again. You must trust me on that one."

She hesitated, but this time for only a moment.

"But that is not the message I want to leave with you today. I cannot complain about anything in my life. I would not change a day of it. I have done exactly as I have pleased. I have travelled the world. I have discovered new insects and birds and mammals. And even at my age I still have a full and rewarding life, and look forward to each new day with a renewed vigor. In fact, my life is so interesting, that friends and associates send me their daughters, as they might to an eccentric aunt, to spend time with me, to see the broader world before their own world closes in and they must assume the role society expects of them. This is a mission I have embraced, because I can help these young women not only have interesting experiences, which are fleeting, but I can also teach them how to see and experience the world for themselves. This is a life-long skill that they can take with them into the world, and even share with their children. All of their lives will be richer for it."

I could not hide my reaction inside the dress. There was not enough of it in which to hide. I wanted to argue that I, for one, was certainly quite capable of seeing the world for myself. That was why I was here, to experience the world outside of the library, the classroom, the laboratory, and even the stuffy confines of Miss Zwinger's hotel room. And I certainly did not need to troop along with a bunch of college-aged school girls. What could she possibly be getting at with that soft, grey look in her eyes? But if I could not read her thoughts, she quickly read mine.

"I want you to take a good hard look at me, Miss Bartram, and ask yourself if this is how you want to spend your life. As I said, I personally would not change a thing. But you and I are not the same person. So please, give it good, hard thought before closing the door on any options."

I felt like I needed to leave, to hide my discomfort which I could feel growing and spreading from my cheeks to my well-exposed chest. I could not look at her, would not, but kept my eyes cast upon the sea of red which surrounded me on the bed.

"Well, you have obviously heard enough," she said. "Let me leave you with one more thought and then I will let you change into your other clothes and prepare for the evening."

As she spoke, she stood and held her own dress which shimmered, almost phosphorescent, in the late afternoon light spilling through the hotel window. She then returned the dress to the wardrobe and closed its door.

"I have always firmly believed that I would meet someone who would appreciate me for who I am, not for what society says I should be. Someone who would be a companion, a colleague, a partner, if you will, in exploring and discovering all that is good and beautiful in the world. I have not given up on that dream. But the reality is that the clock keeps ticking. As I have grown older, the chances of that happening now are very slim indeed. Do not travel down a dead-end road, Miss Bartram, unless you are absolutely convinced that you will be content with the road's destination."

And with that she reached over, raised my face to look into hers, smiled, kissed me lightly on the cheek, and handed me my still damp clothes.

"You better get ready," she said. "It's getting late. And you have a big evening ahead of you."

Jessie, can you believe what is happening to me here? I have always been so confident, so resolute in the direction my life was headed. Now I find myself like one of those sightseers who ventures too close to a geyser, only to discover that the earth on which she is treading is not at all the thick crust she has grown to expect in life but is rather thin and unstable, causing the ground to unexpectedly drop out from underneath her, casting her into a hot, bottomless pool. Once the earth collapses like that underneath a visitor in the Park, very few, I am told, manage to escape with their lives.

Miss Zwinger's parting advice was to dance. With everyone who asks me. So dance I will, even with Lester if he will condescend to it, and hope that the bottom does not fall out from underneath me. Or him!

I so wish you could be here, and see me now. You would not recognize me. I am, I fear, utterly transformed. But I believe you would be proud of me none the less. And proud of our friendship.

I miss you, Jessie. But I must tell Lester tonight that, in spite of Professor Merriam's expressed desires, I am not yet ready to return home.

With the greatest affection,
    your friend,
        Alex

———◆◆◆———

Andrew Rutherford, Ph.D.
c/o Lake Hotel
Yellowstone National Park
July 4, 1898

Robert Healey
Lake Hotel
Yellowstone National Park

My dear President,
    Must decline offer to meet at hotel for dinner. Prefer to avoid fireworks—both personal & those staged for tourists. With Aber's

wife in Park to take him home, should hasten promised demise of camp & Merriam's return to college business.

Meantime, will hole up here, safe & sound in temp. camp of count's crew, while said count off shooting things in Park. Most generous folk. Fine food & liquor cabinet. When count's away, peasants will play.

Will, however, take up kind offer to travel with party back to campus. Message telling when and where to meet can be left c/o hotel. Weather station packed & ready to go.

Visit if time & inclination allow. Must meet Edgar, new friend & constant companion. He will call new ag building home. Guaranteed to amaze all who meet him.

Your most successful servant,
Andrew Rutherford, Ph.D.

Lester King
Lake Hotel
Yellowstone National Park
July 4, 1898

Dear Jessica,

It is with mixed emotions that I must report I have withdrawn from the evening's festivities and the role of Alex's protector. Downstairs I can still hear much revelry and merriment accompanied by the Women's Orchestra from Butte, Montana. But I, for one, am not feeling in the least bit merry.

Alex, by her behavior and outright refusal to do as I have instructed, has all but informed me of her true intentions. She says she does not plan to return to New York until the end of summer. Seeing her here, I realize I must insist that she return now, if not to campus then to the home of her parents, for her own wellbeing. From what Philip Aber has told me, the expedition will not last the month since he intends to withdraw funding once he is back in Washington. Better Alex returns in my company than be forced to travel on her own a week or two after I leave. If she refuses to accompany me, I can assure you she risks more than our mutual understanding.

Jessica, I wish you could see her now. I fear you would not recognize her in the least. There is a wildness about her demeanor which is unsettling. Some might even say frightening. And tonight, thanks to a spinster at the hotel who has pulled a dress out of her own questionable past and forced it upon Alex, she is wearing a red silk dress which outright flaunts respectability. I will not try to disguise my disgust from you who will understand my concern. The dress is the color of blood.

Rather than sit and enjoy the music in the company of refined society, Alex has taken to flirting and flying, table to table, group to group, introducing me with great enthusiasm to lustful hayseeds and lustless aging poets alike. And without any sign of courtesy toward me, she insults my company and good nature by dancing with any man who will have her, abandoning me to the company of Howard Merriam, the man responsible for this misadventure, while she dances with the president of Merriam's land grant college. The president is a man ill suited for such a task, lacking both grace and stature, yet with Alex as a partner he was able to twirl around the dance floor for a full five minutes, defying nature and his short, fleshy physique.

I must admit that Merriam is more sensible than I first gave him credit. He is about my age, although he appears older, his sad, weary face peering from behind spectacles. I fear his lassitude is in part from the constant responsibility of tracking the whereabouts of Alex, a task he assures me he takes to heart. She is very adventuresome, he used that word, and though he appears to approve of her high spirits, he suggested that her actions here have led to more than one serious concern since her arrival.

When pressed, Merriam is the first to admit that he made a mistake inviting Alex to accompany the expedition, referring to some kind of misunderstanding. He used that word, too. But he is impressed by Alex's contributions to the collection now that she is in Yellowstone Park, saying he hopes to use their work to make a systematic study of the plant life in these, the Park's earliest days. Merriam is a man who appears to be dedicated to his work and those under his command, even if his general melancholia makes him, I believe, unfit to lead them.

While sitting there in the hotel ballroom, dancers all around us, we were joined by two of Merriam's other colleagues from the land grant college, a William Gleick, who has just returned from the Smithsonian, and a Daniel Peacock, an entomologist, who has been working in the backcountry for the duration of their stay. It is hard to imagine three such disparate souls being friends, but good friends, in spite of their differences, they appear to be.

Unlike Merriam, Gleick is outgoing and bold in his nature, confident and sure of himself and his place in the world. Older by a few years than the other three of us, he has the annoying habit of smoothing back his long, greying hair away from his face, while he speaks with contempt of Philip Aber whose wife Gleick accompanied from Washington to the National Park.

Peacock, on the other hand, is hard-pressed to sit still, squinting and blinking in the bright lights of the ballroom chandeliers, his eyes darting each and every way as he forever pulls at his collar as if it were choking him. He only sat still when Alex was escorted back to the table by the college president. Once she was seated, Peacock shared a theory about the development of plant and animal life in Yellowstone National Park, which he referred to as a vast volcanic sea. He used those words. Alex was intent in her listening to Peacock's far-fetched tale, while Gleick and Merriam strategized to one side about how to salvage the already doomed expedition. I heard it with my own ears, I wanted to warn them, but it is better if they learn of Aber's plans for the expedition from the man himself.

Unable or at least unwilling to join in the conversation with Gleick and Merriam, I tried to query Peacock regarding his postulations about the history of the Park's geological and biological development. But each time I raised a question about his theory that the Park was being populated in waves which would, over time, reach its highest and most remote sections, Alex gave me such a severe reprimand in her demeanor, that I opted to excuse myself and leave the party altogether.

Before leaving, I asked Alex if she would care to accompany me and, in my asking, let her know of my concerns. She, however, declined, saying she found the atmosphere in the ballroom stifling, she used that word, and for that reason intended to go outside for air. She stood up as I did, shook hands with her usual familiarity with all at our table, and then shook hands with me as well. She then began her slow but deliberate retreat from the room, headed for the hotel verandah, all but defying me to forbid it. I refused to make our struggle public in such a wanton fashion, but opted instead to retreat. I will confront her in earnest, but prefer to do so in private, at my earliest opportunity. This behavior of hers has gone far enough.

As I was leaving the ballroom, I could see Merriam excuse himself from the table and then he, too, went out onto the verandah, no doubt in pursuit of Alex. Perhaps he will talk some sense into her, since she is dead set against listening to my good counsel.

Left on their own, without the attention of Alex, Peacock fidgeted in his chair, gulped his wine, and departed, while Gleick scanned the room for others to impress. Seeing Philip Aber's wife enter the room without an escort, as there had been no sign of her husband all day, Gleick smoothed his hair one last time and hurried to Mrs. Aber's side, offering his arm. I must say his gallantry is something to admire.

I have all but decided to leave the Park at the earliest opportunity. I will write to you then to let you know of my specific plans, and whether or not Alex will accompany me home. I can also let you know at that time what the best option is for informing Alex's parents of her decision.

Yours,

Lester King

H. G. Merriam
c/o Lake Hotel
Yellowstone National Park
July 5, 1898

My dearest Mother,

We have experienced a most wondrous 4th of July here in Yellowstone National Park. Perhaps because we are in territory protected by the Nation, rather than owned by any individual state, it is all the more important to celebrate our independence. Whatever the reason, both the human and natural elements have been at their most dramatic and beautiful.

The day was sunny and warm, fine holiday conditions, which were interrupted only late in the day by dark clouds rolling in across the horizon, followed by a storm which swept across the distant shore of the lake. We watched this display of nature, Miss Bartram, Mrs. Eversman, and I, from the widow walk atop the hotel, while below us, in the ballroom, the all female orchestra played like angels, sweet and haunting melodies which drifted into the night.

Miss Bartram was unusually radiant throughout the evening, having abandoned her customary field clothes for a dress which is most becoming. Unexpectedly so. Watching her dance with the captain, the rancher who has shown particular attention to Miss Bartram since our arrival at the hotel, John Wylloe, an elderly naturalist and poet in residence here, and even President Healey who, I am hoping, will take an equal interest in Miss Bartram as a potential employee of the college as he did in her as a dance part-ner, I could not help but feel the slightest tinge of longing that I, too, might have the pleasure of holding her, ever so briefly, in my arms. But just as I summoned the courage to ask her to dance, she slipped outside and joined Mrs. Eversman, who was on the hotel roof watching the evening settle like a blanket upon the lake. See-ing Miss Bartram there against the darkening sky, with the sun casting last-minute patches of light on the mountains around us, I could not bring myself to ask her. She was much too beautiful. Besides, it would be presumptuous of me to make the request, considering my position. So I asked, instead, Mrs. Eversman, a sweet, mild-mannered widow who, dressed in grey suiting, looked pale and almost forgotten next to Miss Bartram.

Mrs. Eversman smiled, twinkled her eyes, and dipped her head into her shoulders so that she almost disappeared. But then, twinkling again, she accepted my arm, and the two of us reluctantly began to take our leave of Miss Bartram; who promised to join us downstairs. As I began to escort Mrs. Eversman from the roof, however, the sky blackened and Miss Bartram let out a gasp.

Turning, Mrs. Eversman and I could see the object of Miss Bartram's amazement. As the sun was about to disappear on the far horizon, it illuminated one mountain and then another, bright white and yellow, while, to the east and south of us, the sky turned a deep red with a tinge of orange. The spectacle was arresting, with the three of us so quieted by the sight, that the only discernible movement was the sweeping of bats in and around the trees surrounding the hotel. Even the music from the ballroom was silenced now, too.

"I fear the music has ended and we have lost our opportunity to dance," I apologized to Mrs. Eversman.

"Oh, this is such sweet entertainment, Professor Merriam," she said with the same apologetic dip of the head. "I am quite content."

And then, as if to complement Mrs. Eversman's good nature, a narrow wisp of a rainbow, all red without a hint of any other color of the spectrum, spanned the southern sky like a thin, brightly burning ember in the dying light. I have never seen such a phenomenon before, and probably never will see the likes of it again.

The three of us stood there at the widow walk railing, transfixed by the showiness of the natural world, when Miss Bartram unexpectedly turned and looked me square in the eye with that same unbending determination I have grown to know so well and, yes, even dread since she arrived in the Park.

"I am not going," she said with great seriousness. "I know you think I should, and probably wish I would, but I will not leave the Park until our work here is completed. I am staying until it is time for us all to go."

Mother, I know I have not always welcomed Miss Bartram's

presence here, and have believed that it would be in her best interest to return home, particularly now that there is someone here to escort her, but I admit with all my heart that I was relieved to hear the news. I started to explain to her that she would indeed be welcome to stay, that her presence in the expedition has been, in fact, a blessing, but Mrs. Eversman drew our attention elsewhere.

"Look," Mrs. Eversman exclaimed, pointing out a large flock of geese noisily working their way across the night sky. "Now that is what I call real music."

Miss Bartram's spirits lifted and, for the first time that I can remember since she joined our party in the Park, she laughed out loud.

By the time the geese were gone, so was the rainbow, and our collective mood. Down below we could hear much laughter as the party goers proceeded onto the boat dock and along the lake with chairs, while one by one, barges and small boats began to cluster off shore, their lanterns casting small pools of light upon the water as they waited for the fireworks to commence.

"I think I have had enough entertainment to last me for a good long while," Mrs. Eversman said, with a shy dip of the head. "I have never cared much for fireworks or other artificial displays."

"I think we have all seen enough," Miss Bartram agreed. "Besides, we cannot afford to stay up too late, can we Professor? There is still so much work to be done."

"Yes, there is much work, Miss Bartram," I assured her. "And you know what I always say, where there is work, there is hope."

And then, offering both arms to my companions and friends, for friends they now seemed to be, I added, "Shall we?" and the three of us descended arm-in-arm to the verandah of the hotel.

I think we would have been content to call it an evening right then, if Rocky Cave, one of the students travelling with our party, had not interrupted us. Rutherford had been poisoned, the young man hurriedly explained. He was in the count's camp and was in desperate need of assistance. The hotel physician was out on the lake, awaiting the fireworks display, and no one could tell the student how to locate him.

"Do you know what the poison was?" Miss Bartram asked.

"Miss Bartram, I'm not sure," the student said. "The count

came back to his camp, found us raiding his supplies, and cut us all off without another drop. So Dr. Rutherford and the driver took to dipping a cup into the barrel of alcohol the count uses for preserving skins. The men who travel with him seem to think the count laces it with something like arsenic to keep them from drinking it. None of them have been willing to tempt their fate and so no one had even given it a try. Dr. Rutherford's hurting pretty bad, Miss Bartram. So is the driver."

"We need a cathartic, sodium sulfate, magnesium sulfate, sorbitol," Miss Bartram told me. "Whatever you can get your hands on here in the hotel. In the meantime, I'll see if there's anything I can do."

The student had a second horse on which Miss Bartram rode away in a flurry of red silk. Since there was no one in the lobby to assist me, and the doors to the hotel clinic were locked, I hurriedly returned to our own camp to see if I could locate Joseph, while Mrs. Eversman promised to watch for the physician's return.

Joseph and his family were eating when I rushed in and did the best to explain to him the situation. Joseph did not hesitate, but grabbed a leather bundle, bridled his horse, and rode off in the direction of the count's camp. I followed behind on foot.

By the time I reached the camp, both Rutherford and the mountain man were bent over, retching the vilest looking substance imaginable, until I thought their entire insides would be expelled with the rest of it. As their stomachs calmed, and they both appeared to be catching their breath, Joseph handed them yet another cup of the liquid which he had kept warming on the fire. The drink promptly started them retching again. It was a horrid sight, not to mention the sound.

Finally, when it appeared that their anguish would never end, Rutherford let out a long guttural moan, and rolled onto his side, while the mountain man staggered off into the trees, followed closely by his dog. Joseph smiled, triumphant, and Miss Bartram energetically shook his hand.

"Thank you," she said. "It appears that they are going to be fine. I can't thank you enough," she said again.

Rather than move Rutherford, we made a temporary bed for him next to the fire, my selfish motive as strong as my utilitarian one. It would be difficult to transport a man of Rutherford's size without his expressed cooperation and, besides, President Healey could not possibly see him in this state if he spent the night away from our own camp and the hotel. I have enough trouble with Healey without him holding Rutherford's bad judgment against me.

The two students agreed to stay with Rutherford throughout the night, keep an eye on his bird which was hiding under a camp table, and keep us informed if Rutherford experienced any additional problems. Miss Bartram seemed convinced that now that their stomachs were empty, both he and the driver would just have to sleep off the side effects of their indiscretions.

Since there was nothing else either of us could do to help, I offered to accompany Miss Bartram back to the hotel where we found Mrs. Eversman, true to her word, perched on the edge of a chair on the verandah still waiting for the arrival of the hotel's physician. Fireworks roared and crashed in the sky all around her.

"I've not yet seen the physician," she apologized. "I tried walking along the lakeshore, but couldn't find anyone there who knew where I might locate him."

I assured her that Dr. Rutherford and the driver would be fine, and that there was little the physician could do now to help them anyway. She was free to retire, if those were her wishes. Mrs. Eversman thanked me and retreated into the hotel.

Miss Bartram stood on the verandah, looking out over the lake for the longest time, and then she, too, turned as if to retire. But she hesitated.

"I have grown very fond of Dr. Rutherford since arriving here, and would have done anything to save him," she told me. "So you must understand me when I say that it was with great reservation that I let Joseph give him that drink. I had the gravest doubts, but felt under the circumstances I had no other option."

She shook her head and the slightest shudder appeared to run through her body.

"It is clear, Professor Merriam, that there is still much in the world I am woefully under educated about. I do hope you will have patience with me while I learn."

And with that, she, too, turned and retreated into the hotel, her dress a blaze of color fading into the distance of the lobby. As for me, I sat on the verandah for what seemed like hours watching the white lights of the boats upon the water, the remaining show of fireworks sputtering in the sky.

Mother, I know my renewed sense of confidence in what I can accomplish this summer is wildly optimistic and unfounded. Bill Gleick tells me Philip Aber plans to withdraw support for the expedition at his earliest opportunity, and yet I cannot help but believe that with Bill's leadership skills and the hard work of Rutherford, Peacock, and Miss Bartram, we will manage to not only salvage the work we have initiated here, but even flourish during the remainder of our stay. I am so confident of the fact, that I have booked my room at the hotel for an additional night, so that I might rest up for the long summer days ahead of us.

My love and sincere devotion,
Howard

WESTERN UNION TELEGRAM

JULY 5, 1898

COL BRADSHAW   YOU WILL NO DOUBT HEAR ABOUT THIS
SOON SO SHOULD KNOW I HAVE DECLINED ALL OFFERS OF
RAILROAD LEASES AND OTHER RIGHTAWAYS IN PARK
SENATOR JACKSON PROMISES A FIGHT BUT MUST TAKE HIS
BATTLE TO WASHINGTON   I WILL NOT BE MOVED
SHOULD KNOW TOO THAT SMITHSONIAN EMPLOYEE HAS
DISAPPEARED ON HORSEBACK WHICH SENATOR CITES AS
PROOF POSITIVE THAT RAIL LINE NEEDED   HOW HE
CONNECTS THE TWO EVENTS IS DIFFICULT TO FATHOM
BUT TRYING TO CREATE MONOPOLY FOR RAILROADS IN
PARK JUST AS NONSENSICAL TO ME   SEARCH PARTY OUT
LOOKING FOR GENTLEMAN   PROBABLY JUST LOST HIS
WAY   WILL KEEP YOU INFORMED
YOURS SINCERELY CAPT A CRAIGHEAD

My dear Jessie,

In true American fashion we have celebrated our independence and now, like our forefathers, must learn how to live with the consequences of our actions. Perhaps the saddest casualty of drawing our collective line in the sand is Philip Aber, who left the hotel yesterday on horseback and has not been seen since. Captain Craighead has organized a search party but Dr. Aber has been gone so long, it is difficult to imagine that they will be able to locate him if he is determined not to be found.

Although the exact reason for his disappearance is unclear to me, seeing William Gleick and Mrs. Aber together last night, I can imagine where the problem lies. Dr. Gleick accompanied Dr. Aber's wife from Washington, and seems to be more familiar with her than just a few days on the train would warrant.

Mrs. Aber is about my age, although she seems much younger, almost like a child in spite of her striking beauty. She stands perfectly tall, with a long neck and thick, black hair which only serves to accentuate the paleness of her complexion and the darkness of her eyes. I would say that she looks like a doll, but she is much too fragile for that description. She is so delicate that she appears to need the arm of a man just to walk from one side of the room to the other. I can understand why Dr. Aber was reluctant to leave her on her own in Washington. He must have feared that without his constant care and attention, she might shatter.

Dr. Gleick certainly seems to think so. He has steadfastly stayed by her side since Dr. Aber's abrupt departure, and has offered to assist her with plans to return to Washington at the earliest opportunity. Why she should arrive in the Park only to leave again without even knowing of her husband's condition is one of those human mysteries about which I am full of speculation but woefully under experienced to draw any conclusions. These are the kinds of human questions to which John Wylloe tells me I need to dedicate more time and observation.

Through Dr. Gleick, Professor Merriam has learned of Philip Aber's plans to withdraw Smithsonian support for the expedition. Although Dr. Gleick initially counseled Professor Merriam to return to campus with President Healey, the Professor will not be persuaded. He is insistent that the expedition can and will be saved. And, more importantly, that it should be.

To prove his point, Professor Merriam invited Dr. Gleick to view and judge our collection for himself. This is where John Wylloe, as wise as he may be about his view of the world, is wrong about mine. It is one thing to worry about all the intricacies of human interactions, and I am certain it can make life easier at times for us all, but there is a much different set of concerns when it comes to science. Here, it is the work that must be allowed to speak for itself without a hint of human emotion.

Dr. Gleick was impressed not only by the quality of our work so far in the Park, but by the sheer quantity of work our small group has been able to accomplish in such a brief period of time. Although he appeared to be interested in, and I can only hope impressed by, the botanical collection, it was the work of Dr. Peacock that caught his eye.

Dr. Peacock, you may remember, began his collecting during the very first days of the expedition, and has made significant progress, most impressive of which is an exhaustive collection of aquatic insects and butterflies, the sheer beauty of which has attracted Dr. Gleick's attention.

They are indeed most spectacular, although Dr. Peacock would no doubt argue with such a description, resenting the attention such showy insects elicit from others. He prefers the diversity of Coleoptera, finding great charm in each intricate mandible, antenna, and diminutive claw, not to mention the spectacular ability beetles demonstrate in adapting to any environment. You can see Dr. Peacock's devotion to his science in the passion with which he collects and displays these strange-looking creatures. For example, he has collected more than two dozen specimens of one such insect, the *Polyphylla decemlineata*, which he has neatly pinned to a hand-inked grid. In such an intricate presentation, these field beetles look almost Egyptian, bringing good luck or beauty or whatever was once believed of their scarab cousins.

To complement the care Dr. Peacock takes in preserving and displaying his work, Dr. Rutherford has developed an elaborative indexing system, which he has integrated into his botanical mapping system, providing a complex picture of the environment in which these plants and insects thrive.

I suspect that at least one of the reasons Dr. Gleick has been so positively impressed by our work is that he has been genuinely surprised to find something so unexpectedly. professional, albeit unique, being organized under such primitive conditions. I am sure he has been equally impressed by the fact that the work is being conducted by Professor Merriam, Dr. Peacock, and especially Dr. Rutherford. Although Dr. Gleick appears to approve of them all as friends, it is clear in the way that he speaks of them that he does not—or at least has not—considered them colleagues or peers.

In any event, after viewing the collection, Dr. Gleick has pledged to write to the director of the Smithsonian on our behalf, discrediting Dr. Aber if necessary, to help secure support for the duration of the expedition. Professor Merriam seems confident that Dr. Gleick has the necessary influence in Washington to positively affect the outcome of our stay, so is making no plans for our work here to be concluded. In fact, the Professor is so convinced that Dr. Aber will no longer pose a problem for us, that he is making plans to move our camp to higher ground.

As Professor Merriam declared his independence from Dr. Aber, so, too, has Dr. Rutherford severed his relationship or at least allegiance to President Healey. Although this is yet another one of those human stories about which I have not yet been fully informed, it appears that Dr. Rutherford has, contrary to his overall appearance and contributions here, been extremely anxious to return to the comforts of home. He had hoped to accompany President Healey back to campus after the 4th of July celebrations and was, in fact, packed and ready to go.

President Healey, who has been a long and outspoken critic of

Professor Merriam and his work, welcomed Dr. Rutherford into his returning party, in spite of Dr. Rutherford's lugubrious condition brought on by his own independent form of celebration. But the president was decidedly not as generous when it came to offering a ride to Dr. Rutherford's bird. Said bird, a *Corvus corax* with an uncanny talent for mimicry, has become like a pet to Dr. Rutherford. He calls him Edgar. And, in spite of his eagerness to return home, Dr. Rutherford will not leave the bird behind.

So this morning when President Healey refused to let the bird be boarded into his wagon, Dr. Rutherford unloaded his own things and morosely returned to camp, climbed into the tent he shares with Professor Merriam, and refused all of our entreaties to come out again. It is probably just as well. Dr. Rutherford had a serious run-in with some potentially deadly alcohol, and will no doubt benefit from some undisturbed rest and relaxation.

I am also happy to report that Captain Craighead has declared his own independence on behalf of the Nation and our National Park. He has steadfastly refused to entertain any additional railroad leases, in effect ending the history of monopolization of the public trust for the profits of a few. Captain Craighead has complex reasoning for his denial, claiming that he was charged to protect the land, and that any additional incursions by the railroad, with their plans to dam the river and make right-of-ways for the railroad to haul both tourists and gold from a mine near the northern border of the Park, will compromise if not outright condemn the natural features of the Park for generations yet to come.

I, for one, am relieved. The sheer ruggedness of Park roadways keeps travel to a minimum, and forces those of us with a sincere desire to partake of the Park's beauties and wonders to leave the wagons behind and travel on our own volition. It is only on foot that you can see, hear, smell, and touch the wonders that are all around us here. Otherwise, you miss too much. In fact, I would argue that you miss it all.

Because wagon travel in the Park can be so arduous, such mode of transport has the additional benefit of creating communities of travellers in the Park. Although I value my independence and solitude as much if not more so than the average American, it is a wondrous experience to bound along the rutted wagon roads side-by-side with American families, European adventurers, and dedicated outdoorsmen alike. Such shared adventures are as much a part of the Park experience as is visiting Old Faithful, both of which, I believe, are equally worthy of protection. I must say, I am deeply impressed by Captain Craighead's courage as well as his independent spirit as he has made a commitment to preserving these experiences for us all.

It is with mixed emotions that I report that I, too, have declared my own independence. Lester has insisted that I accompany him back to New York, citing the threatened withdrawal of support for our work here and the uncivilized conditions in which I am living and working. He gave me no choice, no options. I must return with him or he will no longer entertain my affections.

That seems such an unreasonable price to have to pay to continue my work here, and I have told him so, but to no avail. I owe so much of who I am to Lester, who was good enough to believe in me and my naturalizing when I was a student with little knowledge and experience. But he cannot now deny me the logical outcome of that encouragement and support.

Miss Zwinger told me I cannot be a student forever, but there is still so much in the world I need to learn about and to study. I would gladly dedicate my life to observation, in effect be a student for life, since there is no way I could possibly learn all there is to know in the very limited time each of us has here on earth.

At times like this, I cannot help but remember Meriwether Lewis who, on his thirtieth birthday, regretted how little he had accomplished at what he considered such a ripe old age. He who had accomplished so much in such a short, sweet lifetime. I can only hope that I might learn and accomplish a mere fraction of what he did, assuming I have the luck and good fortune to be on earth a much longer period of time.

But to accomplish that I need my freedom—to explore, to observe, to experience the natural world, a world rich with possibilities if only we open our eyes to it. And an opportunity to develop into the scientist I know I can become. I certainly cannot limit myself to one man's vision of how and when I should see the world. I may not know which road I will follow in the months ahead, but I know for certain I am not willing to retreat along a path I know so well. At least not yet. Perhaps Miss Zwinger's advice would have been more relevant had she said I cannot be *Lester's* student forever.

Lester is preparing to depart as I write. He is so angry at me that I am not at all certain that he will even bother to say goodbye. This all seems a very high price for the opportunity to continue working, but it is one which I feel it is necessary to pay. I should have expected it. Lester's world is so black and white, and I am just now beginning to see that the world is, in fact, colored with many shades of grey.

I hope you and your family are looking forward to each new day there, as I look forward with increasing enthusiasm to mine.

Your ever determined friend,
    Alex

Howard Merriam
c/o Lake Hotel
Yellowstone National Park
July 6, 1898

Dear Mother,

With the Independence Day celebration behind us, and our party rested and ready to go, we are now awaiting news of Philip Aber and whether or not he will continue to support the completion of our work. The delay is maddening, but there is little I can do but wait. Sadly, I am at the mercy of those who do not understand or appreciate the work that I am doing. I fear this will always be my lot.

Bill Gleick, however, has been very supportive and, having once encouraged me to return home, is now counseling me to complete my stay. He has written to Washington on my behalf, and has suggested to me in private that he has the necessary influence with the director to guarantee continued support. I can only hope that this is true.

My plan is to break camp and proceed across the Park's central plateau. Because we will be following an abandoned road rarely used anymore by tourists and other travellers, Joseph has agreed to accompany our party into the field. I welcome his continued participation as there is still so much I would like to learn about his botanical knowledge, and Bill Gleick assures me that Philip Aber will no longer pose a problem for me in that regard. I hate to think the continuing success of our expedition is dependent on Philip Aber's professional downfall but I will leave that to Bill. If Gleick feels he must discredit Aber to save our work here, so be it. The pursuit of truth has always been more important than the career and reputation of one individual. And in this case in particular, the man has done little, as far as I can tell, to pursue the truth himself.

In the meantime, I have just learned that the wagon in which President Healey was riding was the subject of a well-planned holdup as it left the hotel. It seems only fitting that we wait at least a day or two, out of respect for the man's position if not the man himself, should he be in need of assistance or consolation.

It is ironic indeed that it would be President Healey's wagon, the last in a train of at least a dozen departing the hotel this morning, that would be stopped by the thieves, given his fondness for tall tales about highwaymen. Apparently, the bandits in question waited at a bend in the road and greeted each wagon as it passed, waving and shouting "come again" as if they were official Park representatives. When the very last wagon entered the clearing, the three men placed bags over their heads and descended upon the travellers, shouting and waving pistols in the air, as they pulled the lone wagon to the side of the road. If the passengers in the wagons ahead heard anything at all, they must have assumed it was all part of the official greeting and gave it little or no additional thought.

The thieves mistakenly picked a wagon of academics and friends, including Miss Bartram's friend and associate from Cornell. Had they selected one with eastern bankers and railwaymen, their pickings might have improved. As it worked out, their rewards were meagre to say the least, resulting in only about twenty dollars and a handful of watches. But the highwaymen still managed to get the best of their victims by insisting that the men remove their trousers and hats, which were dutifully gathered up and removed by one of the marauders who thanked them kindly before riding away.

One by one, President Healey's party staggered back to the hotel, as well exposed as they were embarrassed. Since Captain Craighead is off with a search party looking for Philip Aber, and no one seems inclined to take any official action until he returns, there is little hope that the bandits will be apprehended. I suppose these are the perils associated with travelling so far from campus, a lecture I am certain to hear from President Healey, if not today then once I return back home.

I tried to relay the story of the president's misfortunes to Rutherford, thinking it might amuse him or at least console him to know what he missed, but Rutherford has yet to speak to me or anyone else. Even his raven gobbles away for treats to no avail. This is the darkest mood I have ever seen in Rutherford. He can be exceedingly contrary about the world, but always outspokenly so. His mood is so black, he has even declined an offered glass of brandy.

Miss Bartram has suggested an afternoon of sightseeing as one possible way to cheer up Rutherford. Apparently he once mentioned a desire to visit the Old Faithful geyser. That seems very unlike Rutherford, who has only spoken of contempt for the Park's thermal properties (except for those in which he can bathe), but I would be willing to try even this if it would lure him out of the tent and back into our party again.

Miss Bartram has also returned to camp, anxious to make up for what she calls lost time. It appears I am forever misreading her intentions and desires. I assumed she would welcome the opportunity to partake of the weekend festivities at the hotel, but to hear her talk now one would assume she considered the weekend as a frivolous waste of her time. Although I have grown to appreciate Miss Bartram and her contributions to our party here, I do not think I will ever learn to understand her.

Peacock has already returned to the field, promising to establish a base camp at a lake he knows of not far from the summit of the road we will be travelling. Assuming we get the approval from Aber or his superiors, we will join Peacock there in a day or two. That is assuming, too, that I can get Rutherford up and ready to go.

I must tell you the foreign count who is in residence in the hotel has spent the weekend in his own form of celebration, roaming the Park in pursuit of wolves, coyotes, and cougars, one of which he dragged into camp by its neck from behind his horse. His pursuit of science, which science he insists it is, borders on outright cruelty. There can be no scientific reason for killing so many of the same animals over and over again.

Captain Craighead has reluctantly allowed removal of the beasts, given the alarming decline of big game animals in the Park. Craighead is the first to acknowledge that elk, bison, and the rest have disappeared from the Park not because of wolves or coyotes—but because of poachers who once roamed the Park. But as the Senator, who was no doubt well rewarded for his eloquence, argued, the law protecting wildlife does not protect animals of "fang or claw," so the count's guns were returned to him over the weekend and he is now free to kill any of these animals that he can find. I fear such slaughter can only bring harm to the Park in the long run. Wait until the gophers start taking over the fields outside of Fort Yellowstone. Then even the Senator might feel some regret.

In the meantime, someone with a cruel sense of humor has taken his own revenge on the count and his idea of science. As the hotel guests were preparing for their return home, the count drove up with his wagons to provide them with one last look at the heaps of carcasses contained therein. Just as he peeled back the canvas covering, a large cannon firecracker blew up next to the wagon, knocking the count clear off his royal feet. I must admit I was much amused. Even his staff could hardly hold back a smile as they hurriedly ran here and there, trying to right the situation—and the count—before something else exploded. I can only hope that if we keep the hotel as the center of our communication with the outside world, we will not have to continue any association with the likes of that count.

As I begin to bring this letter to a close, I realize I have not asked after you or your situation. It is not, you must believe me, for lack of caring. I have such a large party under my protection here, and they consume so much of my time and all of my worry. These are new responsibilities for me, ones which I do not much enjoy and with which I am just now learning to cope. But please believe me when I say that even though my time is so consumed, I think of you often while I am here. And I do so hope that you are well.

Captain Craighead has promised us horses for our time away from the hotel. Since the students will no doubt be anxious for any excuse to return to civilization, even if it is just to transport the mail, plan on hearing from me from our backcountry camp, even if it is not as regularly as you and I both might wish.

All my love,
    Howard

<hr />

William Gleick, Ph.D.
Lake Hotel
Yellowstone National Park
July 7, 1898

Dr. Roger Johnson
Smithsonian Institution
Washington
District of Columbia

Dear Sir,

It is with great sadness that I write to inform you that after disappearing on the afternoon of July 4, Philip Aber was found late yesterday, having fallen into one of the Park's unmarked thermal pools in the upper geyser basin. He was badly burned over most of his body and although the Park's medical staff at the hotel fought valiantly to save his life, there was little they could do as much of the flesh on his lower body was already beginning to fall away from the bone. He died this morning, at 8:23, in the arms of his beloved wife. I have made arrangements for Mrs. Aber to return to Washington with his remains. I will accompany her there, as she is in no fit condition to travel on her own.

I have, as you requested, visited the camp of Howard Merriam. As you must be aware, he and his companions are colleagues of mine and so my opinion of their work is subject to our collegial relationship. However, in this case, such friendship has proven to be an encumbrance since I have had little by which to judge Merriam's work but his ineffectual presence on campus.

I must report I was extremely impressed with what I found in Merriam's possession, and recommend without reservation the continuation of their funding for the duration of their stay. With limited personnel and resources, they have systematically collected and documented the flora of large geographic areas, using techniques which are most impressive and which bring credit to themselves and to the Smithsonian. In addition, an entomologist travelling with the party has collected a spectacular sampling of winged insects which, I believe, will be of great research interest to the Smithsonian. I know that public displays are of little interest to you, but I am confident that these Yellowstone insects will fascinate scientists, the general public, and anyone else who has the good fortune to view them.

Knowing of your interest in this particular field of study, I have asked for—and been granted—the opportunity to take the bulk of the entomological collection with me when I return to Washington in the morning. The botanical collection designated for the Smithsonian will follow at a later date, most likely when the party returns to Bozeman at the end of the summer and they have had an opportunity to sort through and document the multiple specimens.

Again, I offer my condolences on the death of Philip Aber. He was, I understand, a productive member of the Smithsonian's scientific community. Sadly, he was under what appears to be debilitating personal pressure, which he was unable to balance with his professional duty and responsibilities to the work he had commissioned here in the Park. I can only hope that his personal weaknesses and his untimely death do not bring this worthy project to an equally untimely end.

Yours most sincerely,
William Gleick

A. E. Bartram
c/o Lake Hotel
Yellowstone National Park
July 10, 1898

My dear parents,

I am writing to inform you that we are departing for the backcountry tomorrow, and to assure you that there is absolutely no reason for concern. We will at no time be more than a day away from services, and will be proceeding along a well-established, albeit rarely travelled, road should we ever need to return.

We are leaving our Yellowstone Lake camp with heavy hearts, having lost the life of our Smithsonian benefactor. Philip Aber was a fine scientist and believed in our work enough to not only support us for the summer, but even to travel to the Park to participate in a small but meaningful way in our success. Sadly, by insisting on travelling to the Park, he apparently lost his wife, and then his life. It seems an excessive price to pay for science, and has made me even more appreciative of each living, breathing day.

As I am certain you will hear from Lester, I, too, have paid a personal price for staying in the Park, and I apologize for any grief or concern that this might cause you. I know how you both feel about Lester; I have felt the same. But as I am certain you will understand, I must continue to find my own way. You have raised me to believe that I can accomplish anything I am determined enough to achieve. I came here with a commitment to work for the duration of the summer, to collect the best possible botanical specimens during that time, and to learn and to grow into the best possible scientist I can become. This is my goal, if not my destiny.

I am also now more committed than ever to Professor Merriam, who has been particularly shaken by Philip Aber's loss. Contrary to what Lester will no doubt tell you, Professor Merriam has proven to be a sound leader with a clear vision of our work, a vision which is only now beginning to be understood and valued by the rest of us. Although the Professor and I have had our disagreements, each day I learn to appreciate his world view, as I believe he is beginning to appreciate mine. I can only hope that by the end of the summer he will have learned to accept me as a colleague, and maybe even as a friend. Perhaps then he can see me, not for who or what he had hoped I would be, but for who I truly am. If and when that happens, I will have succeeded here beyond my wildest dreams.

Given our location, I will not be able to correspond with you or Jessie as frequently as I have in the past. I promise, however, to do my utmost to keep you informed about my progress here in the Park. And please, do not worry. I am doing fine. In fact, in spite of the great loss of Dr. Aber, and of Lester, too, I am doing very well indeed.

My love to you both,
Alex

4. Epilobium angustifolium

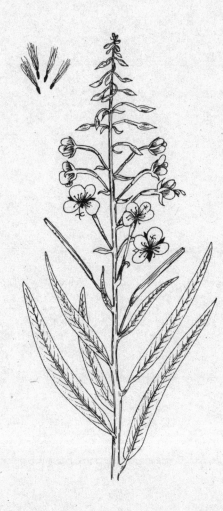

Mother,

I apologize for the delay in corresponding and for any unnecessary worry my silence may have caused. This has been a difficult, if not debilitating, time for me, and it has taken me longer than I could have ever imagined to sort through the implications of those difficulties.

As a result of Philip Aber's disappearance and subsequent death, I have experienced an unexpected and overwhelming sense of despair, finding myself in the deepest, darkest emotional trough I have ever encountered. As I was too blind and selfish to see, while he was making my professional life hell, Philip Aber was living through a personal hell of his own. That the continuation of the expedition should be contingent on someone else's personal loss is difficult for me to accept. That the expedition ended up costing Philip Aber his life is almost more than I can withstand. I am quite certain that had I known Philip Aber's true situation, and understood my small but undeniable responsibility for it, I would not have been able to justify the continuation of our work. Unable to morally defend myself and my party, I would have had no choice but to return home under the critical eye of President Healey.

I cannot tell you how grateful I am, therefore, for the friendship and support of Bill Gleick and my other colleagues here in the Park. After complaining bitterly about having to look after Rutherford and the rest, I find myself now in the position of having to acknowledge that without the constant distraction of their day-to-day demands I do not think I could have endured.

Gleick has proven to be the expedition's strongest supporter and, as it has turned out, its ultimate salvation. Once he departed from the Park, returning to Washington with Philip Aber's remains and Aber's widow, he called upon the director of the Smithsonian and successfully argued for our continued support. The meeting was beneficial for Gleick, as well. He is so familiar with our work and the other interests of Philip Aber, that he was asked to stay on with the Smithsonian, which he has agreed to do, at least through the end of the summer. I would not be surprised, however, if he decides to relocate to the Capital permanently.

I am equally grateful and indebted to all of those in our party who have stood by me through all of my personal ups and downs and the collective sense of uncertainty about the future of our expedition. Peacock, as always, seems oblivious to it all, but Rutherford and Miss Bartram, in spite of their own individual setbacks and losses, have made great sacrifices on my behalf and on behalf of our work here in the Park. It is because of them and the others—even the cook and the driver have done their share— that I am more determined than ever to go on.

My dear friend Andy Rutherford has proven his loyalty time and again, first by agreeing, in direct opposition to his nature, to accompany me to the Park, and now consenting to remain, even though he so clearly longs to be back home. I would like to believe that Rutherford has experienced, perhaps for the first time in his life, the joys and companionship of scientific endeavors, not to mention the satisfaction which derives from beginning to study and understand the natural world. More likely, it is the unexpected pleasure he has experienced as he methodically attempts to teach a raven to mimic human speech—as futile and foolish as his attempts might be. In either case, his willingness to sacrifice his own comforts for our common good is heartwarming, and has helped me sort through—and put into perspective—my own sorrows.

Even though Rutherford has made the commitment to stay through the duration of the summer, his mood has been fragile at best. In fact, for days after President Healey refused to transport Rutherford's bird, Rutherford, in turn, refused to speak to any of us. Not even to Miss Bartram, with whom he has established a particular rapport. It was not until Miss Bartram angered him with her continual glowing comments about the Lewis and Clark expedition that he was drawn back into our party again.

Theirs is an interesting friendship. Up until the tragedies at the Lake Hotel, Rutherford and Miss Bartram spent many evenings arguing around the campfire about the merits and limitations of the Lewis and Clark expedition, about which they are both knowledgeable and highly opinionated. Miss Bartram is extremely well informed about Lewis' contributions to the botanical sciences, having studied his work at great length in Philadelphia, but she also lists with great enthusiasm the expedition's hundreds of other non-botanical discoveries—the western tanager, the broad-tailed hummingbird, the cutthroat trout, the grizzly bear, the mule deer, and even the lowly jack rabbit—all of which were new to the scientific establishment and most of which were described in great detail by Lewis, even if he did not employ the scientific terminology or, I dare say, the spelling preferred by Miss Bartram. Lewis even went so far as to box up a prairie dog, four magpies, and a grouse and sent them live, over land, river, and sea, to Thomas Jefferson. Can you imagine? Both the prairie dog and one of the magpies survived their four-month journey and arrived in good health in Washington where they were displayed in Independence Hall for politicians and scientists alike.

These discoveries and other accomplishments of the expedition impress Rutherford not at all. He points to the fact that Lewis was charged by President Jefferson to maintain strict weather reports, recording the speed and direction of the wind, temperature, access and recess of frosts, &c, an assignment at which, by Rutherford's account, Lewis failed miserably. For months on end, Lewis did not even bother to keep a daily journal, one of the first signs of a weak character. Worse yet, Lewis broke his last thermometer, to hear Rutherford tell it, out of personal spite or sloth or both.

When Miss Bartram counters that Lewis' horse had, in fact, lost its footing in the snow when the sole surviving thermometer was broken on their return journey, Rutherford is deaf to the facts of the case. Miss Bartram also notes that the loss of the thermometer caused great consternation to Lewis, who took even the most insignificant setbacks to heart, but Rutherford refuses to acknowledge the truths of Miss Bartram's evaluation of Meriwether Lewis' character. On the contrary, he dismisses her explanations as non-scientific, advising her to focus on the results of the case, and quit making so many excuses for the man and his motives.

When I consider the passion Rutherford exhibits in these arguments I cannot help but think that when it comes right down to it, my dear friend is but a common phenologist at heart—as was Thomas Jefferson, I should add, lest you think it a malady of a smaller mind. Regardless of his beliefs, Rutherford apparently has made a perfunctory review of the Biddle and Coues editions of the expedition journals and, finding them lacking in the meteorological sciences, has nothing but contempt for Lewis and his men. He even goes so far as to make gross allegations about Lewis' supposed melancholia and his inability to inspire or lead, a weakness Lewis himself acknowledged, to hear Rutherford tell the story, when he illegally shared leadership with Clark. It was Clark who took command and responsibility for choosing the majority of the men who travelled with the expedition—a choice key to the success of the expedition, Rutherford argues.

But Lewis was not just a poor leader and inconsistent journalist, Rutherford takes great pleasure in noting. Worse yet, Meriwether Lewis was a drunk. Now this is an odd argument indeed for a man like Rutherford to be making, but who am I to judge? I barely get along with my colleagues much less understand their true natures.

The same cannot be said about Miss Bartram, who knows how to bring out the best in Rutherford. In fact, in this particular instance, she was the only member of our party capable of bringing him out at all. As I noted earlier, Rutherford has been suffering from a melancholia of his own, refusing to speak—or drink I might add—since his falling out with President Healey. I believe he was ready and, in fact, anxious, to return to campus and to what he considers a somewhat normal life. He was not prepared, however, to leave behind his bird.

Please realize that I relate the following story without any disrespect to you or your friends, Mother. To understand it, however, I must first point out that unlike other women, Miss Bartram is not one to repeat herself. She is well spoken and, like Rutherford, extremely opinionated, but she does not go on and on about a topic like many women have a tendency to do. So it was surprising and, I dare say, even amusing, to hear her say time and again one night at dinner that our encampment near a high country lake made her feel just like a modern Lewis and Clark. About the third or fourth time she made this very same declaration, Rutherford grunted, the first sound we had heard from him in days. Miss Bartram then turned and asked our cook, Kim Li, if he, too, did not feel as if he were travelling into the wilderness with Lewis and Clark.

Rutherford could tolerate her gibes no longer. He charged into an elaborate diatribe about how Miss Bartram was well aware that the Lewis and Clark expedition was wildly over rated. They never accomplished any of their objectives. They never found the Northwest Passage for which they were commissioned. That they managed to survive at all was only thanks to the good graces of the Indian tribes they encountered along the way, many of which lived to regret their generosity. And yet, he raged, both Lewis and Clark were lavishly rewarded with land and prestigious government appointments upon their return. To make matters worse, their so-called triumphs are celebrated to this day. They even name college buildings after them both, he added with a contemptuous snort.

As abruptly as he had started, Rutherford silently returned his attention to his unfinished dinner, pushing at a piece of potato with his knife. When it appeared we had heard the last from him on the subject, he turned to Miss Bartram and added in not much more than a whisper, "No one ever celebrated or rewarded my failures," he said.

We were all silenced by the declaration, which Miss Bartram acknowledged with a sad smile and the slightest nod of her head. She reached across the table and touched Rutherford ever so softly on the hand.

What could have been an uncomfortable moment for us all was transformed when Rutherford's raven took advantage of the lull in the conversation, hopped onto the table, and gobbled like a turkey. Rutherford set his dinner plate down on the ground, an act for which he had been soundly reprimanded by Kim Li in the past. This time, however, Kim Li chose to ignore it and, as the raven hopped back down again to pick at the remains of the meal,

Rutherford, without another word, retreated to his tent. But the spell had been broken, and by morning Rutherford was back, talking as if nothing had happened, and letting us know he was ready to get back to work.

Miss Bartram has also proven to be of great moral fortitude to me as she has helped me regain my own enthusiasm for our work here in the Park. Sensing my despair over the death of Philip Aber, she suggested that I consider dedicating the expedition to Aber's memory, noting that should we not complete our assignment, we would in effect allow Aber's death to be in vain. It was such a gentle, sweet-natured suggestion, that I was almost moved to tears. Funny how such a small token can mean so much. It has motivated me to do my utmost to see this project through to completion, no matter what the personal cost.

I realize now that I could not ask for a better colleague and friend than Miss Bartram. Since setting up our new camp, she has intensified her already impressive level of work, setting forth without complaint at the break of dawn and only returning to camp at nightfall, determined to squeeze each and every collecting moment from these long summer days. Thanks to Captain Craighead, we have a stable of horses which browse contentedly on the luxuriant grasses around the boundary of the lake where we are camped, but Miss Bartram prefers to travel by foot, afraid she will miss something if, in her words, she travels so far from the ground.

This may be motivated, at least in part, by the fact that she has been told by that Montana rancher, who makes an effort to visit our camp from time to time, that white variations of the ubiquitous fringed gentian exist in this stretch of the backcountry. The dominant blue variety is in bloom alongside creekbeds and drainages. We see them everywhere we collect, especially in and near thermal activity where they seem to thrive. To date, however, there have been no signs of an alba variation, but Miss Bartram is not deterred. Since finding that early-blooming bitterroot, she seems willing to believe anything that rancher tells her, and is convinced that she will locate a white one eventually.

She also seems to have warmed to the traditional botanical knowledge of Joseph, who has established his own camp adjacent to ours. I believe Miss Bartram was raised in an enlightened family for she seems true of heart, and unencumbered by the degrading view of so many others of our race who seem to think racial superiority is their birthright. And yet, in spite of the fact that she appears to appreciate our common humanity, Miss Bartram has been, up to now, openly contemptuous of Joseph's botanical knowledge—or, I should say, my appreciation of it. It is clear she has been conditioned since her earliest days in school to believe that there is but one view of the world, that seen through the lens of the eastern scientific establishment. That kind of academic indoctrination, like religion, is difficult if not impossible to escape.

Still, having written that, I find that after she witnessed the miraculous cure of Rutherford, who, she informs me, could have easily succumbed to the poison he imbibed on the 4th of July, she has been watching Joseph and me closely as we discuss plant uses while in the field. She does not speak of it, at least not to me, but I can sense a previously unseen interest there. She has even gone so far as to befriend Joseph's wife, Sara, and their two small children, offering them gifts of a bound journal, loose sheets of paper, paints, and colored pencils, much to their amazement and joy.

Miss Bartram has also renewed friendships established while in the Mammoth Hot Springs area. Last night, Miss Zwinger unexpectedly arrived in our camp with the entourage of young women who accompany her, along with the naturalist and poet, John Wylloe. It was Miss Bartram who asked if they might be allowed to stay so that they, too, might enjoy the wonders of our camp's remote location. I wholeheartedly agreed, even before I knew that Miss Zwinger and Mr. Wylloe had transported their own equipment and provisions, and intended to more than pay for their own expenses while in our camp. I must say, our visitors' unexpected but much appreciated generosity, coupled with Miss Zwinger's seemingly endless supply of excellent wine, has already done much to improve the quality of our living conditions, not to mention the positive effect all the female attention and companionship have had on Rutherford and the boys.

In spite of Rutherford's lack of respect for his accomplishments, I cannot help but wonder how Meriwether Lewis ever managed to accomplish what he did with so many different men for whom he was responsible. I can hardly manage with my small mission, and we have all the luxuries and advantages of the modern-day world. What would I do if I had to leave all of that behind and travel against the current for thousands of miles with three squads of men, a Frenchman, a slave, and an Indian with child? Not even in my wildest dreams could I imagine myself succeeding.

The truth is that even with my own meagre group to look after, I have often found myself overwhelmed and discouraged by day-to-day events. And yet, in spite of all my shortcomings and personal and professional falterings, my party to a man (and yes, to a woman) has been so good to me in my hour of need. I now understand that as I focused all of my energy on caring for them, trying to guarantee the safety and success of each member of our group, they were, in reality, looking after me. I cannot tell you how blessed I now realize I have been throughout this ordeal. I can only hope that I deserve their care and concern. I hope, too, that I can yet earn their respect. And their love.

Your most humbled son,
Howard

———— ❖ ————

A. E. Bartram
c/o Lake Hotel
Yellowstone National Park
July 28, 1898

Dear Jessie,

I know I warned you and my parents that my correspondence would be erratic once we left our camp adjoining the Lake Hotel, but I still feel the need to open this letter with an apology. I must admit in all truthfulness that I have had ample time to write, too much time given the Professor's extended absences, but so far there has been no opportunity to get mail to the hotel for posting. I was told this morning, however, that the two students and the driver will be going to the hotel for mail and supplies, so I am packaging my specimens and field notes for posting to Lester (I can only assume that he will continue to care for them until my return in the fall), and thought I should take the opportunity to write to let you know of my situation here.

We have established a camp of operations next to a small mountain lake. The lake shoreline is rocky and devoid of trees, making it ill suited for a campsite, so Professor Merriam, following Dr. Peacock's lead, chose instead a grassy meadow not far from where the lake is fed by a high mountain creek. Joseph, who accompanied us with his wife, Sara, and their two children, selected a site on even higher ground, their tipi standing like a solitary sentinel above and beyond our camp. The mountain man, still as contrary as ever, made his own solitary encampment further along the shore of the lake, next to a make-shift cabin used during the winter months by cavalrymen patrolling on snowshoes for poachers in the Park.

Not that we need a cavalry cabin to remind us of the impending change of the weather. Although winter is still months away, just this morning we woke to a thin layer of frost as we emerged from our tents, groggy and cold. But we were invigorated, too, as we sipped hot coffee and made plans for the day, all of us wrapped in blankets and buffalo robes, our breath punctuating the chilly air in soft white clouds.

I cannot tell you what a relief it is to report that we are making plans, and working again as a party. When we first arrived at this site, after leaving our camp near the Lake Hotel, the news of Philip Aber's death still weighed heavily on Professor Merriam's heart. Dr. Aber was considered an expert in the diminutive high-elevation adaptation of the flora of the world, so the Professor, in his grief, seemed almost obsessed with the need to contribute to Dr. Aber's Smithsonian collection and to continue the man's work, as if the Professor had a role in his demise or could have somehow anticipated and, thus, prevented his death.

Professor Merriam and Joseph would disappear for days at a time, the Professor either unable or unwilling to accept the assistance or companionship of others in our party. Both the distances to be travelled and the dangers posed were too great to share, he maintained. This may or may not have been true. Regardless, I felt compelled to be quite forthright with the Professor, concerned that he did not understand the risks he was taking with his person and, by extension, with his party. But no matter what I said, or how I pleaded with him to think of the others if not himself, he was deaf to my protestations. I think he longed for and, quite honestly, needed the time away, just as Dr. Rutherford required a few days of silence before finally consenting to fully rejoin our group.

With the Professor absent from camp, and with no specific demands placed upon his time, Dr. Rutherford has found his own peace here in the backcountry. Since his near run in with death and subsequent purgation at the count's camp, Dr. Rutherford has given up all form of alcoholic beverages and has, instead, substituted other venues of entertainment. When we first set up our new camp, and the Professor had, by default, left us to our own devices, Dr. Rutherford started reciting, with much drama and intonation I should add, the poetry of Edgar Allan Poe. Although he has not said as much, it is clear that Dr. Rutherford hopes to teach his *Corvus corax* to say "never more" in addition to "pretty bird," an undertaking to which Dr. Rutherford is most dedicated, in spite of the Professor's obvious disdain. So far, however, the only sign that the pet Corvie appreciates Dr. Rutherford's dramatic readings is that it hops around, flaps its wings, and gobbles like a turkey at every chance it gets.

The two students seem to enjoy Dr. Rutherford's recitations of Poe as much as, if not more so than, the raven and, since the mishap at the count's camp, have proven themselves to be Dr. Rutherford's most devoted assistants. The boys have helped Dr. Rutherford re-establish his weather station at our new camp, and one day surprised him with a primitive atrium for the bird. Not that the raven needs a cage to restrain it. It seems quite content to stay in camp close by Dr. Rutherford's side, at least when it is not poking around in our tents in search of shiny objects to steal and cache in his new home.

One night at dinner, when the Professor and Joseph were back from the field, Joseph told Dr. Rutherford a story, probably based more on Indian myth than on reality, about ravens travelling with wolves, living on the remains of pack kills. According to Joseph, who tells these stories in all seriousness, ravens have what he refers to as a keen sense of humor. He even claims to have seen the birds tease and torment the wolves until they give futile chase, which Joseph refers to, again with a great earnestness accentuated by his simple, straight-forward English, as a raven's version of play. Even if this reported behavior is true, there must be a more logical explanation. Perhaps its quizzical nature is tied to its survival.

Whatever the scientific explanation behind the Indian's tales, Dr. Rutherford now keeps a close look out for wolves, and when he does leave camp, even for short periods of time, he locks the bird in its new home. If nothing else, he feels better knowing that the raven is safe from predation—although I cannot imagine what creature would be interested in killing or eating a raven. But who am I to say what is a reasonable precaution for Dr. Rutherford to take? The bird means the world to him.

As for me, I have tried to take advantage of the Professor's absence and the new-found freedom it has provided, but for the first time since arriving in the Park, I have felt uneasy wandering too far from camp on my own. Part of my underlying discomfort has been, I am certain, a feeling of being set adrift with Lester's abrupt departure. I have no regrets. I made the correct choice in that regard. But just because a decision is right for all concerned does not make the consequences of that decision any more palatable. Suddenly my future seems so uncertain. Of course, that uncertainty is ripe with a universe of new possibilities!

But there is more to my uneasiness than regret, and the loss of someone I have held so dear. I have always believed that my companions, with the odd exception of the driver, have acted with the best intentions towards me as a woman, and I have never feared for my personal integrity or safety in their company. And yet, without the routine the Professor brings to each day, I have found myself cautious in a way that I have never been before. I am ashamed to admit that this primitive and illogical fear sometimes renders me powerless. I rage against it but to no avail.

This discomfort is caused, I am most certain, by the mountain man driver's hostility towards me. I have always felt wary in his presence, knowing that he never welcomed me into the party. If his reticence had been based on my abilities, I simply would have worked harder to demonstrate my worth, as I hope I have proven myself to Professor Merriam and his friends. But as I have gained the acceptance of the others in our party, I seem to have alienated the driver even more. Since his animosity is based solely upon my sex, there is nothing whatsoever that I can do but keep my distance from him, as he has done from me. But now, in such a remote location, where we are thrown together in all but the most intimate activities, I can sense his aggression at all hours of the day. He is clearly one of those men who resent the company of women in any form of society outside their own beds.

One night after dinner, when Professor Merriam was gone from camp, and I was illustrating a specimen of what I believe to be, by Coulter's description, a *Dryas octopetala*, I overheard the driver tell Dr. Rutherford the most gruesome and graphic story of a young woman who had been killed by a bear. Although the story was clearly intended for my benefit, and the driver told the tale in a voice loud enough to ensure I would hear every detail, it was Dr. Rutherford who was transfixed.

"What happened?" he wanted to know.

"Hard to tell," the driver replied flatly. "Out where she shouldn't a been, I guess. Pickin' berries or some such thing. Women don't belong in this kinda country, and that's a fact."

The driver spat into the fire and stared in my direction as if awaiting a response. I refused to even acknowledge him. There was no point in giving him even that small bit of satisfaction. But Dr. Rutherford, already worried about wolves, could not let the story drop.

"So then what? What did you do?" he asked.

"Not much I could do," he said. "Dug a hole and put what was left of her in it. Couldn't tell no one. There was no one 'round to tell."

Again the driver spat and waited for a response.

Dr. Rutherford let out a mild groan, and looked around for his raven, which was scavenging in the dirt under the table. Without another word, Dr. Rutherford scooped up the bird, tucked it safely under his arm, and retreated to his tent, while the driver casually poured himself another cup of coffee. When still I said nothing, the driver sullenly retreated to his tent on the shore of the lake.

Jessie, why is it that some men in this world so despise women? What have we ever done to them as a sex that makes them feel they must dominate and suppress our good natures and willingness to contribute equally to the world? Why do they feel the need to demean us, belittle us, make us fear for our lives?

These questions haunt me but, not being the questions of science, I fear they will never be answered by the likes of me. The best I can do is ignore the blunt ignorance of these men when they are minor irritants, and do my best to circumvent them when and if they try to pose a significant threat.

But given these conditions, you can imagine how relieved I was when Mr. Wylloe and Miss Zwinger and her charges arrived unannounced in camp, seeking what they referred to as a more primitive base for the duration of their stay. I more than welcomed their company, and urged Professor Merriam upon his return from the field to let them remain. After the driver's cowardly attempt to terrorize me, I found even the giddy laughter of the young women splashing in the creekbeds a welcomed relief. An additional benefit of their female presence is that it has forced the mountain man to withdraw even further from our camp, since he appears unable to enjoy anything other than his own bad-tempered company. And that of his dog, which doesn't talk, much less talk back.

Miss Zwinger's arrival has had an even more significant result. With his new responsibility for visitors, Professor Merriam has returned to camp full time, reasserting his leadership and direction. With little ceremony or explanation, last night he requested that Dr. Rutherford and I join him and Joseph tomorrow morning in the field. I cannot tell you how relieved his request made me feel. Not only am I anxious to be truly productive again, but I must admit that I have missed the Professor's good nature and companionship.

I am most relieved to report that no harm has come to the Professor during his solitary pursuits. But even I must admit that his imprudent behavior has resulted in ample rewards. He has returned to camp from his most recent extended outing with multiple specimens, including one unknown to Coulter, an alpine variation of *Lewisia rediviva*. Instead of twelve brightly colored petals, with no visible basal leaves, this specimen has seven pale-colored petals growing concurrently with multiple fleshy leaves. It is a rare beauty indeed and, when I said as much to the Professor, he generously offered to add it to my personal collection if I would share with him my documentation. This was such an unexpected gesture that I leaned over and kissed him, right on the cheek. He, in turn, was so startled by my own imprudent behavior that he removed his glasses and commenced polishing, muttering something about finding another specimen at his earliest opportunity.

Jessie, he is such a sweet colleague and companion. I am so pleased that he is back with us, and is ready to resume our collective work. I cannot tell you how fortunate it was for all of us that he put together this Yellowstone Park expedition. And how lucky I feel that he has chosen me to be a member of it. Even if he did so at first under a gross misunderstanding.

Please tell my parents that I am well, and miss them both more than I can say. I miss you, too. You are such a good friend to me. I am lucky indeed to have someone like you with whom I can share all of my confidential stories and concerns. And, in time, I hope all my successes.

Yours most sincerely,
Alex

———◆———

Howard Merriam
c/o Lake Hotel
Yellowstone National Park
August 14, 1898

Dr. William Gleick
Smithsonian Institution
Washington, D.C.

Dear Bill,
The boys are riding down to the hotel this morning for supplies, so I thought I should use this opportunity to assure you that all is

well with the expedition, and that our work is proceeding not as planned—I do not seem to be able to "plan" anything—but at least it is proceeding with good results. Because we now are keeping such long, hard-working days, Rutherford sulks, and calls these the dogged days of summer. I prefer Miss Bartram's classification. She looks around our high country camp with just the slightest hint of a smile on her lips and refers to our time here as the days of heaven.

We have made significant progress in spite of the weather which has been cool, sometimes even icy in the early morning hours, and oppressively hot as the day wears on. Insects, particularly mosquitoes, are a constant bother. We battle them day and night. Most days, the sky turns cloudy and the air cools by midday. Storms roll in from the south and west, first blackening the horizon and then advancing overhead with strong winds, heavy rain, and sometimes even hail.

More than once Miss Bartram and I have found ourselves huddled under a tree, seeking protection from these meteorological outbursts, concerned not so much for our persons, but for our specimens, the rain is so sudden and threatening. Miss Bartram has often used these occasions to politely point out what she considers to be the inadequate methods I employ to transport and store my specimens. She says this, I should add, without a hint of personal criticism. While she efficiently carries her specimens in layers of blotting paper in a metal vasculum, I prefer to wrap mine in paper, securing them with string, with the intention of preparing them for proper storage upon my return. She is correct, of course, when she notes that the conditions of the Park demand the greatest diligence when it comes to caring for our collection. I owe it to both you and the memory of Philip Aber, she maintains. Perhaps she is correct about that as well.

That I can listen to and learn from Miss Bartram in areas of scientific protocol should suggest to you that our relationship has indeed matured. So it was with great interest and not a little concern that I noted the arrival of the rancher, Ralph Clancy, to our dinner table the other evening. He came, as has been his habit all along, with a supply of fresh beef for our cook. He also carried beaded hatbands for the boys, sweet-smelling tobacco for Andy Rutherford, a heavy compass for me, and a hand-forged trowel marked with his ranch's Flying-C brand and a bouquet of flowers for Miss Bartram. The flowers themselves were of little botanical interest, but you could tell she was pleased by the gifts none the less. As for me, I felt I had been transported back to the Crow reservation where wives are exchanged for what appear to be mere trifles. I was so upset I could not even savor my steak, which Kim Li, after all these months, is finally learning how to prepare.

Clancy spent that evening in camp telling stories about his land near Helena, of his family who not only survived but prospered after the winter of 1887 when most cattlemen lost everything they had, and of the freshwater streams which crisscross his land, creating ideal landscapes for cultivating both animals and plants. And for raising strong and healthy families, he added, looking directly at Miss Bartram, who did not even attempt to avert her eyes.

Clancy is a gregarious and talented storyteller, blessed with both an intelligent wit and a fine appreciation of nature. Having fought in the U.S. Army, he is a man of the world. Having spent most of his life on his ranch in Montana, he is also a man of the land. I could not help but suffer a growing resentment at his continued presence at my party's table.

When he took Miss Bartram aside under the guise of showing her something he had stored in his wagon, I withdrew to my tent with an underlying feeling of dread. I lit a lantern and tried to read, but my mind kept returning to one of the many campfire battles Rutherford and Miss Bartram had waged over the contributions of Meriwether Lewis and his western expedition. On the evening in question, Miss Bartram had argued that Lewis was the father of descriptive flora in the West. I remembered listening intently as she presented her point of view. She is an eloquent speaker, in spite of her great passion for the subject, which, in a lesser mind, might inhibit her ability to logically debate her position. Rutherford, on the other hand, countered that Lewis could never have led a mule across the street much less survived the journey to and from the West without the constancy and good counsel of Captain Clark, who was the real leader of men. And, as a maker of maps, it was Clark who had set the direction of the journey, Rutherford had added.

As I remembered their passionate sparring, both of them refusing to give an inch, I could not help but notice that I was much like the Meriwether Lewis that Rutherford was so fond of describing. I, too, have failed miserably at so many steps along the way while you, my dear friend, are so much like the valiant William Clark. You have been the real leader this summer, have helped set the sights, have mapped our course of action, and have secured our expedition's survival and success. I cannot tell you how grateful I am.

Now, however, I find myself in the unique position of no longer needing a leader, or a map. After all, thanks to the generosity of the rancher, I now have my own compass! Our journey, thanks to your generiosity, vision, and leadership when it was most needed, is well charted and secure. What I now need is someone to help me accomplish our expedition's goals. I absolutely must be certain I have all that I need to return to campus and prepare a definitive volume of Rocky Mountain Botany.

For the first time, I am having serious doubts that I can complete that part of the journey on my own. But this is a task unsuited to a William Clark, as critical to our initial success as you have been. For the next stage of the journey, what I really need is a Bartram. Bill, I need Miss Bartram to stay so we can finish our work here together. But not only do I need her. In all honesty, I want her to stay.

I admit that I often have been contemptuous towards Miss Bartram. I have treated her like a child. Worse yet, I have ignored her for long periods of time, acting as if, in this self-contained world of men and science, she simply did not exist. When she first arrived, I hoped that she would understand the difficulty of my position and, understanding that, follow the proper course of action and, on her own volition, return home.

Now, if given the chance, I would fall upon my knees and give her my word of honor that I would do all in my power to improve my treatment of her and atone for the worst of my actions. Sadly,

I doubt that she would listen to me now. Or, even if she would, I doubt that she would believe what I have to say. So I will give you my word instead. I promise with all my heart to do my utmost to earn her respect for the duration of our stay here. I will do so, that is, if it is not too late, and I can yet convince her to remain with the expedition at least until we break this camp. I cannot promise more. I wish that I could.

I hope that you are well, and you are enjoying life in our Nation's Capital. I also hope that you are planning to relocate to that city, although not a day will pass that I will not miss your good company and counsel. Washington will value your abilities far more than President Healey ever could, and the Smithsonian will be a good and suitable home for a man with your intelligence and skills. Should you decide to return to Montana, however, and it is by chance before we depart from the Park, I do hope that you will visit our camp on your way back home. I want very much for you to see the scientific results of your vision and your unbending support.

My best regards,
Howard

———•◦•———

A. E. Bartram
c/o Lake Hotel
Yellowstone National Park
August 14, 1898

Dear Jessica,

I hope you have been keeping my parents informed about my good health and wellbeing and that they are satisfied that no harm has come to me here. My life and my work are both going exceedingly well, in spite of the weather which, of necessity, forms the backdrop to everything we do. While I had the opportunity, I wanted to share a few events which might be of interest. You might want to share some of them with my father, as well.

One afternoon, while the Professor and Joseph were cataloging specimens and I was taking advantage of a few hours on my own, I set up an easel just beyond the clearing where Joseph and Sara have established their camp. The day was unusually hot, as the weather has been in the late afternoons, and the sky was awash in a milky white cover of cloud.

As I worked, I could hear thunder rumbling in the distance but before long, the wind picked up and thin lines of lightning cut through the blackness that advanced from the south. The sky overhead suddenly turned grey, then black, the temperature plummeted, and rain started falling in large, globular drops. As I hurriedly repacked my supplies and readied for the short walk back to camp, the wind continued to bluster, now carrying what appeared, at first glance, to be snow.

The shortest route back to the safety of my tent was directly through Joseph's camp, which I had avoided on my way out, thinking his family would want their privacy. But hail the size of pebbles was now pelting the earth, so I hurried directly through the Indian camp as I headed back towards my own. Sara and her children would no doubt be safely ensconced in their own tent, I reasoned, and would not witness my intrusion. Besides, even a few extra minutes in this weather could easily cost me my afternoon's work, something I was not willing to sacrifice for what I considered to be a simple courtesy of questionable value to any of those concerned.

Sara and her two children were indeed safe inside their tipi but they were not hidden away. Rather, they sat at the tipi opening, watching the advance of the storm. All three watched as I rushed into the clearing where they were camped. I acknowledged my presence with an apologetic smile, intending to hurry right past them, but as I did so a large explosion cracked a nearby tree and the wind picked up a branch of it and carried it like paper overhead. The oldest child gasped. I was never certain if it was the thunder, which was deafening, or if the bough just missed me in its flight. Perhaps it was both. Whatever the cause of the child's expressed concern, Sara rushed from the tipi and grabbed me by the arm. My first instinct was to resist, since my own camp was only a few hundred feet away, but since I was rude enough to intrude on her privacy, I felt it would have been doubly rude to refuse her offer of shelter and respite from the storm, so I allowed her to lead me into her family's home.

I had visited Joseph and his family on a couple of occasions, bearing small gifts for his wife and their children. At the time, I wanted Joseph to know that, contrary to my earlier behavior and demeanor, I appreciated his knowledge and that his actions that evening at the lake had, without a doubt, saved the lives of Dr. Rutherford and our driver. But because these earlier visits to his camp were brief, mere courtesies really, I had not taken the time to fully appreciate the way he and his family lived. I now had an opportunity to look around.

Unlike Professor Merriam's hospital tent, which is a large rectangle of uniform height giving the impression of a room set aside for solitary confinement, the tipi I entered with Sara is of a conical shape, with a small fire pit at the center, and a ceiling which rises maybe twenty-five or thirty feet into the air. The family sleeping skins are laid out on one side, opposite some tools and supplies stacked neatly against the tipi shell. In spite of the awkwardness of my arrival, and the fact that I was a stranger in their home, I felt comfortable as I settled into the dwelling. Even the moaning of the trees in the wind overhead could not penetrate the homey warmth of that large, circular room.

At first neither Sara nor I had much to say to the other. I was grateful, of course, for her hospitality, and I told her so, but she sat perfectly still, almost immobile, looking out past me at the now retreating storm. She has long hair, the deep blue-black of Dr. Rutherford's Corvid, and she has a detached way of looking that makes her appear as if she were far away, or not quite of this world.

As the weather calmed, and the hail changed to a light but steady rain, I thanked her again for her courtesy, and began to take my leave.

"It is my pleasure to assist you," she said. "You have been most generous to my husband, and appreciative of his science stories. For that I am grateful."

Jessie, I can admit to you alone that I was stunned that she had spoken so clearly to me. And in such perfect English. I am not so prejudiced to think her dumb or incapable of speech. It is just that

I had never imagined that she would have anything to say to me. It turns out that she had much to say, from which I hope I am able to learn.

As a light rain continued to fall, Sara shared her own stories, about how, when she was very young, she was sent away to a missionary school, not to learn white man ways, as she referred to them, but to learn to be a leader in her tribe. Unlike white families, she explained without the slightest hint of condescension, Crow families value their women. They are considered important to the foundation of society.

Ironically, it is the value of women that puts them at risk. Although men and women do marry, the wives of other men can be highly prized and, according to Sara, can be taken away—in essence stolen—if another man has what Sara referred to as a prior claim. She then revealed the real reason she and Joseph have been travelling for so long with us in the Park—Sara had learned from her sister that a tribal leader was planning to kidnap her and make her his wife.

"This man had already taken the wife of a friend," she told me, "and was planning to steal me as well. I love my husband and my family," she said. "I made the decision I would not go."

I was shocked at such a confession. But you know me, Jessie. I can never stay silenced for long. I had to know what she could do to prevent being taken away.

"I told Joseph I would not go without a fight," she said flatly. "This put my husband in a difficult situation, considering the man's claim, so he agreed that we should leave. He said we would go gather medicine. Collect materials for knives and tools. And we would wait until the man lost his interest."

In spite of her willingness to share these confidences, she still looked at me as if I were miles away. She never smiled. In fact, she never really acknowledged it was me to whom she was speaking.

"So how will you know it is safe for you to go home?" I asked.

"We will return when it is time," she told me. "When we are done here, we will go home. By then the man should understand that I will not leave with him and that I plan to stay with my husband. That should be the end of it."

She said this with such conviction that I dared not question her further. But, Jessie, can you imagine? How could anyone live with those fears? She is like property, to be stolen by any man who wishes to claim her. But when I consider the young women travelling with Miss Zwinger, many of whom will be, when it comes right down to it, purchased by the highest bidder, I cannot pass judgment on Sara and her kind. I now see for myself what my father has maintained all along to be true. Native people may live in a different world from ours, but it is not an inferior one. I admit that I have been quick to condemn Joseph for what I have perceived to be his primitive beliefs, but he and his wife are not savages, as their detractors would have us believe. Or at least they are no more savage in their world than we are in ours.

When I readied myself to leave, Sara looked at me with a piercing familiarity, and then invited me to visit again. "Do not wait on the weather," she advised, looking at me directly for the first time.

Jessie, you would not believe her strength and demeanor. She puts most women I know to shame. Myself included. I know I have had my prejudices, no more than ignorance really, to overcome in this world. I am beginning to see that I need to learn how to recognize what is good and kind and true in each individual's view of the world. I can only hope that my own primitive beliefs will not stand in the way.

But there has been more to my experiences here than just a long-overdue opening of my eyes. My spirit has been opened as well. The other day Professor Merriam, Dr. Rutherford, Joseph, the two students, and I left camp early and headed out under a vaporous cover of cloud. Steam was rising from the creekbed we followed, mixing with the fog and mist, transforming the world around us into a seeming fairy land of sparkling white. In spite of the damp and cold we were all in excellent spirits, calling out to each other like children in the mist, as we worked our way through the damp, thick undergrowth.

As we cleared a rocky outcropping, and the creekbed took a turn to the south, we found ourselves on the edge of an expansive high mountain meadow awash in color. Even Dr. Rutherford, who reluctantly had agreed to join us on this outing, and who had lost his good humor about half way up the mountainous climb, was overwhelmed by the sight.

Lupinus argenteus, Castilleja miniata, Geranium viscosissimum, and *Perideridia Gairdneri* painted a field with bright blue, red, pink, and occasional white brush strokes against a sea of low-lying mist and green as far as the eye could see. As if to intensify the moment for us alone, just as we entered the meadow, the sun rose past a ridge to our east, and glistened against the thin blanket of ice which was spread across the field. I looked at my colleagues and I could see that they, too, felt as I did. This was the moment for which all of us, each in our own way, had been waiting. We stood silent, as if in prayer or meditation, and then slowly, one by one, we went to work.

Everything was wet with the mist and icy dew, which numbed my hands and fingers as if I were collecting under ice water, but there was simply not enough time to wait for the sun to warm the day. Dr. Rutherford joined me, along with Rocky, and the three of us commenced collecting on the far western reaches of the meadow where, we reasoned, the sun would be the warmest, while Professor Merriam, Joseph, and the other student treaded through the crunchy grass to collect along the clearing nearest to the creek.

As we worked, it occurred to me that this might be ideal conditions to see *Ursus horribilis,* and I mistakenly mentioned the fact to Dr. Rutherford.

"Grizzly bears?" he asked. "Here?"

"Can't you imagine them living here?" I asked him. "It seems like perfect country for bears. Look at those berries. And all that decaying wood along the line of trees."

Dr. Rutherford turned pale. He had no desire to see wildlife and, after the mountain man's tale, was determined to avoid seeing bears, any bear, at just about any cost.

We all worked diligently throughout the morning, except for Dr. Rutherford who was forever keeping a lookout over his shoulder for marauding bears. Finally, around noon, with the sun and temperature rising, we made our way back to the shady creekbed to decide how next to proceed.

Professor Merriam suggested that, after eating lunch, we ascend the rocky ledge to the east of us, and search the ridge for additional alpine variations. This particular ledge did not present a risk or climbing challenge to any one of us, however, Dr. Rutherford, still leery of bears and unwilling to climb any farther, voted against the idea. He suggested instead that we return to camp, noting that it had been a long and exhausting day and that we could always collect along the streambed as we headed home.

Professor Merriam then turned to me and requested that I voice my preference. I was surprised that he would ask and, because my opinion had never before been solicited, I found myself unprepared to offer one. Jessie, can you imagine it? I did not have an opinion! Instead, I assured Professor Merriam that I would be content with either decision.

The Professor nodded and suggested that we eat our lunch. "It's always easier to make plans on a full stomach than an empty one," he said.

Dr. Rutherford grunted in agreement and, as we removed our bread and cold meat from our field bags, he excused himself and retreated into the privacy of the woods.

Before I had time to spread my cloth upon my lap, we all heard Dr. Rutherford's loud hollering as he came rushing through the trees.

"I heard it, I saw it," he shouted, valiantly trying to pull his trousers from around his ankles as he ran.

"Up there. I saw it," he cried again. "It was huge, walking, back there, through the trees."

As Dr. Rutherford splashed to the other side of the creek, we all sat still for a moment and tried to sharpen our eyes and ears in the direction he was pointing.

"There, there, did you hear it? That crashing. Did you hear it?"

We could indeed hear something moving through the underbrush. It was hardly a crashing, but it was approaching, slowly, cautiously, on the far side of the creek. We hastily returned our lunches to our cases and stood, the five of us, peering into the shadowy darkness on the other side of the creek, while Dr. Rutherford buttoned his trousers.

"I told you we should go back to camp," Dr. Rutherford shouted. "I told you."

On many occasions, Dr. Peacock has assured me that the bears we are most likely to encounter here and throughout the Park feeding at the garbage pits and begging outside of the hotels are not particularly dangerous unless, of course, you interfere with their young. Grizzlies are another story, but since they prefer to avoid contact with humans at almost any cost, even they pose little threat. Naturally, since *U. horribilis* are less adapted to human contact and interaction, I have become more determined than ever to see one before returning home.

"We should go see what it is," I suggested to Professor Merriam. "It could be a grizzly," I added, "and there aren't many opportunities to see one in the Park."

"Miss Bartram," the Professor responded, "I know you have great curiosity when it comes to bears, but I would prefer for the safety of us all that you remain with the group. At least until we understand what we're dealing with here."

He looked around the small clearing where we were now huddled together, and added, "Perhaps we should move to open ground where we can see the animal better if it does continue to advance."

I was disappointed by yet another example of the Professor's lack of interest in anything outside of medical botany and common names, but we could hear the bear or whatever it was moving just above us now, where the streambed took a turn to the south, so I reluctantly joined my party as they re-entered the open basin. From our new location, we could still see nothing, but we could hear a splashing, as if the creature were following our path down the creek.

Rutherford became even more agitated as he realized we were now standing in an open area with little or no protection. Should the bear decide to attack, we would have nowhere to hide.

"We have to go," he warned. "Up there. Onto that ridge."

Professor Merriam cast me a sly look to ascertain whether or not I understood that this was the very same ridge that only moments before Dr. Rutherford had refused to climb.

"Well, I suppose that would work," he said with a shrug.

As we gathered our things in preparation for the ascent, the bushes along the creekbed shuddered briefly and Dr. Rutherford panicked.

"There, there," he cried. "There it is."

Now we could all see a large shape, just through the trees, as it moved alongside or, more likely, through the water. Then we heard it grumble, groan, and then—swear.

Dr. Rutherford was stunned but he identified the sounds immediately.

For the first time, at least in my hearing, Dr. Rutherford swore in return and then added, "Peacock. I should have known."

We all let out a collective sigh of relief, and laughed, the exaggerated laughter of salvation, for saved we believed ourselves to be. We also laughed at Dr. Rutherford. We could not help ourselves, we were all so happy to be alive.

Hearing us, Dr. Peacock emerged from the trees, carrying his collecting net and tins and blinking in the bright sun. Rutherford was instantly vindicated since it was easy for us all to imagine making a similar mistake. At first glance, Peacock looked every part the bear, with hair and beard filthy and matted from an extended stay in the field. And we could not help but notice, as he approached our small group, that he smelled much like a wild beast, too.

As for Dr. Rutherford, he was initially shaken by the situation and had little to say on our descent back to camp. But by the time we arrived, and settled in for our evening meal, he turned the story to his own advantage, telling of how we all quaked in our boots at the piercing cry of the wild Rocky Mountain peacock "Goddammittohell!" as it stumbled along the river banks in search of bugs.

I have since noticed, however, that Dr. Rutherford is more committed than ever to avoiding the backcountry, preferring instead to stay in camp and log in, dry, and care for our botanical specimens. Since we have such an extensive collection now, the Professor has agreed that Dr. Rutherford's contributions in this regard are critical, even if Dr. Rutherford opts to spend most of his time not working on the collection but rather in deep philosophical, albeit one-sided, debates with his *Corvus corax* which follows him everywhere like a dog.

While I am sharing all of my stories, I must tell you, too, that Ralph Clancy, the rancher I have written to you about in the past, has asked me to stay in Montana and to travel with him to his family's ranch. To be honest, I would love to stay. I am so happy here. But marriage for me now would limit my ability to explore all the rich new possibilities that are awaiting for me and my new career. And children, as blessed as they would be, would steal that part of my future away. If I have learned anything from my conversation with Sara, and my extended stay here in the Park, it is that women can and should take charge of their lives. Sara has done so by removing herself from the traditions of her tribe. I intend to learn from her wisdom and remove myself, at least for the time being, from the traditions of mine.

So you see, I am well, happy, and enjoying my life here to the fullest. You can also be assured that even when I try to see bears in the backcountry, the only hairy beasts I encounter in the woods are members of my own party. There is hardly any danger in that!

I do so hope you are well.

My love to you and your dear, sweet family,

Alex

--- ◆ ---

Andrew Rutherford, Ph.D.
c/o Lake Hotel
Yellowstone National Park
August 14, 1898

Robert Healey
President
Agricultural College &c.
Bozeman, Mont.

Dear Sir,

Returning to campus by end of month. Securing necessary permits to remove raven from Park. Seeking yr. kind permission to establish bird sanctuary & research facility at experiment station on campus. Will personally provide for bird's room & board, so no out-of-pocket expense to you or college.

Will observe, investigate, & report signs of raven intelligence. Could put Mont. College on higher ed. map. Travellers from around world will visit to see bird like at Tower of London.

Timing critical. Ravens, I'm told, may soon go way of P. pigeons and C. geese. Destined to die out with destruction of W. wolves.

I await your kind reply.

Yours most sincerely,

    Andrew Rutherford, Ph.D.

———— •◦• ————

Howard Merriam
c/o Lake Hotel
Yellowstone National Park
August 25, 1898

William Gleick
Smithsonian Institution
Washington
District of Columbia

Dear Bill,

I am writing to inform you that I have received today an ultimatum from President Healey. We must all return to campus by the end of the month or face certain dismissal. We are now in the process of breaking down our backcountry camp, and will be returning to our original campsite near the Lake Hotel within the week. From there we will prepare ourselves and our collection for our return to Bozeman.

Although we could have spent, at minimum, another three weeks in the field, I am still most satisfied with the results of our work. We have, I believe, assembled a very good representative botanical collection, one which the Smithsonian should be most pleased to receive. Philip Aber's supporters should be more than satisfied with the Rocky Mountain alpine varieties we have collected to supplement his European specimens. In this small way I hope to ensure that his work continues, even now that he is gone.

I will do my utmost to classify, document, and ship everything to you (or Aber's permanent successor should you be foolish enough to decline their most generous offer) by the end of the year. I will also pry additional duplicates from Peacock's beetles and other bugs which are taking up far too much space as far as Rutherford is concerned. Based on what you have told me of the Director's research, the sheer volume and variety of specimens Peacock has collected are certain to be an enormous success.

Before leaving the Park, we will take at least a day, if not two, to allow everyone an opportunity for some sightseeing. For some unknown reason, Rutherford has become fixated upon visiting Old Faithful. He speaks of it often, and plans to visit the upper geyser basin before we depart. Miss Zwinger has invited Miss Bartram to join her for a hike to the top of Mount Washburn to partake of the view. John Wylloe has volunteered to accompany them on the outing, as has Joseph. Their temporary absence from camp allows me the time I need to wrap up any loose ends before we depart.

Jake Packard offered to drive the group to their destination, but I must confess, I still do not trust the man outside of my sight. There still lingers in him a general hostility towards us all. I assume this is based on my decision to let Miss Bartram stay with the expedition. Or perhaps it was the ban on alcohol in camp, with which he has never bothered to comply. In either case, or both, our driver has not been happy with his situation here, so it is best to keep him busy and his mind off other things. Besides, I might need him for last-minute transport. At least that is what I have said.

Having complained yet again about the difficulty of managing or, more to the point, mismanaging those in my employ, I must tell you that if I have learned anything on this expedition it is that, with the exception of Jake Packard who is not unlike that unruly dog of his and requires a short leash, it is best to leave the rest of them alone, to be themselves, and to expect nothing more of them than what they, themselves, are willing or are able to give. When I have not constrained them, it turns out that each in their own way has much to contribute.

Rutherford, I am now the first to admit, has turned out to be a fine scientist, albeit one of a slightly different stripe. He has captured a raven, which he keeps as a pet, although he insists on calling his observations of the bird "research." Because the bird has a natural proclivity for mimicry, Rutherford has dedicated the summer to teaching the raven to talk. Although I have been openly contemptuous, Rutherford continues to be fascinated by the bird's every caw, quork, and turkey-like gobble. I am doubtful that Rutherford will garner any results from his so-called experiment, but I cannot for one minute question his dedication or commitment to the work as he has defined it.

Because of all the attention it receives, the raven has become so tame it is becoming a bit of a pest, nightly hopping onto the dinner table, where it preens itself and dips its head from side to side eyeing the food on our plates. Then it gobbles until one of us foolishly rewards this misbehavior by tossing it something to eat. The bird also has taken to pecking through our equipment, carrying away interesting-looking objects in its beak. Just last week it hopped off with one of my smaller pocket glasses. When it started getting into the collection, however, I really did have to protest.

I must warn you as both a colleague and a friend that, should you decide to remain at the Smithsonian Institution, I am certain Rutherford will contact you about his proposed raven research. He considers you his "friend in Washington" and seems to think that that is all he needs to ensure financial support. I have not yet informed him that President Healey has written to me directly, outright forbidding me to transport or in any other way assist Rutherford as he tries to return to campus with that bird. My gut instinct tells me, however, that the news will not alter Rutherford's plans in the least. I doubt that he will give a minute's thought to anything the president or I forbid him to do when it comes to that raven.

Miss Bartram, too, has turned out to be another fine addition to our group, proving herself to be invaluable to the success of our work. I am beginning to see now, as I could have never foreseen when she arrived, that her perspective on illustrating flora in its natural environs contributes much to our understanding of the plant life in the Park. Because she is committed to both illustrating as well as collecting, she has often worked day and night to ensure that she has the time to contribute fully to both. Seeing her as I do now, it was with great sadness that I learned from the president that he will not entertain even a small salary to allow her to continue her work on the collection upon our return. I can only hope that you will do whatever it takes to ensure that her illustrations and documentations, when they arrive at the Smithsonian, are well cared for since there does not appear to be a place for her or her work at the college.

That is not to say that Miss Bartram and I do not still have our differences. I fear she still views me as a bit of a dilettante or even a fool in my approach to science. In fact, she grows quite impatient with me when I try to discuss with her my ideas about the nature of science in the modern-day world.

The other day, Peacock, knowing of my interest, told me of a high mountain basin, a few miles from our camp, which was showing the impact of fire on plant life. Because it would take almost a full day to reach the site he described, and because I could not in good conscience insist that Miss Bartram stay behind with Rutherford, I invited along Miss Zwinger (who had recently sent her charges home so that she might spend these waning days of the summer exploring the Park on her own). I also invited the naturalist and poet, John Wylloe, who has been spending some time with us in camp and has demonstrated an interest in our work. Their presence, I hoped, would counter any thought of impropriety of my travelling overnight with Miss Bartram, since Rutherford insists that he is now too busy readying the collection for the trip home to travel into the field. I think the real reason is that he is terrified by the prospect of encountering a foraging bear, but he would never outright admit that. At least not to me.

Anyway, both Miss Zwinger and Wylloe accepted my invitation, thinking of it as an end-of-summer adventure, and the six of us (including Joseph and Rocky, who also volunteered), headed out early the next morning in the direction Peacock had indicated.

The day was particularly fine, with high, thin clouds and no wind. It was an easy hike, but even so it took us most of the day to reach our destination, an open basin on the edge of a pine forest where the underbrush had been cleared by fire just as Peacock had described it. The fire had also felled most of the aging trees, resulting in an eye-pleasing mixture of newly emerging pines, grasses, and flowering plants. A thick wash of fireweed spread along one side of the meadow, intermixed here and there with the young saplings.

As soon as we entered the clearing, Miss Bartram eyed something of interest and commenced collecting. I chose to work where the fireweed was particularly dense, even though it meant climbing in and around the trunks of fallen trees. Both John Wylloe and Miss Zwinger offered to help, but I was really not keen on supervising them so, as I worked, the two of them wandered off for the afternoon to watch a golden eagle circling the basin in search of food.

That night, after a rewarding afternoon of collecting and a satisfactory dinner around the campfire, we opened the third bottle of Miss Zwinger's wine and I started to explain how the heat of forest fires releases the seeds from the cones of the lodgepole pines, as it makes way for new plant life like the fireweed.

"*Epilobium angustifolium,*" Miss Bartram, sipping her wine from a coffee cup, corrected. The Latin slipped easily off her tongue.

It was a beautiful night—warm, with the stars bright and clear. Much too lovely to argue about nomenclature with Miss Bartram. Apparently Miss Zwinger agreed, because she, too, interrupted, noting that the Northern Cross was beginning to rise in the sky.

"Cygnus, the Swan," Wylloe countered without the slightest hint of irony.

"The Crow people call that constellation Goose Above," I explained, happy to learn that it was not just me and Miss Bartram who argued over the proper names of things. "They see it as a sign that the geese will soon be headed south."

Miss Zwinger leaned back, perhaps to better detect the shape of the constellations we were naming.

"Some say they look at the stars, and the vastness and uncertainty of the universe make them feel insignificant," she said. "But I have always felt the reverse. Compared to the stars, the world around us is so much closer. So much more immediate somehow. I look at the stars and cannot help but feel bigger. Or maybe it is that the world seems to be just that much more alive."

Some believe, I pointed out, that the stars exert great influence on us and our actions.

"Well, Professor Merriam, we know that is nonsense, now don't we?" Miss Zwinger replied. "Just calling those stars the Northern Cross is silly enough, when you think about it. Just a handful of stars floating in space, not looking like much of anything."

"Maybe that is how we appear to them," I said, not in the least bit believing it, of course, but it was late, and we were all a bit dreamy lying there under the clear mountain sky.

Now I should have expected it. John Wylloe certainly did because he was chuckling to himself in anticipation. I did not make the comment to upset her, but Miss Bartram could not let such a meaningless and harmless statement stand.

"Professor Merriam, please," she chided me from across the fire. "Surely you do not believe that. You really should not say something so frivolous in the presence of our guests. They may not know that you are jesting and might take you seriously."

To keep the peace, I apologized to all present for my careless remark, but I could not help but add that we must all be careful not to assume that we hold the only key to understanding the ways of the world. Our idea of science was, after all, promoted by those who steadfastly believe that the world was created in six days by an all-knowing and all-seeing god.

This last comment went unchallenged by Miss Bartram, who had withdrawn far enough away from the light of the fire that it was difficult to see if she was even still present, much less paying attention to what was being said. Perhaps she had already fallen asleep.

I can almost guarantee it was the wine, which Miss Zwinger had poured liberally into our cups, but whatever the cause, I could not stop myself from firing another round into the darkness.

"I think that most of us here would say that our collective world view is based, in one way or another, on science rather than religion or myth. By the way, I include Joseph in this grouping because the Crow are fine scientists. Their understanding of the stars, the natural world, even their religion is based on centuries of observation and results, not on blind belief. The Crow are a very pragmatic people when it comes to these kinds of questions."

Still there was no word of protest from Miss Bartram, so I continued.

"But what is science, really, but another means of looking at the stars, just as Miss Zwinger so eloquently pointed out, and bringing some order, meaning, and, ultimately, predictability to the universe? Isn't that what the Crow do when they see the starry goose flying south? They know that fall is coming and start preparing themselves for the winter ahead."

"Professor Merriam, you are deliberately trying to provoke me," Miss Bartram called out from beyond the light of the fire. "You have no right to say that myth and science are the same."

Miss Bartram leaned back toward the group with great earnestness, her wine-filled coffee cup in hand.

"I do not mean to be impertinent," she continued, "but are you saying that the constellations somehow affect the seasons?" As she said this she suppressed a laugh, but I could not tell if she was thinking the whole notion humorous or simply preposterous. Knowing Miss Bartram, I assumed the latter.

"No, I'm saying nothing of the sort," I protested. "What I am saying is that science, myth, and religion all enable each of us in our own way, depending upon how we were raised and the books we were given to read at an early age, to bring order to what is otherwise a very chaotic-seeming world. It appears that it is in our nature as a species to construct these kinds of stories."

"As the much maligned visitor in this camp, I find that now I must intercede," John Wylloe said. "I agree with Miss Bartram that there is a great difference between scientific truth, that which can be observed empirically, and the fanciful stories you make up out of conjecture and wishful thinking. And you will never convince me otherwise."

Wylloe spoke with such certainty and authority, it was as if that should be enough to end the conversation right there.

"We are a species that likes to name things," Miss Zwinger noted, perhaps to cool off the increasingly heated exchange. "I will give you that," she added, not indicating to whom it was given.

Miss Bartram ignored them both and leaned questioningly in my direction.

"So, Professor, are you arguing that science, myth, and religion are all true?" This time I could clearly hear the incredulity in her voice.

"No," I defended myself. "I'm saying they are all useful. I don't know that much about religious beliefs, but I do know that the constellation Goose Above predicts the arrival of winter, Miss Bartram. And I can assure you that if you live in Crow country, and you ignore its arrival in the night sky, you do so at your own peril."

I cannot be certain if it was my last comment, or Joseph's distant "hmmm" of approval, that bothered Miss Bartram more, but she was now so agitated that it seemed to be all that she could do to keep from jumping over the fire at me.

"Professor Merriam, now you really do go too far," she cried. "Please, do not jest like this in the presence of our guests."

Our words volleyed back and forth over the campfire which sizzled and crackled between us in the deepening dark, until John Wylloe felt compelled to once again intercede.

"As a guest," he said, "it might be useful, at least for me, if you defined the nature of your disagreement. Are you saying, Miss Bartram, that you do not feel it is good form to question the nature of science in the presence of amateurs? Is that the heart of your argument?"

"No, of course not," Miss Bartram replied forcefully. "It is that

Professor Merriam is a man of influence and, as such, has great power over us all." She said that in all earnestness. "I certainly hope that he would not, on a whim, say that the stars influence our behavior or the weather or other such nonsense as Miss Zwinger rightly calls it. Because he is a man of science, someone might take him seriously."

At this comment, one of the logs in the fire let out a loud pop, sending shimmers of sparks into the night. As Wylloe poked at the fire with the toe of his boot, re-settling the logs, Miss Zwinger re-joined the conversation.

"Well, I certainly do not take him seriously," she said with much conviction, at which John Wylloe laughed loudly, helping us all to relax once again.

"I meant no offense, Professor Merriam," Miss Zwinger added. "I only meant to say that I assumed that you were just trying to be friendly. You know, making small talk around the campfire."

I assured her no offense was taken, but I also felt compelled to bring some order to the now chaotic nature of our conversation.

"Think of it this way," I offered. "We look at the stars and take what, from our perspective, are random points of light and make them into pictures. Now some make up stories associated with those pictures, which you may or may not believe, while others make up stories to tell us where the points of light came from in the first place. But in both of these cases, the universe seems less random if you name or in some other way describe the origin of the stars. Would you agree with that, Miss Bartram?"

"Well," she hesitated. "I would agree that when Miss Zwinger points out the Northern Cross, I can look to the sky and know precisely which stars she is talking about. When Mr. Wylloe calls it a swan, it gets more problematic. But I can say in all honesty that I do not see a goose flying south. That is beyond me."

"Now, I am not saying, Miss Bartram, that you should see a cross or a swan or whatever the stars are supposed to be," I countered. "What I am saying is that in the masses of stars that confront us nightly, there are a handful of them which have been grouped by a common name and that grouping helps us to conveniently identify them. For example, over there, where the Greeks saw a crown, Miss Bartram, the Crow people see a campsite, and when it is directly overhead they know it is time to meet all the families of their tribe. It really doesn't matter, does it, what we call them, or how we use them to measure distance or time. It is that we gather them in some meaningful pattern, give them a name upon which we can all agree, and with that common understanding, we can converse intelligently about the world."

Miss Zwinger, who seemed to be wool-gathering by the side of the fire, now leaned forward, the light and shadows of the fire dancing across her face.

"Well, then I would say that you are describing all of science. For isn't that what you do? Gather bits of information in the universe you are studying and classify them for the purposes of identification and scientific discourse?"

"Oh," Miss Bartram cried out as if in pain. "Not you, too. Miss Zwinger, please. Don't encourage him."

Now it was Miss Zwinger who laughed. "And to think this all started by my noting a cross of stars rising on the horizon. I can't thank you enough, both of you, for inviting me along on this trip. It has been a wonderful, but long and tiring day. I fear I do not have your youthful stamina, so I think it's time for me to call it a day."

With that, Miss Zwinger unrolled her bedding to one side of the fire and bid us all a good night.

"The world is filled with such wonder and uncertainty," I said to Miss Bartram as she, too, busied herself with her bed roll. "If we can bring some order to it through science or even religion or myth, all of our lives can be equally full of wonder."

She looked up at me then and, with great seriousness, said, "I will not argue with any of what I have heard you say tonight, Professor, if you will agree that when Miss Zwinger calls a grouping of stars the Northern Cross, it might be confusing to Mr. Wylloe who knows it as Cygnus the Swan. And it would be even more confusing to Joseph who calls it Goose Above. Can you agree to that?"

"Of course, of course," I agreed, blind to the trap she was setting. "It would be very confusing if the three of them wanted to discuss a grouping of stars. Particularly if they could not point them out to one another in the nighttime sky as we have done here tonight."

"Then would you also agree that it is very confusing to me when you insist on calling *Epilobium angustifolium* by its common name which could be referring to any number of plants? You must understand that I often do not have a clue what you are talking about."

At this John Wylloe laughed heartily, stood, and excused himself. We could hear his good-natured chuckles as he busied himself laying out his buffalo skins at a discreet distance from the fire.

I looked at Miss Bartram, who returned my gaze with that same intense, serious, passionate look of hers. I could not help but smile.

"Of course," I said to her. "I would be most happy to give you your scientific nomenclature. What is more, I would happily use it from now on whenever I speak to you about our work here."

That should have been the end of it but, blame it on the wine, I could not leave it at that. I had to make one slight correction to my declaration.

"I would use your terminology on a daily basis," I said, pausing for effect, "if, that is, I could pronounce it."

With both Miss Zwinger and Mr. Wylloe chuckling in their beds, and Miss Bartram nodding with a resigned smile, we all retired for the evening, each of us in our own good humor, sleeping under a canopy of stars which we named and brought order to in our own individual ways.

Bill, I have to tell you that in spite of all the difficulties and the very tragic loss of Philip Aber, this has been a most successful and rewarding summer for me here on both a personal and professional level. I hope it turns out equally successful and rewarding for you there.

My best regards,
Howard

A. E. Bartram
c/o Lake Hotel
Yellowstone National Park
August 28, 1898

Dear Jessie,

Our days in our Nation's Park are slowly drawing to a close. I can sense it in the land, which is turning golden as it readies itself for fall, in the air, which has grown cool as it promises winter, and in the spirit of our group, which grows warmer by the day as we learn, each and every one of us, to become more accepting of the strengths and weaknesses and strange passions of our colleagues and friends.

We have re-established our old camp near the hotel, as we busy ourselves for the return trip home. There is a sadness in these preparations, but a gentle joyousness, too, as we acknowledge our friendships and all the kindnesses we have received from one another. That I must say goodbye to this wondrous place, and all the wonderful people I have been associated with here, almost breaks my heart. But Professor Merriam has assured me that he will attempt another expedition in the spring, perhaps in an unexplored northern part of the state. If successful in raising the necessary funds, he will invite me back as a contributor. So, even though my field work in the Park must end, it appears that my career as a botanist is just now beginning. This means, of course, that I no longer have a reason to return to Cornell. Given the awkwardness of my parting from Lester, perhaps it is just as well. I need to move forward with my career—and my life—and not return to where I have already been.

Before leaving, Miss Zwinger, John Wylloe, Joseph Not-afraid, and I left camp for one last grand view of the Park before going our separate ways. The early morning weather was cool and windy but cloudless, so it was with great anticipation that we set out at dawn for our last mountain hike. Fortunately for Mr. Wylloe, we were able to hitch our horses to the back of a coach for most of the journey. It is a long ride and Mr. Wylloe's thin, bony frame is ill-suited to spending a day in the saddle, even with a strategically placed pillow. So when I asked if we might leave the horses behind for the final ascent up the trail, he was the first to eagerly agree.

We tied our horses next to an open marshy area with the most spectacular display of *Mimulus Lewisii* I have seen since entering the Park. These bright pink flowers were intermixed with *Orthocarpus tenuifolius*, *Achillea lanulosa*, *Aster conspicuus*, and some species of *Haplopappus*, bright and beautiful in a ravine on the side of the road. Of course I could not pass up the opportunity to collect, even if for just a moment or two. Joseph also indicated an interest in the *Achillea*, which he proceeded to harvest with great precision. Miss Zwinger, sympathetic to us both, offered to hike ahead with John Wylloe, who was in desperate need of stretching his legs. The two of them suggested we meet again further on the trail at our convenience. This was an arrangement to which Joseph and I both eagerly agreed.

A small hawk circled overhead and then vanished as our two companions slowly disappeared over the first clearing. Joseph, too, soon disappeared waist deep and then deeper into the green. From time to time I could hear the horses settle from one foot to another as they nuzzled in the grass, but otherwise the only sound was a slight breeze which stirred the tree branches overhead, and the trickle of water at the unseen center of this flowery bog.

I waded through the marsh until the ground underfoot became too soft to comfortably travel, at which point I commenced collecting, heading uphill so that I would eventually be reunited with my companions. I must have lost track of time, for it seemed like only after a moment or two that I was distracted by a noise a little further up the hill.

Thinking it was Joseph, I advanced in the direction of the sound, which was louder now, followed by a splash and a crashing sound as if a tree had fallen or had been thrown into the swampy ground. I know I should have been more cautious, but in reality, I was simply curious. I wondered what Joseph was doing or, if it was not Joseph, who or what it could be. Rather than return to the trail, which in retrospect would have been the more prudent course, I ventured along the waterway in the direction of the sound.

Then I saw it, an adult *U. horribilis*, not more than 100 feet away. It was, in all honesty, not horrible at all, but beautiful, digging with its claws and rooting with its snout in the mud, the silver tips of its fur wavering back and forth in a dappled wash of sunlight and shadow. Because I was standing across the water and upwind from the beast, it did not hear or see me, so I watched with what I assumed to be immunity. Of course, I was foolish not to retreat. But at the time, I was simply transfixed, completely unaware of any danger. I stood my ground until the wind shifted slightly, and the bear lifted its head.

Because its chest and front legs were wet from digging in the mud, I could see its thick muscles ripple and stretch under its fur as the beast probed the air with its nose, first away from the creek, swooping with its head and grunting, and then, with another swoop, nosing downstream in my direction. I suppose then that I really should have been frightened, because it was pointing its nose in my direction, but before I even had time to comprehend what was happening, the bear was gone. It abruptly turned, charged up the hill—and was gone.

From up the hill I could hear Joseph singing as he collected, unaware of the danger to himself and to the others. Now I really was frightened, because the direction the bear was headed, as far as I could tell, was towards Joseph and the path being followed by Miss Zwinger and Mr. Wylloe.

I scrambled up the boggy bank to alert Joseph.

"Grizzly," I called to him. He smiled but kept singing. "We need to alert the others," I said, now panicked at the thought of the bear charging directly into the path of Miss Zwinger and Mr. Wylloe. Joseph smiled and nodded again.

"Now," I shouted.

"Hmmm," he said, without much conviction, but he did follow me back up the trail.

My heart was pounding, not from having seen the bear, but at the prospect of inadvertently seeing it again. Joseph's loud, insistent droning, which seemed to keep him calm, only served to heighten my own sense of uneasiness and dread. What if it was his death song, I could not help but wonder.

I realized then how Professor Merriam must have felt time and again when I disappeared from the group or went off in the foolish pursuit of bears or elusive white flowers. He takes our safety and wellbeing so personally. What a burden I have been to him.

We hurried up the trail, Joseph much less hurried in the ascent than I was, until we encountered our companions, who were sitting, side by side, silently watching a family of *Ovis canadensis*. My calling out to alert the pair and, I dare say, Joseph's unusually loud singing, sent the bighorns skittering across the rocks, and over the side of the mountain, much to our friends' consternation.

When I tried to explain that we were concerned about a bear, a grizzly, they were both, still, unimpressed. They had not seen it, they both informed me flatly. Again, Joseph smiled and nodded, having finished his song.

"Well, Miss Bartram," John Wylloe said to me, still weary from the long ride and perturbed that I had scared off the sheep. "I hope that your curiosity about bears is satisfied?"

I could not help but laugh at the comment, recalling that Meriwether Lewis had said something very similar to his troops, although it took several life-threatening encounters to satiate their curiosity. Joseph laughed, too, right out loud, which for him is unusual.

As we followed the trail to the summit, I tried to tell Miss Zwinger and Mr. Wylloe about the bear, how it had looked, what it was doing, how I had surprised it there (or it had surprised me), and how under no circumstances should any of them tell the Professor of my encounter, but neither Mr. Wylloe nor Miss Zwinger was at all interested in what I had to say. They were much more fascinated by the bighorn sheep they had encountered, and the animals' apparent lack of fear. The sheep just stood there, close enough to touch, they kept repeating, until I scared them off with all my commotion.

Joseph was in an unusually good humor, singing again, but this time contentedly to himself. His pleasure with the day, or maybe he was pleased with his own collecting, helped smooth our personal rough edges and buoy us beyond the timberline and onto the summit. We stood there, the four of us, all so different and yet all so very much the same, for a long, silent time, the gusty wind whipping our hair and clothes and the wisps of clouds overhead. It was as if we were at the top of the world, or at the center of the universe, surveying all that we had created. Or, in Professor Merriam's way of viewing the world, all that we had named.

I missed the Professor then, knowing that I would miss him when I had to leave for home, and wished with all my heart that he could have seen the vista that stretched out around us: the canyons, the rivers, the lakes, the steaming geysers, even the Teton Mountains miles and miles to the south. It is our Nation's greatest wonder and through some miracle of selflessness in a country too often built on greed, the Yellowstone Park will be preserved for generations to come. Even someone like Capt. Craighead, who has little or no interest in the natural world, has dedicated himself and his career in opposition to those interested in exploiting rather than protecting this national treasure.

Someone who had visited this same spot years before had constructed a monument of rocks piled from the rubble on the summit. Joseph took a small pebble and, circling the pile once, placed it near the top, careful not to disturb the others. It seemed such a fitting tribute, that I, too, added a small stone to the pile before following the others down the trail. Funny how these rituals seem to make more sense to me now.

By the time we finally reached our campsite at the end of the day, we learned that Dr. Rutherford had postponed his own sightseeing so that he could host a farewell party. While we had been gone, Dr. Rutherford and the students had spent the morning in the hotel purchasing food, drink, and souvenirs for us all, including spoons and little weathered stones which had been painted yellow and hand lettered with the word Wonderland. He had even commissioned a photographer to take our portraits down by the lake.

In addition, he had enlisted the assistance of Kim Li who, up to this point, had maintained a healthy distance from, if not respect for, Dr. Rutherford. The two of them worked together in the afternoon to, in Dr. Rutherford's words, "spruce up" the campsite with Kim Li's bright red and gold Chinese cloths and paper lanterns from China and Butte, candles, paper and fabric garlands which were strewn throughout the trees, and large bouquets of the ubiquitous family Compositae which now blooms in golden profusion everywhere you look. Dr. Rutherford even went so far as to fill a lovely porcelain vase, also from Kim Li's collection, with the bright yellow sprays of *Mimulus guttatus* which, he informed me with great pride, he had found (and I quote!) "just like the Prof said I would, lilting with their little monkey faces down by the creek where it spills into the lake." We may make a scientist of Dr. Rutherford yet, even if he insists on following the Professor's misguided path of common nomenclature.

As we re-entered camp, Kim Li stirred large pots of fragrant foods and coached along a cast iron oven of real bread, rather than his usual skillet biscuits, infusing the pine-scented woods with its soft, warm perfume. Dr. Rutherford, in the meantime, was orchestrating his portraits at a makeshift studio he and the photographer had arranged down by the lake. Anxious to take advantage of the late afternoon light, Dr. Rutherford made sure the students hurried us along.

After riding and climbing for miles through dirt and dust and creekbeds, we all protested, feeling filthy as well as weary. Dr. Rutherford told us we could each have 20 minutes, maximum he said, to prepare ourselves. Miss Zwinger made a quick visit to the hotel, Joseph returned to his camp, and John Wylloe carried a towel and a clean shirt down to the lake, while I decided to take one of the horses to a nearby hotsprings where Dr. Rutherford and the students had arranged logs into yet another makeshift bath. I could at least wash my face and weary legs in the warm water if not enjoy a real soak which, I admit, I could have used after the ride and hike and the excitement of the day. But, I was expected back in camp for Dr. Rutherford's photography sessions and celebration, so I quickly washed and dried myself, slipped into my one clean shirtwaist, squeezed out my hair, and hurried back to the lake. I could always soak in warm water when I was once again back home.

Professor Merriam was standing next to the photographer, his hair slicked back making it appear almost brown in spite of its naturally golden color. Even his clothes were cleaned and pressed. In his arms he held a small bundle tied with string. I left the horse in the shade of the trees, and walked out across the rocky shore-line to greet him and Dr. Rutherford, who also looked well-combed and tidy in his freshly pressed suit. Joseph and Sara were both wearing a full set of beaded buckskins, and their distant but all-knowing smiles. Dr. Peacock, who had already had his photograph taken, sat off to one side on a rock, blinking in the late afternoon sun.

Miss Zwinger, having sat for her portrait, too, was now wading barefoot along the lakeshore, laughing with John Wylloe who had his photograph taken with his fishing pole in hand. He now crept along the lakeshore in Miss Zwinger's wake, casting a diminutive fly upon the surface of the water, looking revived in spite of the long day. In fact, he seemed to be thoroughly enjoying himself, even though Miss Zwinger's enthusiastic splashing almost guaranteed that he would catch no fish.

As I walked towards my friends and colleagues, I pushed at my clothes, trying to bring them into some semblance of order, and hastily pulled back my hair which was falling damp and loose around my shoulders. With one more tug on my jacket, and a last-minute smoothing of my skirt, I presented myself, with some hesitation, to my friends.

"I'm sorry I'm late," I said to them as I walked forward. Both the Professor and Dr. Rutherford turned and smiled in my direction. In spite of myself, I started fussing with my hair. I could not help it, the two of them looked so polished in the late afternoon light.

"I hope I look good enough," I said, again apologizing. Now I was nervously playing with a button on my jacket, like an insecure school girl, smoothing and straightening my clothes. Jessie, you would have laughed if you could have seen me, I was so flustered.

Dr. Rutherford strode forward, confident and smelling of soap.

"Nonsense," he cried, taking me by the arm. "You look lovely. Now sit here," he said, leading me to a log bench that he had set up lakeside in front of the camera.

I did the best that I could to ready myself, sitting where I was told, straightening my clothes, pinning back some loose strands of still damp hair, when Professor Merriam walked over to me with his bundle.

"I thought you might like this," he said, handing me the package.

Afraid I might upset his schedule even more, I looked to Dr. Rutherford for instructions. He smiled, beamed really, in approval. I untied the string and opened the folds of paper across my lap. Inside, wrapped in a wet cloth and chips of ice, was a fresh bouquet of *Gentiana detonsa,* pure white, just as it had been described to me. And, the plants had been removed with most of the root structure still intact!

I looked again to Dr. Rutherford, but he nodded in the direction of the Professor, who was busy wiping some dirt or dust from his boot.

"Ready?" the photographer asked from under his cloth hood.

"In a minute," Dr. Rutherford replied, taking away the damp wrappings, but leaving the flowers in my lap. With the sun casting long shadows across the water, John Wylloe swirling long loops of fishing line above his head, Miss Zwinger splashing like a child in the late afternoon light, Dr. Peacock squinting at a bug which had just entered into his line of vision, and Professor Merriam thoughtfully kicking at the water-worn stones at his feet, and while Dr. Rutherford, Joseph, and Sara stood watching to one side, smiling as if they knew more than the rest of us combined, and with me cradling the bouquet of white gentian like a child in my arms, I could hear the photographer's shutter slowly open and close, capturing my image, our summer, all of us, permanently, like magic, within his light-sensitive box.

Later, we all sat at the long camp table—the Professor, Dr. Rutherford, Dr. Peacock, Joseph Not-afraid and his family, the two students, Rocky and Stony, Mrs. Eversman, Miss Zwinger, John Wylloe, Ralph Clancy who donated steaks for the occasion, all my colleagues and good and kind friends, joined together for the flavorful dinner stirred up for the occasion by Kim Li, who sat with us at the table for the first time as well. Even the surly mountain man driver, washed and combed, joined us briefly, his dog sitting quietly at his feet. He seemed to relish the good food if not outright enjoy our good company.

With the night sky growing black and starry, the moon rippling a ribbon of light across the wind-whipped surface of the lake, and the lanterns, hanging from the trees around our camp, flickering in the breeze, our campsite was transformed into a special, fantastical place. I cannot remember enjoying a meal or celebration, as Dr. Rutherford likes to call it, more than I did that evening.

And then, as if to make a perfect evening even more wonderful, transforming the occasion into something I am certain none of us will ever forget for as long as we live, Dr. Rutherford's raven jumped onto the table, looked this way and that at all the sumptuous food laid out before it, and said, as clearly as I can write it here on the page, "never more." Then it uttered a couple of odd-sounding quorks, gobbled like a turkey, and stood there, its head turning from side to side, waiting for its greasy reward.

We laughed and laughed, all of us, friends. Joseph was laughing so hard he slapped his palms on the table, and Kim Li, in spite of the fact that he was forever shooing the bird away from his cooking, was so amused he kept dabbing with a rag at the corners of his eyes. He then cut a chunk of fat from one of the steaks and held it out to the raven, which hopped right up to him without fear and carried the prize off without hesitation.

It was an amazing performance. Dr. Rutherford was at first so shocked that he kept looking to the rest of us for confirmation. When he was satisfied that he had indeed heard what he thought he had heard, and that we had all heard it, too, the man smiled and laughed and smiled again, until tears flooded his eyes and he had to excuse himself from the table.

If that was the happiest I have ever seen Dr. Rutherford, it was beyond a doubt the most perplexed that I have ever seen the Professor. He, too, shook his head and acted as if he did not believe his own ears. But if he had his doubts, he, too, was laughing.

Jessie, I will miss them and this wonderful place, this Wonderland, with all my heart. I am happy that I will soon be able to see you and my dear family, but my colleagues here have become a family of sorts for me, too. I cannot tell you how sorry I am that it is time for me to leave them all behind.

I will see you soon.

In the meantime,

All my love,

Alex

A. E. Bartram
c/o Lake Hotel
Yellowstone National Park
August 30, 1898

Jessie:

I am writing to you rather than to my parents to let you know that I may not be coming home yet as planned. Something terrible has happened, and I do not yet know how it will affect my return. Or my stay.

Just the other night, after the party orchestrated by Dr. Rutherford and Kim Li, we all took to our beds with great humor. With the possible exception of Dr. Rutherford, who no longer imbibes, I think we were all looking forward to a good night's sleep to wear off the deleterious effects of Miss Zwinger's excellent wine as well as our long day of sightseeing.

The following morning, Dr. Rutherford's raven awoke early as is its habit and, finding no one up yet to feed it, hopped off in search of food. It did not have to venture far, for in the next clearing the count has established his own camp where he has amassed a malodorous pile of coyote, wolf, and big cat carcasses. Eyeing the carrion, the raven, which has grown accustomed to human interaction and is fearless in situations most wild birds would avoid, started to tear at the decaying flesh. One of the young men in the camp was making coffee, saw the bird, and pitched a handful of rocks in its direction, but since Kim Li is forever throwing something at the raven while it eats, the bird apparently hopped back, waited a moment, and then resumed feeding without any reserve.

It was then that the count entered the camp to prepare his men for another day of exploration, as he insists on calling his slaughter. Seeing the raven pecking away at his plunder, the count did not hesitate. He pulled a gun from his saddle, took aim at the bird, which had a hunk of putrid coyote flesh hanging from its beak, and killed it in a single shot. In actual fact the count did not shoot the bird so much as explode it, since he used so much firepower there was not much left except for some gore and a handful of feathers which fluttered here and there in the wind. The count could have killed an elephant with that gun.

Dr. Rutherford learned of the raven's death at breakfast, after the Professor and Joseph Not-afraid had already left camp for the day. He was numbed by the news, sitting at the fire, tears streaming down his ruddy face. Except for a shudder which racked his body from time to time and the occasional cloud of smoke which burst from his pipe, he sat there motionless, showing little sign of life.

The mountain man driver, in what can only be viewed as an act of compassion, joined him and offered a swig from his bottle. At first, Dr. Rutherford ignored him, preferring to stare into the fire, but as the driver finally shrugged and stood to take his leave, Dr. Rutherford changed his mind and took a long pull from the jug. Then he took another.

The mountain man reached down and, with a gentle flutter of his hand, patted Dr. Rutherford on the shoulder. He left him there with the bottle, as if he understood the depth of Dr. Rutherford's despair. Then the driver and his dog, which he had tied to a rope to save his pet from a similar fate, walked back to the edge of the trees to his own tent, which is located apart from the rest of ours. The mountain man tied the dog firmly to the tent's central post and disappeared inside.

In the meantime, Dr. Rutherford got up, staggered around, and removed himself to the trees. When he returned to the fire, he stumbled, sat back down, added another stack of logs to the fire in spite of the fact that the morning was already quite warm, and commenced sobbing and drinking again. Jessie, I wished so badly that I could help him but there was little that I could do. I sat with him for a while, thinking he might like to talk about the bird, remember it somehow, acknowledge all the wonderful things he had done in training it, but my presence only seemed to heighten Dr. Rutherford's grief. He did not seem to be able to do anything other than drink and throw more and more logs onto the fire. When I was sure he could not cry another tear, he silently sobbed and drank some more. It broke my heart to see him in such a state.

I took my sketch pad and field journal and set out for the lake, telling the students where they could find me if the Professor and Joseph should return before lunch, or if they needed my help with Dr. Rutherford. Then, like in a dream, I retraced our steps along the well-worn path down to the water, where only hours before we had walked with such joy. Then I, too, started crying. I cried for Dr. Rutherford, for his clever and, yes, intelligent *Corvus corax*, for the Professor who takes such pains to look out for us all, and for the ill-humored mountain man driver who had shown that even he had an ounce if not a pound of compassion. And I cried for myself, I loved them all so.

I sat there on a bluff overlooking the water as the passenger boat made its way slowly back to shore and the wind churned the surface of the water, whipping at my hair, my clothes, my tears. I cannot tell you how long I sat there, I was so lost in my grief. But suddenly, one of the students was running down the hill, a bucket in each hand, warning me of a fire. Soon others were shouting, running down from the hotel carrying buckets and bottles and anything else that could be dipped into the lake and carried back up the hill into the woods. Then the driver rushed out of the woods with a large metal basin, which he carried waist deep into the lake and pulled back up the hill, slopping water as he hurried past.

The wind was now fierce and unruly. I stood up, shaking free of my reverie, and saw that the wind was blowing large gusts of smoke into the sky. I picked up my journal and sketch pad and joined the rush of cavalrymen and hotel guests all hurrying along the trail with water in hand. When I reached our clearing I found our entire campsite was ablaze. My tent, my books, my blankets—they were all gone. Kim Li's tent was also destroyed, burned to the ground, with pots and pans standing next to piles of smoldering rubble strewn here and there on the now scorched earth.

The large white tent which Dr. Rutherford and the Professor had called home for the summer was burning wildly, in spite of the ineffective shower being sprayed at it from all directions by the volunteers. The more water they threw onto the blaze, the more fiercely the wind seemed to blow, whipping the fire into the nearby brush and up and into the forest canopy, spreading the inferno overhead and up the hill in the direction of the mountain man's tent.

Over the shouts and clamor of those trying to contain the fire, I could hear the dog howling after its master, who was at the lake retrieving more water. I look back on my actions now, and am certain that if the Professor hears of how I behaved he will never forgive me, for as the large white tent he shared with Dr. Rutherford and the collection were being ravaged in the gusty wind, I did nothing to try and stop it. Instead, without any thought or hesitation, I ran up the hill to where the trees circled the clearing and pulled loose the mountain man's dog. I was not thinking clearly but I knew I could not bear the thought of another creature being killed, or another man's spirit being broken.

Once untied, the dog ran yapping down the hill, narrowly escaping a fiery branch which momentarily caught my skirt ablaze. I unblushingly tore it off and beat it on the ground and then turned to a small fire that was burning off to the left of me, and beat at that, too. This was no time to be worried about convention.

As I turned down the hill, the wind picked up the last shreds of the Professor's tent and lifted it, like a flaming flag, into the branches of a tree where it sizzled and sparked, starting yet another fire in the branches overhead. The smooth piece of ground where the tent had been pitched now burned freely without the tent to enclose it, the two cots no more than charred remains. In the center stood a stack of boxes—our summer's work ready and awaiting the trip back home.

The volunteers, having retreated from the flaming tent as it burst past them into the sky, ran forward again with a solitary bucket of water. But it was too late. The boxes sizzled and smoked and then they, too, exploded into flame, just as the branches from the tree above fell smoking and blazing, adding even more fuel to the fire.

With my skirt in hand, I rushed forward and tried beating at the flames which were consuming the boxes. I was so close to the fire that I could smell Dr. Peacock's preservative, mixed with the smoke and the sour smell of burning wool. I think I could even smell burning hair. Others grabbed blankets and buffalo robes, while more volunteers rushed forward with buckets from the lake. But in spite of their valiant attempts, the fire only seemed to sizzle momentarily before the wind set fire to more branches, which fell flaming from overhead, turning back the volunteers and re-fueling the fire.

The cavalrymen, having dealt with emergencies like this in the past, methodically moved past our camp, and up the hill to the road, where they worked their way back down again, dousing or beating out each small burst of flame before it could spread. By the time they reached the remains of our camp, they had the fire well under control. We had lost our battle at the campsite, but the cavalrymen, it was clear, had won the war.

It was then that my thoughts turned to Dr. Rutherford. What if he had been in the tent? I cried out at my stupidity, having freed a dog when a human life could have been at risk. But Rocky, who stood surveying the wreckage, assured me that Dr. Rutherford was gone. Unable to walk very well, he told me, Dr. Rutherford had taken the wagon, just as Kim Li's tent had burst into flame.

"He told me that all was lost," the student informed me with a sad shake of his head. "He said he could not help it. There was too much wind. I tried to enlist his assistance fighting the fire, but he just kept crying. He was pretty drunk."

The student did not know where Dr. Rutherford was headed, but thinking of Dr. Aber's demise, I knew that given his condition it was critical that I find him before it got dark. And then there was the Professor who had yet to return to camp. Who would tell him? I wondered. Although I was still not thinking clearly, it seemed to make the most sense to deal with Dr. Rutherford first. He would be in the gravest danger.

I took one of the cavalry horses, which were still tied up down by the lake, and headed out on the road to the upper geyser basin. This section of the road is new and, thus, easy to travel, and the horse, having been tied up over night and, no doubt agitated by the fire, was more than willing to hurry right along. After a long, hard ride, of which I can remember very little, I entered the geyser basin clearing, dismounted, and led my horse along the indicated path. I know Park visitors walk around and even right up to the geysers, but I also know that they fall in, too.

The afternoon was waning and there were only a handful of visitors waiting for Old Faithful. One man walked from tourist to tourist with a logbook in hand, indicating how long they would have to wait for the geyser's next display. Upon hearing the news, one young woman shrugged and walked back to a crudely constructed log building with a rickety front porch, aptly known as the Shack Hotel.

Dr. Rutherford was a more dedicated observer. He had tied the horses to a log bench off to one side of the geyser's cone, where he patiently waited, hunched over, his head in his hands. I tied my horse to the opposite end, and joined him on the bench.

We sat there, the two of us, neither knowing what to say to the other, until, finally, the man with the journal stepped forward and cried, "It's time."

As predicted, within a minute a small puff of watery steam was exhaled from the ground, disappeared, and then was followed by another gasp, and then another. When I began to think that there was nothing more to the famous geyser than a predictable wisp or two of steam, a large blast of water burst from the cone, retreated, and then re-emerged, strewing water and steam 200 or so feet into the air. The wind carried the water in drifts across the clearing.

Dr. Rutherford, his face softened by drink and despair, looked up at the spectacle with dispassion. When the water finally retreated after three or four minutes with a last gasp or two of steam, he took the unlit pipe from his mouth and stared into its bowl.

"I never was that reliable, you know," he said. "I always wanted to be, but I never could stay with any one project long enough. Or maybe I was not meant to be the kind of person anyone would ever want to depend on to accomplish anything in life."

I wanted to protest, to reassure him somehow, but I knew, too, that Dr. Rutherford needed to have his say about whatever it was that was on his mind.

"My family always said I was not to be trusted," he finally said. "I have spent my entire adult life proving them right. I failed miserably when I farmed the family land. Then I had this idea that I could redeem myself by teaching others how to successfully ranch and farm. There is so much land, so much opportunity in the West. Maybe if I helped others to succeed . . ."

His voice trailed off, and he shook his head sadly. Then he laughed.

"Only thing I ever proved was that they were right. All of them. I can't succeed. Not at anything. Couldn't even get Merriam back to agriculture except by mistake. One big mistake." He stared into the bowl of his pipe. "That's my life all right. One giant mistake."

He laughed softly, emptied the pipe at his feet, and methodically began refilling it. Steam and water rose and fell along the horizon as other geysers erupted in the distance. The air smelled faintly of sulphur.

"Well," he finally said. "Looks like President Healey will get what he wants out of life." He relit his pipe and stood up, sighing. Then he looked at me.

"What happened to your skirts?" he asked.

I looked down at my ragged, filthy petticoat and shrugged.

"The fire," I explained.

"Was there anything left?"

"No," I had to tell him. "Most everything is gone."

He looked at me once more, his eyes red and weary, and then he, too, shrugged and went to untie his horses.

"I guess we should get back then."

I nodded.

As he stood there next to the wagon, he pointed out a glass building adjoining the rickety hotel.

"They use the water from the geysers to heat that greenhouse.

Grow vegetables for the tourists. Right here in the Park. Amazing how ingenious people can be when they put their minds to it, isn't it?"

Tears welled up again in his eyes. His face was flushed.

"Miss Bartram, it's all been a terrible mistake. A terrible, terrible mistake."

"I know," I tried to assure him. "I know."

By the time we returned to what was left of our campsite, the Professor had withdrawn to the hotel and would not speak to any of us about what we should be doing. He knows we cannot stay. We no longer have a camp. On the other hand, I cannot imagine leaving, when we could still salvage at least a week or two of work.

Until we hear from the Professor, Kim Li and I have joined Joseph Not-afraid and his family, who have graciously opened their camp to us. We are a sad sight indeed, with nothing but the ragged clothes on our back, but they have been more than accommodating. They refer to us as their science clan.

Dr. Rutherford is so devastated by his loss and his guilt, that he refused to join us, and has instead taken one of the driver's buffalo robes down to the lake. I think he plans to spend the night on the lakeshore alone, and leave for Bozeman in the morning.

As we left the geyser basin, I told Dr. Rutherford that I understood how all of this could have happened. That I understood how much he loved his bird, and understood his grief, and understood that this was all a terrible mistake. But the truth is that I do not understand any of it at all. I wish that I did.

As soon as I know what our situation is here, I will write to you again. Please do not tell my parents any more than you think prudent for them to know. On second thought, you might tactfully ask them to forward some money—it looks like I might need it to get home.

Love,
Alex

5. Rosa Woodsii

WESTERN UNION TELEGRAM

SEPTEMBER 1, 1898

DEAR SIR   APPRECIATE NEWS OF SENATOR ALIGNING
WITH RAILROADS   BATTLE LINES DRAWN   AM MORE
DEDICATED THAN EVER TO PARKS PROTECTION   BOTANY
EXPEDITION DRAWING TO CLOSE AFTER MAJOR SETBACK
HAVE INVITED THEM TO RETURN NEXT SUMMER FOR
EXTENDED STAY   HAVE EXPELLED FOREIGN COUNT AND
BANNED FROM PARK FOR LIFE
CAPT ALEXANDER CRAIGHEAD

Howard Merriam
Yellowstone National Park
September 1, 1898

My dearest Mother,

I can only hope that I have written to you with at least some good news while I have been here in the Park, otherwise I fear you will think me permanently afflicted with melancholia and be disinclined to believe what I am about to write. I must inform you of the saddest news, but I want to first assure you that we may yet be able to rise, phoenix-like, from our ashes. At least that is my sincerest desire.

We have had a horrendous accident, which has brought our work to a sad and untimely end. Our camp, our collection, our work—all have been destroyed by an unexpected fire. Joseph and I were away from camp for the morning, and by the time we returned there was nothing left. Even the principal members of our party were gone. Only the cook and driver had stayed, busy cleaning up the charred remains of the tents and the other gear for which they would no doubt be held responsible once they return to Butte. I did notice, however, that the driver had taken the time to clean up what remained of our books and other personal effects, including Miss Bartram's field bag, which had miraculously escaped the fate of the fire.

Neither Li nor Packard spoke to me when I entered the camp, which was just as well because they would have found that I was speechless. I looked at the smoldering rubble but I could not see. I knew that I should stay and help and be there when Miss Bartram and Rutherford and the others returned, but I could not do it. Ironically, I had just written to Bill Gleick about what a great leader I was becoming as a result of our time here in the Park. The sad reality is that, when faced with this loss, I was so devastated I could barely lead myself away from the charred remains of our camp.

Without thinking, I retreated to the hotel and sat by myself in a rented room staring out across the lake. That evening I saw Rutherford return and stagger down to the lakeshore, clutching his journal to his chest. He, too, just sat and stared, perched on the same log bench we had used for our portraits only a day before. It now seemed as if those smiling, happy people were from somewhere months, if not years, ago in our collective past.

As darkness fell, I could also see Joseph's small western-style campfire on the clearing above the lake, but I could not tell at such a distance if any of the others were with him. I knew I should join them, help them somehow, provide them with some guidance or assurances, but I could not at that moment even help myself.

I took out my field journal, which I carry with me everywhere (thank your God it was not destroyed!), and blindly thumbed through its weathered pages. I did not have the heart to read it, but instead let my eye wander across a word or a phrase or a simple field sketch until I was carried back through the summer. There was the day we found the fragile forget-me-nots growing high above the timberline. I had roughly sketched them there in my journal, next to my notes, but in my mind's eye I could still see Miss Bartram's eloquent pen and ink illustration, which captured even the minute hairs on the tightly matted leaves.

Then there was the time we encountered the gentians flowering in the snow next to the thermal pools and, later, those elusive white gentians Joseph discovered, and was good enough to show me where I could find them for myself. I will always remember how beautiful Miss Bartram looked there on the lake, the white flowers in her lap, and how gracious she was to leave behind the orchid, against her better judgment, so as not to offend. She is a scientist clearly committed to her discipline, but she is also, it now appears, a woman with a heart.

It was only after looking back through my field notes that I began to fully appreciate how much we had accomplished in such a short period of time. I may not be good at understanding the human element, but I must give myself at least some credit for adequately managing the logistics of a difficult and trying scientific expedition in the field.

If only I had developed similar skills to anticipate and prevent the fire! And oh, how I wished that there was something I could do for my friends and colleagues so that they, too, might see and appreciate the small but significant gains we all had made in such a fleeting period of time.

It was then that my thoughts turned to my dear friend, Andy Rutherford. When I first learned of the fire, and Rutherford's role in it, I was absolutely certain that I could never forgive him, accident or not. But he, too, must be suffering. Rutherford had finally learned, first hand, the joys of science and research, only to have that pest of a bird of his destroyed by a predatory European.

And our dear Miss Bartram. I wondered how she was faring. I thought of all her hard work and dedication, and the courage she demonstrated travelling so far on her own. She, too, must be feeling the loss of it all. She is young, I tried to assure myself, but, like the rest of us, she has lost so much. How can she ever fully recover? There was always the slight chance that Bill Gleick might be able to provide her with some opportunity at the Smithsonian. And, if she managed to salvage her field notes, she might, perhaps, be able to prepare a publication for the scientific press. These possibilities might sustain her. Rutherford, too, for that matter. He had, after all, saved his journal. He was sitting at the lake with it clutched to his chest.

I realized then that there was, in fact, something I could give to them both. There was still so much work to be done and, as I have always told them, where there is work, there is hope. With that hope I, too, had the courage to face them and, if not lead them, to at least lead myself from the safe confines of my room and down to the lake.

I found Rutherford still on his bench, slumped under a buffalo blanket, sucking on his unlit pipe. I joined him, and without any ceremony asked him matter of factly for his field notes.

"It was an accident," he said without looking up. "You must believe me. There was just too much wind."

"It may very well have been an accident," I replied, "but that does not make it excusable. I must tell you, Andy, that when I learned about the fire this afternoon, I did not think I could ever forgive you. We have all worked too hard to have everything destroyed like this."

I waited a moment, the two of us sitting there in the dark looking out over the lake, and then continued. "But we have had enough loss already, without losing friendships. So now I think I will forgive you, but only under one condition."

Rutherford looked at me briefly.

"I will forgive you," I told him, "but only if you managed to save your journal."

"It's here," he said pulling the logbook out from under the blanket.

"And the maps?" I asked, still speaking with as little emotion as I could manage given his condition. He looked terrible.

"They're in there," he replied. "You know, they're not much." At this he grimaced, and handed me the battered book. "Just an idea I had, really."

As he self-consciously focused on refilling his pipe, I flipped through the pages of his journal. Not only had Rutherford documented the day-to-day details of our collecting along with his thrice-daily weather reports, he had also kept hour-by-hour descriptions of his bird's vocalizing, making minute distinctions between each quork, quack, queek, and, of course, each gobble. He had also taken to sketching and describing the bird's different behaviors as well. I must admit, the sketches were good. Excellent likenesses of the bird in a variety of poses—dominated by the act of begging for food.

"An idea?" I asked as he commenced puffing.

Rutherford turned toward me on the bench. Even in the darkness, he looked beaten, his face ravaged by grief. He took the pipe from his mouth and sighed at the futility of his ever having a worthwhile idea in his life.

"Well, yes," he said finally. "I had this idea that I would use those maps and our collection to document plant life combined with temperature, climate, altitude, and the like. And then, using that information, I would be able to predict what would grow in various regions of the state. You know, from an agricultural perspective," he added.

I could sense a dampened excitement in his voice. It was as if just the thought of his idea was enough to rekindle his enthusiasm. Or at least bring it to a flicker.

"So that was your idea?" I queried.

"I know, it's foolish, but that's what I was thinking at the time." He sighed again and turned away. "Everything seems so hopeless now."

"Well," I finally said, handing him back the journal. "I think it's a wonderful idea. A sound scientific idea. One that you should plan on developing when we get back to campus."

He looked at me, the faint light of enthusiasm still flickering in his eyes, eager and ready to be re-ignited, but he was terrified, too, that my encouragement was offered in jest. He managed a weak smile.

"Are you serious?" he asked.

I assured him I was very serious. We needed to have something concrete to show for our work here. Rutherford's idea, if he thought he could realize it, was more than enough to justify our trip. Not to mention the fact that President Healey would, no doubt, be enthusiastic about such a practical, economic application. Even Healey might be appeased. Now that really would be an accomplishment.

Rutherford sucked on his pipe and looked out over the lake for the longest time. The wind had blown the night sky free of clouds, and I could clearly make out Goose Above flying south for the winter. It was time for all of us to get ready to head back home.

"And what about the raven? Edgar?" I had to ask. "Do you have any ideas about that work?"

Rutherford shook his head. "I don't know," he said flatly. "I don't know."

"Well, think about it," I advised. "You have done too much work to drop it now. You had an idea once. Something about teaching a wild bird to talk as I recall. You proved me wrong, that's for sure. Let's not forget that."

As I stood to leave, I reached out and instinctively patted Rutherford on the back. He turned, and in an emotional display that made me feel at first uncomfortable but also relieved, Rutherford embraced me and thanked me for all that I had done.

"I will make it up to you, I promise," he said, his voice raspy with emotion. "I promise you I will. I owe you that much at least."

I turned then to look for Miss Bartram. I owed her much more than a pat on the back. Or an embrace. But I did not know how to offer it. I could only hope, as I walked up the hill that she, too, had an idea. But before I could reach Joseph's camp, I encountered Mrs. Eversman, sitting on a fallen tree trunk, surveying the damage at our fire-scarred camp.

"Professor Merriam," she said, with an apologetic dip of the head. "I do not mean to intrude, but I was hoping I could return these to Miss Bartram." She indicated a small bundle in her lap.

"She was kind enough to share these specimens with me the other night at dinner. I thought perhaps she might want them back now." She smiled and shrugged. "They are no longer duplicates, right? So I was thinking . . ." Again she paused, her attention focused inwardly as if trying to discover the right words. "There are only a dozen or so samples, but maybe she could use them to start again?"

I assured her, for assurances were what she seemed to be needing, that Miss Bartram would be most grateful to receive the specimens. I then asked Mrs. Eversman if she would like to accompany me so that she might personally return them.

"Oh, no, I really do not wish to disturb her. Or you," she added quickly. "I would not know what to say to her, except that I am so sorry that this has happened. Please, would you give these to her?"

She crept towards me, the package held before her like a shield. "I would be most grateful if you would do this for me."

I took the package and, as if this simple act had set her free, Mrs. Eversman nodded, smiled, shrugged, and promptly disappeared down the trail like a timid, wild bird. I looked at the small, neat bundle in my hand, and could not help but smile. Perhaps this was the "idea" I needed.

Joseph had re-established his camp on a secluded bluff overlooking the lake. When I arrived, the inhabitants all looked weary and battle worn, but they were all sitting together, a family of sorts, going about their day-to-day lives. Except for the large tipi, it could have been any other domestic campsite in the Park. Miss Bartram was sitting by the campfire, looking through a ledger book that sat open on her blanket-covered lap. On one side sat Joseph's two small children, leaning towards her to get a better look at the book. On her other side sat Joseph's wife, Sara, straight backed and beautiful, keeping a wary eye on the fire.

Our camp table, which had been moved to Joseph's clearing, was where Kim Li, wrapped in an old buffalo robe, now sat, carefully watching Joseph as he stripped the leaves from a pile of yarrow. The driver's dog, tied to one of the legs of the table, yapped and wagged its tail at my approach. Joseph nodded in my direction but continued his work.

"Did you know," I said to Miss Bartram, thinking this the perfect opportunity to note our compatibility when it comes to the botanical sciences, "that Achilles used the yarrow plant to stop the bleeding of his soldiers' wounds at the battle of Troy, and that is why you refer to the plant as *Achillea?*"

I pronounced the scientific nomenclature perfectly, but Miss Bartram looked up at me as if she had no idea what I was talking about.

"*Achillea*, Miss Bartram. It provides insight into the plant's use. In this case, it is the scientific name that resonates with history. It's the kind of information I'm working to document, to ensure that traditional plant uses are not lost to us forever."

As I walked over to the fire to join her, the two children ran to their mother, who did not even acknowledge my presence. She did not leave, this was her home after all, but simply continued her campfire watch. The younger child, a girl, clambered into her mother's lap, while the older child stood beside her, keeping a close watch.

"We have not lost anything," Miss Bartram said as if she were paying no attention at all to me. "It's all here, in this book," she said, indicating the open journal on her lap.

As usual, Miss Bartram caught me off guard. She clearly had ideas of her own. I looked at the journal, expecting to see Miss Bartram's field notes, but instead saw a brightly colored drawing of our campsite by the lake. We were all there in the drawing, just as we had been the night of Rutherford's celebration—the night before the fire. In more exactness and artfulness than a photograph could have ever captured, there was Miss Bartram, Rutherford, Kim Li, Joseph and his family, and all of our visitors that evening, including Miss Zwinger, Mrs. Eversman, and Mr. Wylloe, all of us sitting around the table which had been draped in red and gold-colored cloths. Not a detail had been missed, from the food on our plates to the exact shape and color of the flowers in the vases. Even Edgar had hopped into the scene, his feathers the bluish black of gun metal as they reflected the lantern lights glistening overhead.

"It's beautiful, isn't it?" Miss Bartram smiled. "And there's more," she added.

She turned to another page, as enchanting as the one before. This one illustrated the diminutive orchid, with Miss Bartram, Joseph, the student, and myself all circled around it in the shade of the trees. In the foreground sat John Wylloe, his hat in his hands, soaking his feet in the stream.

Next she showed me a picture in which she was collecting monkeyflowers in a narrow ravine. On a rocky crag above her, Miss Zwinger and Mr. Wylloe sat next to a placid looking family of bighorn sheep. On the road between the two was Joseph, who appeared to be shouting, frightening off a grizzly bear which was bounding down the mountain on the opposite side.

"You never told me you encountered a bear," I said.

"There are some things, Professor, that it is best that you do not know," was Miss Bartram's instant reply. But studying the drawing she added, "I did think it odd, though, Joseph's singing."

As I examined the picture, she looked closely at me, as if she were trying to read what was hidden in my face. I doubt there was anything left there to read.

"Isn't it strange, Professor, how as scientists we become so focused on what is close at hand, that we often miss the real picture?"

These drawings captured our shared experience with such clarity and objectivity, that I could not help but smile at Miss Bartram's question. Then I laughed as I realized Miss Bartram was right. We had not lost everything after all. Our summer was captured in our field journals and there, in the drawings in her book.

"Miss Bartram, you never cease to amaze me," I said finally. "These pictures are truly a work of art."

"But it isn't my work," she quickly corrected. "It was Joseph and Sara. They did this. It is a gift. For all of us. They did this for us because we are their science clan," she added with seriousness.

At this the tall Indian woman looked at me again, and stood to leave.

"There should always be a light that comes of the darkness," she said, in perfect boarding school English. "That is the Indian way. Your people pray at night, because they are afraid of entering the darkness. We say our thanks in the last moments before the dawn, when you cannot see the face of that which approaches. We are not afraid of darkness because we know it comes before the light."

"I didn't know she spoke English," I said as Sara and her children left the campfire to join her husband and Kim Li at the table.

"That's probably because she did not know that you cared."

Again, Miss Bartram gave me that look of hers which I find so unsettling, because inevitably I find myself unable to respond.

"Once again I find I must thank you, Professor," Miss Bartram finally said. "I know that I will never abandon my commitment to science. It is not only my life. It is my passion. But now I understand that there is more to the world than I have been able to discover through the limited perspective of science."

She indicated the journal still open across her lap and then nodded in the direction of Joseph who was showing Kim Li how to properly prepare the yarrow leaves for storage.

"The world is so vast and so unbelievably beautiful," she added, "it is difficult at times to see the whole universe of possibilities. So we only look at parts of it at a time. Like the photographs Dr. Rutherford commissioned the other day. Each is as useful and true to the experiences of the real world as the other, but they do not show the whole picture. I know that now."

Miss Bartram closed the journal and then handed it to me as if in confirmation of what she had learned. I, in turn, handed to her the parcel I was still holding.

"I saw Mrs. Eversman on my way up here," I explained. "She wanted to return these. I guess she did not want the fire to be a total loss for you."

Miss Bartram took the package into her own blanket-covered lap and held it there, her attention focused elsewhere.

"It's too bad that I wasn't generous or thoughtful enough to give some of my duplicates to friends," I said. But Miss Bartram was not listening. She skimmed her hand across the surface of the package, almost caressing the paper and twine in which the specimens were wrapped.

Again at a loss as to how to respond to her, I intended to return my attention to the ledger book but was distracted by the barking of the mountain man's dog. The dog strained at its leash, leaping with each bark, in the direction of something or someone approaching Joseph's camp.

"Where is that Rutherford?" Peacock demanded, entering the clearing carrying a large load covered in a waterproofed tarp. He was followed by the mountain man who carried an equally large bundle.

"I was just in your camp, Merriam, and couldn't find any sign of him. Couldn't find any sign of anyone." He quickly scanned the area of Joseph's camp. "I guess that's because you are all up here," he added, momentarily appeased.

Peacock placed his cumbrous package gently onto the ground

and slid out from under another large bundle which he had ingeniously strapped to his back. He squinted and blinked in our direction.

"So where is the son of a b——?" he said, his original mood returning. "Excuse me Miss Bartram," he added, "but Rutherford has my bugs. Where did he put them? There's nothing left at the camp."

"No," I confirmed. "There is nothing left at the camp."

Peacock squinted and blinked again, as if trying to comprehend what I was telling him.

"You mean the specimens, too?" he asked.

"All of it," I replied. "Gone." There was no other way to say it. "Everything was lost."

Peacock blinked and grunted. "I knew I should never leave any of my bugs with that Rutherford," he said.

"Well," I tried to correct him, "it wasn't really Rutherford's fault."

I tried again to explain that it had been an accident, and to remind him that a good portion of his collection had been forwarded to Washington anyway so it was out of harm's way, but Peacock was not interested in hearing it.

"I told you, didn't I?" he said blinking with great conviction. "But no. You insisted that Rutherford would take good care of our work. That he was dedicated." He blinked and grunted, and began untying the first bundle. He grunted again to make certain I understood exactly what he thought of my so-called judge of character.

"Well, all I can say is that it's a good thing I didn't listen to you," he added, pulling one small paper-wrapped tin case after another from within the larger bundle. He stacked them neatly into a series of orderly rows.

"Found this great cave. Just the thing for long-term storage. Dry. Isolated. You know, there are a lot of interesting places in this Park. You should get out of camp more often, Merriam."

Miss Bartram looked at me to ascertain if I fully understood what Peacock was saying. I understood perfectly. Then she laughed, wiping at her eyes, as Peacock grumbled and blinked at us from across the fire. I also laughed, and then I, too, had to remove my spectacles and rub at my eyes.

"Never give your best specimens to someone else to look after," Peacock chided me. "You know that, Merriam."

He then asked Kim Li for some better packing material.

"I need to get these ready to go back home," he explained.

I tried again to put in a word of defense for Rutherford, but Peacock was still not interested in anything I had to say in that regard.

"So what about the two of you?" Peacock demanded, squinting at us over the fire. "Where did you stash the best of your collections?"

I shrugged. "We were all supposed to be in this together," I reminded him.

"Hmmm," he grunted and blinked again.

"You, too, Miss B?" he wanted to know.

"Yes," she confirmed. But then, still holding the small package of specimens on her lap, she added, "Well, no, as a matter of fact, I do have duplicates. Yes, I do."

She nodded with a grave authority hoping, I'm sure, to discourage any more negative comments from Peacock.

"See," Peacock said to me. "A real scientist. What did I tell you?"

And then, looking around the camp, he added, "So where's the other woman? The one with the wine? It's been a long day. I could use something good to drink."

At this, the mountain man untied his dog as if to leave, but before departing he walked over to Miss Bartram and towered over her in that silent, hostile way that he has. I prepared myself for the worst, even though I knew I would be no match for him if he tried something foolish. But he said nothing. Rather, he crouched down and in a single, unexplained gesture, presented her with a solitary, late-blooming wild rose. And then, without a word, he stood again and retreated, his dog wagging its tail by his side.

So, you see, Mother, we have gone through the worst together, and I am now more confident than ever that if given the time to salvage what is left of our work, we can and will be a party again. We can all return to campus now, knowing that each of us in our way has the opportunity to draw upon the richness of our experiences here to produce meaningful work. Just the prospect of that work gives me much hope.

As for Miss Bartram, I have suffered greatly, unable to ascertain how best to assist her. I cannot tell you how much I have longed for her to accompany us back to campus, but when considering the possibility I must admit that I have nothing there to realistically offer her. President Healey has made it perfectly clear that he will not support an assistant in my office, even if it were Miss Bartram, whose company he clearly enjoyed at the hotel. But then, the president would probably decline to support me if given the opportunity, and I am a member of his agricultural experiment station—albeit a reluctant one.

I am certainly in no position to invite Miss Bartram to stay in Montana without some promise of appropriate work and support. My rooms in Bozeman are inadequate, not to mention ill-suited, to entertain the company of a woman as much as I might like to have her by my side. Instead, I have asked Bill Gleick if he might offer her some opportunity should he decide to stay at the Smithsonian. If nothing else, I was hoping he might provide her with time and perhaps an extra stipend to reproduce her field notes and illustrations before forwarding them to the Smithsonian as we had promised she would do. I was resigned to the fact that if that was all that I could do for her, it would have to be enough, even though she deserves so much more.

So you can imagine my relief and, yes, my joy, when I learned that Bill Gleick had contacted President Healey on his own behalf and, through some shrewd negotiations, has managed to work out an arrangement which benefits us all. First, Gleick requested an annual leave from the college so that he might remain in Washington for the remainder of the year. Reluctant to make a commitment to the Smithsonian in the long run, Gleick has instead offered to stay through a transition period to help them adapt to Philip Aber's death. At the end of the year, he has promised to reconsider his options, both personal and professional.

When presented with Gleick's request for a leave, the president was less than enthusiastic, arguing that Gleick is needed on campus, and that he relies on Gleick and his assistance. Besides, the president argued, in these early days of the college, every penny that is given to support outsiders is a penny he, the president, would prefer to keep in the college construction fund.

Now the president is wise when it comes to finances, and knows perfectly well that he can use Gleick's salary to hire someone at a much lower rate. But Gleick is also shrewd when it comes to these kinds of negotiations and, pretending not to understand the options, proposed an alternative that the president was hard pressed to refuse. The Smithsonian would support Miss Bartram as Gleick's replacement for the year, with the one condition that she be provided with adequate time to document and catalogue the specimens from the Park. This was an arrangement to which President Healey was more than willing to agree. Apparently if Miss Bartram is to assist the president—and not me—he has no objections whatsoever and is more than willing to provide her with the time she needs to pursue her professional obligations to the Smithsonian and to Bill.

And Miss Bartram will need plenty of time, for it turns out there is still much work to be done and an extensive collection with which to work. Even before we knew about the arrangements that Bill Gleick was making, Miss Bartram had made arrangements of her own. Unbeknownst to me or anyone else in our party, Miss Bartram has routinely shipped multiple specimens and illustrations to Cornell for safekeeping. She has since asked that those specimens be sent directly to the college for cataloging. Once again, Peacock was right. Miss Bartram is a fine and thoughtful scientist, with foresight and a level of professionalism which put us all to shame. Bill Gleick suggests that when we forward the Smithsonian's portion of those specimens to the Institution, that we formally refer to it as the Bartram Collection. I agreed with all my heart.

When I told Miss Bartram that she was invited to stay in Bozeman for the year, not as my assistant but in a position of her own, she took both my hands into hers and thanked me so sincerely, you would have thought I had bestowed upon her the world's greatest gift. She warmly embraced me, giving me hope that Miss

Bartram is no longer as contemptuous of me as I had once believed. Of course, I cannot read too much into that spontaneous action, as she embraced Rutherford and Peacock, as well. They were as flattered and flustered by her attentions as I was at the time. But even though I cannot be so presumptuous to assume that she thinks highly of me, there may be a slight possibility that she does not think I am totally without promise as a scientist—or as a man. That alone gives me great hope as we prepare for our journey home.

Rutherford, too, faces the return trip with a renewed sense of optimism. As we were making our final preparations, Joseph approached the wagon carrying a large wooden crate. He asked permission to put it on board, and I told him that he had my permission, but that he must first check with Rutherford, to ensure that it was agreeable to him as well.

"What is it?" Rutherford asked, his lack of interest communicated by the tone of his voice. Although Rutherford has tried his best to help us prepare for our return, I can tell that his heart is not in it. I know he must be anxious to get back home, but since the fire and the sad loss of his bird, he has not shown much interest in anything he does.

"I don't know," I told him. "Something Joseph wants us to transport to Bozeman. You better see what it is."

Rutherford shot me an impatient look. "You know we can't take artifacts out of the Park. Even if they are for Joseph." He took the pipe from his mouth and waved it at me. "We will be detained," he warned. "I don't care how friendly you think you are with that captain."

"I know," I assured him. "That's why I want your advice before we decide how to proceed."

Rutherford sighed and walked heavily to the back side of the wagon where Joseph had deposited the crate. He sighed again and peered inside it. Two adult and two juvenile ravens looked back at him, their thick, black beaks curiously probing the spaces between the wooden slats.

I could see tears well up in Rutherford's eyes as he retreated behind a cloud of tobacco smoke.

As Rutherford regained his composure, Joseph joined him and, in an effective combination of Crow and English, informed Rutherford that the adults were a male and a female, a breeding pair. The juveniles, he believed, were also a male and a female. I have been told that even experts have a difficult time distinguishing the sex of ravens of any age, but knowing Joseph as I now do, I do not care what the experts say. If he believes the birds to be two males and two females, I believe that he is right.

"Can we take them with us?" Rutherford finally asked.

"Fine with me," I said. "You have Captain Craighead's permission, isn't that correct? I am not planning to look in the box to see if you have stuffed more than one bird in there. Besides, as it stands now, any idiot with a gun can shoot these birds with immunity. Even in the Park. Seems like they would have a much better future with you."

Rutherford nodded. The two students now joined him, peering into the crate, excitedly describing the aviary they would help him build. They could enclose a full acre if he wanted. They could even include bushes and trees. It could be everything Rutherford ever dreamed of, they enthused, and more. And, the two suggested, they would locate it on Rutherford's family land outside of Bozeman. They would live out there, the two of them, so that Rutherford would not have to travel back and forth every day. They would even test some of Rutherford's ideas about agriculture and plant growth and temperature, and help him manage the land while they continued with their own studies on campus.

"Like scientists," the one student said. "We could live like scientists on the land, and have our own research facility."

"And establish a real weather station," the other added. "And we would check it twice a day."

Rutherford puffed thoughtfully on his pipe.

"Three times," the other student corrected.

Rutherford smiled. Then, taking the pipe from his mouth, he reached over and closely examined the birds, poking one of his ruddy fingers through the slats of the crate, as if to stroke one of the ravens on the head or rump, like he used to do with his other bird. At first, all four birds withdrew, wary of the intrusion, but then one of them, the biggest, hopped up to Rutherford's finger, eyed it from side to side, and took a cautious taste. It squawked its disapproval and hopped back again.

"Edgar," Rutherford said. "That one's name is Edgar."

I know now for certain that Joseph's wife is right. There is a light that comes from darkness. After all, it does so every morning of every day.

All my love,
  Howard

A. E. Bartram
Mammoth Hot Springs
Yellowstone National Park
September 1, 1898

Dear Jessie,

I have just a moment to write one last letter from Yellowstone, to mark the end of my field work and my summer here. The Professor, in an unusually ebullient mood, has arranged for our transport to Bozeman by train, so we are now all getting ready to depart.

The driver, Kim Li, and the two students have agreed to transport the wagon, supplies, and Dr. Rutherford's four new birds back to Bozeman. The rancher, Ralph Clancy, has offered to accompany them since he, too, is headed home for the season. Joseph and his family will leave us here, preferring to travel less populated routes through the mountains, while Miss Zwinger and Mr. Wylloe will continue the journey as far as Livingston at which point they will leave us to board an eastbound train. You can never be certain where a road—or a train trip—will carry you, but it appears that Miss Zwinger embarks on that journey with more than a general sense of expectation, and a new measure of contentment which is clear to all in her demeanor.

Mr. Wylloe seems equally sanguine about life, although he promises to advise his readers thinking of travelling to Yellowstone Park to look instead to their own backyards if they want to experience the workings of the real world. A robin building its nest, a bee flitting from plant to plant, an apple tree swelling, budding, and seemingly overnight bursting into flower, a constellation rising in the summer sky—these insignificant events of life make Mr. Wylloe's heart sing. Or so he says.

I, too, leave the Park with a new sense of contentment. This is so unfamiliar to me that I am still learning to accept it. Just the other morning, so that I might better understand and plan for my fate, I asked the Professor if there was any chance at all that he might allow me to return to the college with him. I could be his assistant, I argued, and help him rebuild the collection. I could reproduce the field notes, and catalogue and classify all that we had accomplished in the Park.

He was at first taken aback by my request, but he was clearly determined to refuse me. Having seen his concerns this summer, I am certain he worries about the personal responsibility for caring for someone like me. He kept insisting that there was nothing in Bozeman which he could offer me.

"But there is much that you can offer," I countered. "We need to rebuild our summer's work. We can do it," I said, "but we need each other to get it done."

The Professor laughed sadly at my impertinence. He thinks I am much too bold, but he is too kind to reprimand me now.

"Miss Bartram, you have managed quite well on your own this summer," was all he would say. "You do not need me."

But Jessie, I really do need him. Looking back through Joseph and Sara's ledger book, I realize I have come such a long way since arriving in the Park, but I still have so much farther to go. Miss Zwinger once advised that I should not embark down a road unless I would be absolutely satisfied with where that road was headed. I will never be satisfied if I return the way that I have travelled, and I am forced to go back to where I have already been.

When I argued this to the Professor, he did not appear in the least bit interested in anything I might want or need. Not that I can blame him. I have been so arrogant and self-centered when it comes to him and his friends, that in retrospect I cannot imagine why he ever let me stay.

His insistence that there is nothing for me in Bozeman only served to fuel my own desires, and my determination not to be sent back home. By the end of our argument about my future, I was practically on my knees. At the height of my argument, the Professor reached out and ever so briefly touched his hand to my cheek. Instinctively, I took his hand in both of mine.

"Please?" I asked. "I don't need to be your assistant," I added. "I could be your companion, a partner, a friend."

But as kind as the Professor was trying to be, he would not budge. In fact, he seemed as determined as he was the day I arrived. And, just as he did that afternoon in the hotel, he removed and wiped his glasses, balanced them back on his nose, and then examined me closely. How I wished that he could see that not only have I become a better scientist during my tenure here, but I have become a better person as well. I have gained a new appreciation and respect for the Professor and his friends, and even for Joseph and Sara and their knowledge of the world. Time and again they have put me and my so-called education to shame. I still prefer the exactness and predictability of the science that I practice, but I am now more than willing to admit that just because it is exact, does not necessarily mean that it is true. So much of what we refer to as science is built on a foundation of pure faith, given to change at a moment's notice of new information. And just because science is based on what we see, it does not necessarily represent what is there.

In acknowledging that, I also realize that I need and want much more. I need to move forward with my botanizing, but I also want to move forward with my life. I do not want Professor Merriam to leave me behind. So you can imagine the joy I felt when he later informed me that I have been offered a most generous salary to prepare and catalogue the remaining collection on behalf of the Smithsonian, and that I will assist President Healey of Montana College while Bill Gleick is on leave. I am pleased to report that the Professor seems quite satisfied with the possibilities of this new arrangement. As am I.

Best yet, someone the Professor met during the Independence Day festivities has forwarded to him two railroad passes for unlimited travel throughout the West. It is not the funding for a new research facility of which he once dreamed, but these passes provide something potentially greater than mortar and bricks. By providing an opportunity to travel and collect, it in essence supports the research itself.

I cannot predict the future, but like Miss Zwinger, I, too, will travel down that narrow, windy road out of the Park with a great sense of expectation. We all have so much work to do, and as the Professor is fond of saying, where there is work, there is hope. Now there is much hope for us all.

I would so love to see you and my family, Jessie, but you must believe me when I tell you that the Professor, Dr. Rutherford, Dr. Peacock, Joseph, Sara, and the rest have become a family of sorts to me here. They are my science clan. And I love them. Each and every one.

I will write to you and my family to let you know what lies ahead. You must travel west, as Thoreau once advised, and experience my new world for yourself as soon as you possibly can. I am more confident than ever that it will be rapture, Jessie. Pure rapture.

All my love,
Alex

A PENGUIN READERS GUIDE TO

LETTERS FROM YELLOWSTONE

Diane Smith

An Introduction to

Letters from Yellowstone

It is the spring of 1898, and Cornell medical student Alexandria Bartram is on her way to the wilds of Montana to pursue her life's passion—botany. Bright and independent-minded, Alex has found that despite her family's hopes for her medical career, she is more interested in plants than in patients. The previous March, she heard about a Smithsonian-sponsored summer field study in Yellowstone National Park and immediately wrote to the trip organizer, Professor Howard Merriam. He accepted her proposal, and Alex anticipates an edifying summer.

What Alex doesn't know is that Merriam's expedition is riddled with problems. "I have put together the barest bones of an expedition," the professor writes to a friend. There is little project funding, still less support from the president of Merriam's college, and two key members of the field party have bailed out at the last minute. The professor, a quiet intellectual who readily admits to weak "people skills" ("I barely get along with my colleagues, let alone understand their true natures," he writes to his mother), is now faced with a small, makeshift field party that consists of an eccentric entomologist, an alcoholic agriculturist, two student interns, and a driver with an attitude problem. On top of all this, Merriam thinks that his Cornell medical student, whom he has never met, and who signs her letters "A. E. Bartram," is a man.

These profound misperceptions form the basis of Diane Smith's unique and warmhearted novel about naturalists and nature at the turn of the century. The story is told entirely through correspondence—an unusual style for a late-twentieth-century novel, but a common one in the nineteenth century, when letters and the telegraph were the most vital forms of personal communication. Smith's elegantly crafted writing bestows each character with a distinctive voice, and through a wide variety of interactions—from Alex and Merriam's debates over scientific methods to Rutherford's determined attempts to teach his pet raven to talk—readers gain insight into the novel's many disparate characters. In their letters to friends, family, and colleagues, Alex, Merriam, and the others describe events from contrasting perspectives, a kaleidoscopic effect that unites the fragments of multiple viewpoints into a multifaceted whole.

The relationship between parts and the whole is crucial to the development of the novel, which begins with a group of strong-minded strangers—each with his or her own separate purpose—who are forced into a partnership that proves more fruitful than any of their personal goals. As the field study progresses through the summer, botanical discoveries, snowstorms, sabotage, and a pivotal Fourth of July celebration are among the many events that compel the group members to cooperate and eventually lose their preconceived ideas about each other.

Throughout the novel, the characters' letters touch on pressing issues of the era, many of which are still with us today, from conservation to Native American displacement to feminism. The story is also a coming-of-age novel, not only for Alex, but for Merriam and the others as well, as they confront their fears and conquer them or, in a few tragic cases, are conquered by them. Brimming with humor, excitement, and the romance of the Yellowstone landscape, Smith's enlightening novel shimmers with discoveries—both human and scientific—that beckon the dawn of a new century.

A Biography of Diane Smith

Diane Smith has lived most of her adult life and a few years of her childhood in Montana, with only brief interruptions to live in San Francisco and London. She studied western and environmental history at the University of Montana, and now specializes in science writing, with an emphasis on public understanding of science and the reform of science education. She also does some travel writing, which often integrates her interests in history and the environment. In her free time, she visits the national parks, volunteers on archaeological and paleontological digs, explores the back roads of Montana, and tries to learn all she can about the natural history of the West.

A Conversation with Diane Smith

What made you decide to write your novel completely in the form of correspondence? What were the challenges and rewards of writing in this format? Would you do it again?

I originally opened *Letters from Yellowstone* with a traditional narrative, following Professor Merriam as he prepares for the expedition and ending the first chapter with the arrival of the letter from Miss Bartram. However, once I wrote that letter, it was clear that the book was coming to life in a way that the preceding fifty or so pages simply had failed to do. I was also interested in investigating the characters' various perspectives on the science of nature—and the nature of science. The letter format allowed the characters to express his or her point of view—as well as their consternation with the beliefs of their colleagues. And yes, I am integrating some letters into my next novel, but since Professor

Merriam and his party have been invited back, I hope to revisit the Park with them again sometime in the future. I assume if I write such a book it would once again be told entirely in the form of letters.

Do you maintain correspondences via letters today? Many people see parallels between the e-mail correspondences of this decade and the relationships that blossomed through the epistolary correspondences of the past. How do you feel about this?

I have to respectfully disagree that communicating electronically is the same as corresponding by mail. Although writing down your thoughts and beliefs and experiences can be revealing to oneself and to others regardless of the medium, I view electronic mail simply as a fast and convenient way to transfer information and data asynchronously. I am a regular user, preferring it to the telephone in most cases because it is so nonintrusive and efficient for getting things done. But electronic mail is not what I would call a reflective medium. We've become so conditioned to having information on demand that, I believe, many of us have lost the simple joy of anticipating the arrival of a letter, and the leisure to consider our reply. And yes, for the last year, I have benefited from such an antiquated correspondence, which I have found to be immensely rewarding. I feel fortunate indeed to have a friend who is even more atavistic than I am when it comes to letter writing.

How did your background in science and the environment help inform your approach to the novel?

Certainly the characters in *Letters from Yellowstone* reflect many of the experiences I have had working in science and engineering, although the specifics of the novel are entirely imagined. My interaction with scientists and mathematicians also provided me with the confidence to teach myself new disciplines, and to open my eyes to the natural world in much the way the characters in the book open themselves to Yellowstone National Park and its environs. I think it's important to point out that I have no training as a scientist. I believe all of us can, and should, develop a very basic understanding and appreciation of science and mathematics. At their heart, both are exquisitely simple and elegant if you can get past the scientific jargon. On the other hand, in the natural world in particular, botanical and other scientific nomenclature can help enrich our understanding. So I agree in general with the statement widely attributed to Linnaeus (although apparently first written by Isidore of Seville) that who knoweth not the names, knoweth not the subject. I guess in the end, I'm sympathetic with both Professor Merriam's and Miss Bartram's points of view.

The novel touches on many late-nineteenth-century political and cultural concerns such as the growth of the railroad, conservation concerns, and Native American issues. How did you research these issues?

I studied nineteenth-century western and environmental history in graduate school, and to this day have a keen interest in the subject, having read and enjoyed a wide variety of historians from Frederick Jackson Turner to contemporary feminists. Aubrey Haines wrote a two-volume history of Yellowstone Park, which helped inform some of the issues debated in the book, while other details were drawn from the many excellent books written by Park archivist Lee H. Whittlesey. In addition, there are a number of great books on the late-nineteenth-century environmentalist movement and on the interpretation of nature; the one which comes to mind first is *The Nature Fakers: Wildlife, Science and Sentiment* by Ralph Lutts. This one covers a slightly later period of time, but is still relevant to the issues of my book. And I will always be deeply indebted to Vine Deloria, whose work questioning the traditional assumptions of science and academia has helped me see the world in new ways.

What made you choose early botanical research in a U.S. national park as the topic for your first novel?

On an unrelated project, working in the special collections library at Montana State University–Bozeman, I discovered photographs of Teddy Roosevelt and John Burroughs in Yellowstone National Park. To this day those images stay with me and, based on seeing those, I started reading about the history of the Park. The Hayden expedition was of particular interest to me. Around the same time, a writer friend suggested botany as a topic, since it was one of the few scientific fields in which women were accepted during the Victorian age. A Hayden-like expedition in the Park seemed a natural extension of those two seemingly disparate ideas and interests.

Andrew Rutherford grows from a blustery curmudgeon to an interesting and sympathetic character during the course of the novel. Did you plan his development from the outset or did he take on a life of his own as you wrote?

I have heard writers say this happens, but I never really believed it until I started writing about Andrew Rutherford, Ph.D. I always envisioned him as being sympathetic by the end of the book, but my initial vision of him was nothing like the character he grew into over the course of writing about that summer in the Park.

Who is your favorite character in the novel? Why?

That's a difficult question, since I feel a certain affinity with all of them—with the possible exception of the mountain man driver. I think I relate best to Miss Bartram and Professor Merriam, but the so-called minor characters—Rutherford, Miss Zwinger, Mrs. Eversman, and even Peacock—never failed to amaze me when I was writing about them. Clearly, I was quite fond of Rutherford's bird, having once been amazed myself by a turkey-gobbling raven in the Park.

What are you working on now?

I am currently at work on another novel tentatively entitled *Evolution*. It, too, uses a unique format to relay the story and is set in the Montana Territories in the late 1800s.

QUESTIONS FOR DISCUSSION

1. Did you like reading a story told completely through correspondence? What were the benefits? The drawbacks?

2. One of the ways we learn about Alex Bartram is by paying attention to the different ways that she writes to different people, such as her parents, her friend Jess, and her colleague Lester. What do we learn about Alex in this way? What can we learn about the other characters from the tone and content of their letters?

3. The epistolary format of this novel means that there is no objective narration: all events are described through the point of view of a particular character. How does this characteristic affect how we experience the novel?

4. A number of telegrams are interspersed among the letters in this novel. How do these affect the pace of the novel?

5. Each of the main characters in this novel is distinctive. Which did you like the best, and why? Which did you dislike, and why? Did you identify with any of the characters?

6. Throughout the novel, Professor Merriam and Alex argue over whether, in academic study, plants should be called by their Latin names or by their familiar names. (For instance, Alex is horrified that Merriam refers to the "*Mimulus Lewisii*" as the "monkeyflower.") What does this argument tell us about the two characters' personalities?

7. At the Lake Hotel Fourth of July celebration, Miss Zwinger tells Alex, "Do not travel down a dead-end road, Miss Bartram, unless you are absolutely convinced that you will be content with the road's destination." What does Miss Zwinger mean? How does her advice affect Alex's future actions?

8. What insights about women's place in society at the turn of the century do the female characters in this novel reveal? What different perspectives do Alex, Miss Zwinger, Mrs. Eversman, and Sarah provide?

9. Smith has divided her novel into five sections, each of which carries the Latin name for a plant as its title. What is the significance of the titles, and the section breaks? How do they affect our experience of the novel?

10. How is the novel's plot affected by controversial political and social issues that stirred the American West in the late nineteenth century? Are any of these issues still relevant today?

11. Toward the end of the novel, Professor Merriam declares that "the world is filled with such wonder and uncertainty. . . . If we can bring some order to it through science or even religion or myth, all of our lives can be equally full of wonder." How does his view contrast with the other characters', especially Alex's? How does his statement relate to the larger themes of the novel?

12. On page 194, in a letter to her friend Jess, Alex describes in detail the moment when her photograph is taken on the last day of the field study. Later, on page 215, while holding the group picture drawn by Joseph and Sarah, Alex remarks to Merriam, "Isn't it strange, Professor, how as scientists we become so focused on what is close at hand, that we often miss the real picture?" What is the connection between these two scenes? What does Alex mean by her statement to Merriam?

13. Whether they know it or not, a romance is blossoming between Alex and Professor Merriam throughout the course of the novel. At what point does Merriam start thinking of Alex in terms that aren't purely professional? When does Alex start doing the same, and why?

For information about other Penguin Readers Guides, please call the Penguin Marketing Department at (800) 778-6425, E-mail at reading@penguinputnam.com or write to us at:

Penguin Marketing Department CC
Readers Guides
375 Hudson Street
New York, NY 10014-3657

Please allow 4–6 weeks for delivery.
To access Penguin Readers Guides on-line, visit Club PPI on our Web site at: http://www.penguinputnam.com

FOR THE BEST IN PAPERBACKS, LOOK FOR THE 🐧

In every corner of the world, on every subject under the sun, Penguin represents quality and variety—the very best in publishing today.

For complete information about books available from Penguin—including Penguin Classics, Penguin Compass, and Puffins—and how to order them, write to us at the appropriate address below. Please note that for copyright reasons the selection of books varies from country to country.

In the United States: Please write to *Penguin Putnam Inc., P.O. Box 12289 Dept. B, Newark, New Jersey 07101-5289* or call 1-800-788-6262.

In the United Kingdom: Please write to *Dept. EP, Penguin Books Ltd, Bath Road, Harmondsworth, West Drayton, Middlesex UB7 0DA.*

In Canada: Please write to *Penguin Books Canada Ltd, 10 Alcorn Avenue, Suite 300, Toronto, Ontario M4V 3B2.*

In Australia: Please write to *Penguin Books Australia Ltd, P.O. Box 257, Ringwood, Victoria 3134.*

In New Zealand: Please write to *Penguin Books (NZ) Ltd, Private Bag 102902, North Shore Mail Centre, Auckland 10.*

In India: Please write to *Penguin Books India Pvt Ltd, 11 Panchsheel Shopping Centre, Panchsheel Park, New Delhi 110 017.*

In the Netherlands: Please write to *Penguin Books Netherlands bv, Postbus 3507, NL-1001 AH Amsterdam.*

In Germany: Please write to *Penguin Books Deutschland GmbH, Metzlerstrasse 26, 60594 Frankfurt am Main.*

In Spain: Please write to *Penguin Books S. A., Bravo Murillo 19, 1° B, 28015 Madrid.*

In Italy: Please write to *Penguin Italia s.r.l., Via Benedetto Croce 2, 20094 Corsico, Milano.*

In France: Please write to *Penguin France, Le Carré Wilson, 62 rue Benjamin Baillaud, 31500 Toulouse.*

In Japan: Please write to *Penguin Books Japan Ltd, Kaneko Building, 2-3-25 Koraku, Bunkyo-Ku, Tokyo 112.*

In South Africa: Please write to *Penguin Books South Africa (Pty) Ltd, Private Bag X14, Parkview, 2122 Johannesburg.*